Olympus Awakening
Gods Among Us

By:

TJ Berry

Fox Fire Publications, LLC 2019

ISBN 13: 978-1-950745-04-3
ISBN 10: 1-950745-04-X

Printed in the U.S.A.
First *Olympus Awakening: Gods Among Us* paperback printing,
December 2019

Acknowledgements

To my mother, the original storyteller in my life. To my uncle, Bobby, who introduced me to the world of comic books, art, and storytelling…without him, I wouldn't be here today. To my siblings, for putting up with all the weird that is me. To my friends and friends who became family, thanks for all the love and support. Last but certainly not least, to JH DeMond…for giving me a whole new world…well, several new worlds to explore.

Fox Fire Publications would like to thank www.SelfPubBookCovers.com/RLSather for this amazing cover.

Gods Among Us Chapters

Chapter 1: Introduction

"I don't understand," Steven says, but claps along with the crowd anyway. He shakes his head. "I don't get it." His brown eyes stick with me for a few seconds too long…for me, at least.

"What's not to get?" I say back to that funny little dimple at the tip of his nose. He runs a hand over his mahogany colored hair, sweeping it back to the left. "This guy cleans up the roughest neighborhoods in town, branches out to help clean up neighborhoods almost as rough, and then gets our fair city declared the safest city in the state. Now, the mayor's giving him a key to the city. Seems simple to me."

"Our fair city?" Steven asks. "I told you that kind of flowery writing will never get you a cover story." He rubs the fuzz around his mouth with a stiff scratching noise. "Aaaaahhhh, nah," he groans. "That's not what I don't get though. I get that the guy deserves a key to the city." He nods unevenly, head bobbing left to right. "What I don't get is the name thing."

Mayor Lane steps up to the podium atop the courthouse steps. Cameras and camera phones, including mine, go up. His white toupee wafts in the breeze, and his too tight collar makes his pale cheeks seem that much more jowly. "Thank you all for coming," he bellows, raising his hands above his head. "I promised our recipient that I would keep this presentation short and sweet."

He smiles and looks behind him. "What this young man has done for our city…is nothing short of miraculous. Thanks to his planning, coordination, and selfless devotion to this cause, he has helped the city of Bevelle be declared the safest city in the state and one of the safest in the country." The crowd applauds. "Thank you. It is because of this, that it gives me great pleasure to give the Key to the City to Five."

"Five?" Steven scoffs. "Really? How is that a name?"

"We checked county records. He legally changed his name to Five ten years ago."

"Yeah, but who does that? And why isn't there any record of what his name used to be?"

"Come on, don't be shy," Mayor Lane says.

"Worse yet, hardly anyone's even seen this guy," Steven grumbles. "And no one's been able to get an interview with him."

"What are you trying to say?"

"I think it's all just a little shady."

"Pfft, you think oatmeal's shady."

A man steps up to the podium…a black man…young…built like a quarterback though…caramel colored skin…light brown eyes…low-cut

Caesar, and a thin goatee…just a little pretty…but very manly. His jeans, t-shirt, and burgundy leather jacket kind of understate the gravitas of the event though.

"Nicole?"

"Huh?"

"What are you doing? Get some pictures."

"Right," I say, lifting my phone again. I start snapping away.

"Are you sure that thing will be able to get print quality pics?"

"It's why I paid extra for the lens I've got attached to it." I point at the small zoom lens attached to the back of my phone. He nods.

The young man shakes the mayor's, who's smiling like the frigging Cheshire cat, hand. He whispers something to the mayor that makes him laugh. He steps up to the microphone, gripping the podium sides with both hands.

"Thank you…um…everyone. This wasn't…just me. It was a group effort. The neighborhoods' leadership, the police and fire departments, and the mayor's office all worked together to make this happen. I'm glad it did…every kid deserves to grow up in a safe neighborhood…and if we all continue working together…we can keep it that way. So, I accept this on behalf of all of them. Thank you again." He backs away from the podium with a wave.

"Humph," Steven groans.

"What?"

"No one is that selfless…I mean, he's getting the Key to the City and all he does is talk about…"

"…all the people that helped…? Yeah, you're right. He must be pure evil."

"Well, you haven't been able to stop staring at him since he stepped up to the podium."

"What? I'm doing my job."

Mayor Lane hands over a plaque with a golden skeleton key affixed to the top. He and Five shake hands again and again cameras flash, sequentially. Five waves as Lane puts an arm around him. I lower my phone.

"What are you doing?"

"Checking the pics. You might be lead on this story, but you're going to put my name on the by-line or no pictures." I scroll through the pictures…not bad, a couple of good shots. I frown. In one, I swear Five was looking directly at my phone.

"You know what would get you a by-line even faster?"

"What?" I moan, still focusing on the picture. "Helping you get an interview with him?"

"Nope, letting me take you to dinner."

I frown and look at him…is look the right word? Nope, I'm glaring. "Why would you want to date a junior copy writer trying to make staff writer? The only reason you even brought me was because all the staff photographers were tied up somewhere else…or don't like you," I add as a mumble.

"Or that's what I told you." I shake my head. "What's not to get? Caramel-colored skin, cute pixie-cut, cinnamon hair, big chocolate eyes…"

"What am I? A woman or a dessert?"

"Either way, I want a taste." I groan and roll my eyes. "Where'd he go?"

"What?"

"That guy Five. Where'd he go?" I look up from my phone and…well, pretty much everyone's looking for him. "He can't have just disappeared."

"He wouldn't've, if you were doing your job instead of flirting with your photographer." He glares this time. "Look, somebody had to have seen which way he went."

I check the gathered police, reporters, and other random onlookers. Everyone seems just as lost as we are…except two men near the center of the crowd. They both look young, mid-twenties maybe…around my age is apparently young to me.

"What are you looking at?"

"Those two," I reply, tipping my head to them. "Those two black guys…well-dressed and manicured…both seem uninterested in the search for the elusive Mr. Five."

"Just Five according to the mayor's bio on him." Steven looks them over and frowns. "So, what about them?"

"Everyone else is looking for him, right? They're not looking for him, because they know where he went, maybe?" The younger one with brighter skin leans toward the other and says something. They both laugh. The taller one with darker skin and eyes…seems focused on something just past the courthouse steps…and the dais past them.

"Follow me." I walk to the right of the courthouse platform.

"Where're you going?" Steven asks, but follows me anyway.

I move around to the parking deck next to the courthouse. "Exactly where they were looking." We cross over into the darkness…and I spot Five, stepping out from behind a car. He straightens his jacket collar and turns away from us. "Come on," I whisper.

"What? Why?"

"So, I can get you that interview and earn my by-line…" I move to follow Five. "…and not have to date you to get it."

"I'll tell you what," Steven says. "He's probably going for a car. I'll go get mine and you call me when you get an idea where he's going."

"What if his car's in here?"

"I'm right around the corner. It'll only be a minute." He turns and runs…well, jogs in his too tight suit.

I look back the way we came in and then after Five. I run through the parking deck, trying to catch up to him. I come to a screeching halt when I hear a noise…it's weird…I'd swear it sounded like a bird…a big one. I sigh and run on. It's not easy running in heeled boots.

I reach the other side of the deck and look around. I know he didn't get into a car. I didn't hear an engine, and he definitely doesn't seem like the electric car type. I spot him rounding the next corner. I run, nearly rolling my ankle, making the turn. He's at the next corner already. Man, he walks fast.

I follow him for four more blocks…before he turns. He's going into the residential part of town, but why is he walking? My phone buzzes. Steven wants to know where I am. I text him back, *the corner of Cedar and 4th Street…heading east.* No response. I wonder if a white boy from a stuck-up prep school would come through the hood.

After two more blocks, Five cuts across a parking lot heading toward a little brick building…no, it's not brick…faux brick…it looks like an old McDonald's…before they moved downtown. I hurry over to the door, with the gold letters *Mack's BBQ* etched on the glass. Directly below that, are the words: *Ribs. Chicken. Sausage. Steak.* Oh, my inner vegan just cringed while my outer carnivore is trying not to drool. I haven't had decent barbecue since I moved south. This stuff smells like dad's grill though.

I text Steven the address, before stepping through the door…with a familiar 'M' molded neared the handle. "Welcome to Mack's," a pretty, young woman behind the counter says. "Can I help you with anything?"

"Um, I'm actually waiting on a friend…" …and stalking the topic of an article for my magazine, but she doesn't need to know that. Yet. She nods and wipes down the counter. I look around Mack's and note that they left most of the original booths in place from when it was a fast food joint. Some of the bricks have been replaced in the tile floor, but it's clean and none of the ones still there are damaged or chipped.

The place is moderately busy…but it's mostly people lingering post-meal. There's no line at the counter. I almost moan when the smell of barbecue chicken, collards, and fresh baked cornbread wafts over to me from a table near the door. Smells like heaven.

The door squeaks behind me. "Hey," Steven says, walking in.

"Hey."

"Ready to get this interview?" I nod. Steven straightens his tie, smooths down his $60 haircut, and does a quick sniff before his right index streaks underneath; not helping the 'he uses coke' rumors. "We're going to get this."

"Yeah," I moan as more of Mack's heavenly cooking carries over from the kitchen. This time it's definitely sausage, cabbage, and more of that delicious smelling cornbread…oh, I wipe the corner of my mouth. What I wouldn't give for a slice of cornbread. Haven't had any of that since last Christmas…where grandma asked me a dozen times where Derrick was while giving me a piece of hers.

Steven looks around. The young girl at the counter looks up. "Welcome to Mack's," she says warmly. I wave, but Steven waves her off. She frowns and turns to the large man in the kitchen.

"Do you see him?" Steven asks.

"Yeah, back corner booth."

He nods and stands on his tiptoes to see him. Five is in the exact same position he was when I walked in. He's just sitting there…staring at the table, not saying anything, no food…he's not even on his phone. He seems focused though. It's kind of like his body is here, but his mind is a million miles away.

"We…are not going to get this interview, are we?" Steven says, after observing him for a couple of seconds.

"I don't think so," I admit. "I mean, he refused to talk to all the networks…even refused to sit down with the governor…the mayor only coaxed him into getting the Key to the City because the neighborhood advocated for it." Steven looks at me. "I do my research."

"Well," Steven says. "We'll never know unless we ask." He marches toward Five…I follow…and the big, bald black man in the back takes notice of both of us. We stop at the end of the aisle, down from him. "He's sitting right there."

"I know, Steven. I'm the one who pointed him out to…" I look at him and he smiles. "Me?" He nods. "You're lead on this story. I told you, I'd help you get the interview."

"Fine."

"You're scared?"

"Of course not, but…" Steven looks at Five. "…he's turned down interviews with every newspaper and magazine from the AJC to the Bevelle Gazette. What makes you think you can help me get this story?"

"Because I have something all of them didn't."

"…hips that don't lie, legs that don't quit, a butt that won't wait, and lips that I just want to suck on all day?"

I snap my fingers and point at him. "White boy, I warned you."

"Warn me again," he says as I turn back to Five. I ignore him and tip my head forward.

He sighs and walks over. I follow close behind. "Excuse me," Steven says when we reach Five's table. Five looks up with just his eyes. They dart from Steven to me and back again. He sits back. "I'm Steven Bender with *Georgia Now Magazine*. How are you, sir?" He extends his hand, and Five just stares at it. "I was wondering if you'd be interested in doing an interview for our magazine…it's a weekly publication, covers middle to north Georgia…we usually publish about 50,000 copies weekly…but of course, most of our coverage is online and on social medi…"

"No interviews," Five says simply.

"…but," Steven continues. "With all due respect, Five…"

"Yeah," Five groans. "The way you just said my name…tells me you have absolutely no respect for me at all."

Steven frowns. "Well, you have a number for a first name…you had a name…and you replaced it with a number. You're probably hiding something and that's why you…"

Five leans forward like he's about to stand up. I put my hand on his shoulder and try to push him back down. He looks at it…but not like, 'why do you have your hand on me?' No, it's more of a surprise for him. I decide to push through.

"He didn't mean any of that. Did you, Steven?" Steven grumbles and turns away. I let out an exasperated sigh. "It's just…can I sit?" Five returns to his seat and tips his head forward. I take the seat across from him.

"It's just…five years ago, you just kind of sprang up out of nowhere. You were unafraid to take on the gangs and the drug dealers in your neighborhood…you bridged gaps within the community…helped get volunteers into the schools to make things better there too…and now you've gotten a key to the city, and no one knows anything about you except your name."

"Maybe, I like it that way."

"You, yeah…but people like me…that are fascinated by someone so…real, so giving…we want to know more. Need to know more." He nods and looks down. "Please, let us in…at least, a little."

"Five?" a husky voice calls from behind Steven. "Are these two harassing you?" It's the man from the kitchen…and he's even bigger without two counters in front of him. He crosses huge arms over his white apron and t-shirt. He stares down a clearly uncomfortable Steven.

"Now," Five whispers. "Mr. Johnson will toss both of you out of here with one word from me…" I grit my teeth. "…and he won't even feel bad about it." I swallow a lump, knowing that he's not lying. That guy's huge and he's probably the owner.

"...but," Five continues whispering. "I'll let you stay if you send your man away."

"He is not my man," I say aloud. Too loud. Five laughs.

"Nah, Mack," Five says above a whisper. "It's fine...HE was just leaving."

"He?" Steven repeats.

"He," I repeat.

Five nods and taps the table. His warm brown eyes seem to drink me in. "I'll talk to you...but just you." His eyes move to Steven. "And only if you go."

Steven looks at me. I nod. "Steven, beat it. I got this." He shakes his head. My eyes bulge, and I nod again. Steven sighs and turns to walk away...but Mack stands obstinately in his way. Steven awkwardly moves around Mack, nearly falling into the booth behind him. Mack watches him warily the entire time, until he's out of the restaurant.

"You want anything, Five?" Mack says.

"I'm good, Mack. Just need a sec to think, you know?" Mack nods. "What about you? Do you want anything...?" Five motions to me as if he's waiting on me to fill-in a blank.

"Nicole."

"You want anything?" Mack repeats in Five's place.

I open my mouth to respond. "Bring her a barbecue bacon cheeseburger on me."

"Um, I don't eat beef or pork." And unfortunately, all soul food cooked in the south is usually cooked with pork.

"Turkey burger with turkey bacon?" Five smirks. "Unless you're a vegetarian."

"I'm not, but I'm not in the mood for a turkey burger."

"Whatever you want," Five says. "It's on me."

"Which really means, it's on me," Mack says with a lighthearted laugh.

"Why you gotta bust me out like that?" Five and Mack continue laughing. I scoff a laugh and shake my head. He seems completely different now. More relaxed, less measured.

"Um, I'll take a turkey Polish...wait, do you have that...?" Mack nods with a confident smirk. "Okay, I'll have a turkey Polish on a bun with barbeque sauce and fries, please."

"No problem," Mack returns. "Drink?"

"Pepsi?"

"Coke, okay?"

I grit my teeth and shake my head. "Sweet tea?" Mack nods and walks away. I come back to Five, who's been staring at me the whole time. "What? I skipped lunch…because I got added to your key ceremony last minute."

He nods.

"So, Five…tell me a little bit about yourself."

He flashes an enigmatic smile, and his cheeks flare red for a second. "What do you wanna know?"

"I guess saying, 'tell me everything' might be too vague?"

"Yeah, doesn't mean I won't though." I smile. He's such a charmer. Crap, I might be starting to like him.

****

I laugh. "How exactly did we get back on me?"

"Well, it's just…I've never seen anyone take down one of Mack's foot-long Polish sausages that fast before."

"Shut up!" I whine.

"Did you even chew?"

I shove him. "Seriously, shut up!" I sigh. "Okay, so maybe not shut up, so much as tell me something about you."

"Okay," he says with a nod. "I…" He cuts off and frowns. He looks out the window and then out the opposite window.

"What? Surprised that it's dark outside already?" He doesn't answer, but his eyes dart around as if he's searching for something. "Well, that's what happens when you stall for over an hour and flirt with your interviewer."

"What? Flirting? Me?" He laughs. "Alright. Yeah. Yeah, I was." He smiles, but it's not the same as when I first sat down. He was flirting then, he's not now. What changed? "I'll tell ya what…" He stands. "…how's about I walk you back to your car and on the way, you can ask me anything you want?"

I stand. "And you'll actually answer some of these questions, this time?"

He shoves his hands into his pockets and bobs his head as he says, "Bet."

"Alright."

He motions to the door, and I lead the way. "Catch ya later, Mack."

"Aight, Five. It was nice meetin' you, Nicole."

"You, too." Five pushes the door open and holds it. "So, where's your car?"

He checks to see if any cars are moving through the parking lot, then ushers me across. "I don't have one. I actually prefer to walk."

"You prefer to walk?" He nods. "Doesn't that take forever? I mean, Bevelle isn't the largest city in Georgia, but it's still pretty big. I've lived here about two years and I've never been to this place."

"Oh, so you live here in town?"

"Yeah, I got a job at *Georgia Now* right out of grad school, and I interned the…" I pause, my mouth still hanging open. "No. We're talking about you now. Asking questions about you."

He laughs.

"So, why'd you do it?"

"Do what?"

"I mean, you just got a Key to the City for cleaning up the neighborhood and all…"

"I did, didn't I?" He pats his pockets. "Now, where'd I put that thing?" He shrugs. "Guess I left it at Mack's."

"That's what I'm talking about. If most people were awarded a Key to the City, they'd be out celebrating, or picking out a spot on their wall to post it…blowing up Twitter…either way, they definitely wouldn't be sitting in a mom and pop restaurant alone."

"Sometimes, I like the quiet of being by myself."

I sigh. "I get that, but…you accomplished something amazing in just five years."

"Just five years…?"

"Yeah." I catch his sleeve. "Why? Why'd you do it? Honest answer."

He nods. "Most honest answer I can give you. I've seen what people who think they're too big for the world do when they get in power. More often than not, they become selfish bullies, obsessed with things going their way. They step on the necks of people weaker than they are and keep pushing down until they get everything they want and then some. No one should be forced to live under someone like that."

"Oh," I moan, realizing that one of us or both of us moved closer. "You said, 'you've seen'…do you mean, from personal experience?"

He laughs it off. "Yeah. I mean me. I used to be petty…kind of a hot-head and constantly, mad at the world for not doing exactly what I wanted it to do." He turns to his left and starts walking again. I move with him. "I had…no empathy…no compassion for anybody that disappointed me. I smacked people around…people got hurt."

"You sound sad."

His jaw clenches. "Well, yeah. I mean, I started seeing how the way I acted affected people…people close to me…people I didn't even know." He shakes his head. "Made me sick…I realized I can't be like that anymore. So, I promised myself that I would not only change me, but I'd change the world around me."

"So, you started the neighborhood clean-up program?"

"Yeah, but that wasn't the start."

"It wasn't?"

"Nah, I started out by opening up a group home five years before that."

"You opened a group home? What do you mean a group home?"

He nods and puts his hands in his jacket pockets. I put mine in my jacket pockets. I hadn't realized how cool it is. Plus, we're already pretty close to downtown again.

"Sometimes kids get in trouble…and…and when they get out of the Juvie Detention Center…well, their options for a home have dried up."

"Dried up? Why would they…?"

He frowns. "Some parents don't like having 'troublemakers' around. Me, I wanted those kids to have some place to come back to…something beyond Juvie or a never-ending rotation of foster homes. Maybe, rehabilitate the kids and help 'em get back on the right track, you know?"

I nod. He talks with so much passion that it's hard not to listen to him.

"So, I bought the old 5th Street Elementary School building off the city…did some renovations…changed most of the classroom spaces into bedrooms and reopened it as a Group Home."

I scoff. "You know. You don't even seem old enough to have all of that going on. No offense."

He laughs. "None taken. You're not the first to say that. A lot of the kids' social workers said the same thing at first.

"Anyway, two of our kids just graduated from high school, something their social workers never thought they'd do. On top of that, they're both going to college."

"Wow, how'd they…?"

"They kept their grades up, one of my rules…and they volunteered their time and helped out around the neighborhood. They got partial scholarships, and I pulled some strings with a charity to help 'em cover the rest. Tre's going to Georgia State now, and Keisha's at Tech."

"Wow. So, you were doing good in your neighborhood before anybody even knew about it?"

"I tried. Some of the kids that came in…" He shakes his head. "…I could see that they had some deeper issues than I could help 'em with that late in the game. There were problems rooted in the community itself, schools…home life…bangers and dealers everywhere. It was like trying to get an angel to go through hell unscathed." Unscathed…? "Not that, I'm comparing the neighborhoods to hell…please don't put that in the article."

"Article?" His eyebrows arch. "Right!" I laugh. "Article. Sorry, it's just…pretty fascinating stuff. You're such a charismatic speaker; do you have any political ambitions?"

"Maybe, not right now though. I still see a couple of areas that can be improved, plus there are other city planners and officials who want to copy the model of Bevelle's clean-up project."

"So, let me get this straight. You don't want any glory for yourself…the Governor wanted to meet with you, and you refused…and you're going to work as a consultant for other city officials." He nods. "And I'm guessing you're not going to charge them a consulting fee?"

"Why would I?"

"I'm starting to think Steven might've been right about you."

"Who's Steven? Is that your boyfriend or something?"

"No. He's...actually the lead, covering your Key to the City award ceremony. He was the guy with me at Mack's."

"Oh, right. Him. Well, what did he say about me?"

"That there's something about you. You seem too good to be true, and that usually means secrets. Also, he thinks you're hiding something."

"And what would that be, huh?"

"Don't get defensive. It just makes you seem guiltier."

"You're right. My fault. Where's your car?" I look around. We're standing on the corner by the courthouse. I didn't pay any attention to where we were going...our surroundings. He could've taken me anywhere, and I wouldn't have said a word.

I throw my hand toward the next block, past the parking deck. He nods and walks with me.

He's quiet. He's eerie quiet. "Hey, I didn't mean to make it seem like I was suspicious of your motives or anything like that. It's just..." I groan. "...I'm used to waiting for the other shoe to drop."

"Don't sweat it," he says, as we reach my car. "This you?" I nod. "Little red Prius?"

I point at him. "Don't knock my car."

He holds his hands up. "Nah, I was just going to say that it's...you. It suits you, like it's your style."

"Uh huh," I moan, moving to the driver side. I unlock the door and open it. He stands on the other side of it. "I don't think I have enough for a full write up, so I may need to call you for a follow up."

"I don't have my phone on me...and I don't remember my number."

"How do you not know your own phone number?"

"New phone...and I never call myself, do I?" I open my mouth, but I don't have anything to put up against his argument. "Exactly," he says in an exaggerated taunt that makes me laugh.

"Fine," I snap, slipping my card out of my back pocket. "Here. My cell's on the back."

He looks the card over. "Nicole Clark. Copy Writer, *Georgia Now Magazine*. Hmm, I was wondering when I would get your whole name."

"Yeah, I bet you were." That weird bird from earlier caws again. I look up at the same time Five does. "So, you heard that too, right? I'm not crazy."

"Yeah," he breathes in a serious tone. "You ever get the feeling like you're being followed? Or watched?"

"More than I like to admit," I reply. I come back to him. "Is that the same feeling you got at Mack's? Is that why you wanted to leave all of a sudden?"

He keeps searching the sky. "Maybe."

"Definitely. Five, what aren't you telling me?" He looks at me…and I don't know. It feels weird. It gives me butterflies, but not…he's gorgeous butterflies…which he is, but that's not why. It feels like he's trying to tell me something without coming out and saying it.

"I should go." He pats my hands on top my door. "Are you alright here?" I nod. That weird bird caws again. A branch crashes down on the hood of the next car, scaring the hell out of me. I put my hand over my heart that feels like it's about to beat out of my chest.

"Yeah," Five says. "I should definitely go." He turns away.

"Five…?" He doesn't look back. He heads toward the parking deck. "That's weird," I purr. I could've sworn he told me he doesn't have a car. I look at the branch lying across the next car's hood as that bird caws again.

I close my door and walk around the front of my car. I pick up the coarse, leafless branch. It looks like it broke…but…I rub my fingers over four…if I didn't know any better, I'd swear they were claw marks. I sigh and look up at the tree. What is going on?

That bird caws over and over again. I look around, but I still can't lay eyes on it. It screeches. I feel a rumble and "OH MY GOD!" I moan as the top three floors of the building next to the parking deck explode, blowing out all the windows as billowy balls of fire escape.

"FIVE?" I scream, but I don't see him. Sirens blare in the distance as black smoke rises from the shattered windows, and the smell of burning carpet and drywall fills the air. Tiny bits of ash waft in the breeze like snowflakes, flittering to the ground. I take out my phone and start snapping pictures, while moving down the street.

A murmur of scattered voices fills the air. Soon, the street floods with people doing the same thing I am, taking pictures and watching in horror.

The police arrive and push everyone back to the opposite sidewalk. The cars evacuate the parking structure as the fire trucks roll in, earsplitting sirens blaring, and lights flashing bright. The fire department go to work, moving like a disturbed bed of ants, running their hoses.

I snap some pics of the police and firemen in action. I get a few of the crowd's reaction, running the gamut from horrified to frightened and every variation between.

"Ma'am," a uniformed officer says. "I need you to move to the other side of…"

I take out my ID badge. "Press."

"Be that as it may, for your safety…" He points to the crowd across the street. I nod and hurry over, while taking a few more pictures. I turn and snap off a few more crowd shots.

I lower my phone and type out a quick email to Ronda and cc Steven. I start filtering through the pics, selecting which ones to upload to *Georgia Now's* cloud. Wait…I go back two pics, because there's no way I saw what I think I just saw.

I gasp…an actual gasp. It's those two guys from the Key ceremony. I turn back to the crowd, where they were standing. They're gone. I move away from the crowd, wandering down the sidewalk.

Going back through the pics, I check the one before that one. They're standing with a third guy. This one has a gray hoodie on, but they face him…as if they're talking. I zoom in trying to get a better look at the third guy and it gets too pixelated.

I go back to the pic after that one and he's gone. There's not even a hint of him in the corner of the frame. I check the time stamps…I took the pics only three seconds apart. There's no way he could've gotten out of this mob that fast.

I look around…and check the building again. What in the hell is going on? Who are those guys? What do they have to do with Five? Are they…following him?

****

Chapter 3: Olympus

I groan. She's worse than the cops are, but oddly not as bad as dad is. "Yes, Ronda, I'm leaving the police station now." She's been questioning me so long I switch my phone to the other, less sweaty ear.

"So, what else can you tell me about the fire?"

"Explosion," I correct. "I had just finished up the first half of my interview with Five. He walked me back to my car and then boom."

"That's disturbing." She hums over the phone. "And these are pictures from right after?" She must be staring at the pics I uploaded…minus the picture of those two guys…and the third guy in the hood.

"Yeah. I was the first on the scene…" I tip my head to the right. "…well, I guess the scene developed around me."

"Alright. We let Deborah clean up your notes, and the story should be online in the next twenty."

"What about the blurb that went out last night?"

"Place holder. It was just something so that we could say our journalist was first on the scene." I nod and unlock my car. "You said you were going to finish up the interview with Five today, right?"

"Yeah, I hope so. I'm headed that way now. He tends to…distract from my line of questioning."

"I'll say," she purrs over the phone. I frown, pausing in my open doorway. "You uploaded your pics from the Key ceremony with the pics of the fire." I groan, pinching the bridge of my nose. "Just be careful. You don't want to be known as THAT reporter."

"What do you mean?"

"The one who sleeps with her subject to get the story."

"Bye!" I snap and end the call. I slide into my car and pull up my phone's GPS. I search for the group home I found online last night. "Mt. Olympus…" I scoff, punching it in. He said it was on 5th Street…and if I really wanted to get lost today, I'd do this without the GPS. I drive through town quickly, listening to every turn-by-turn direction…even when it has to recalculate after taking me down a road that's a dead end now because of construction, according the Moors Construction sign.

After I get around the construction project, the way seems straightforward. I pull up to a huge red brick building with ten concrete gray steps leading up to the front door. Sadly, those steps are a good way from the curb out front.

I sigh, pulling up my park brake. I climb out and notice the big sign next to the stairs that reads, "Mt. Olympus Children's Home." I walk around the car. I hear kids playing in the distance and see a whole other gathering of kids running down the sidewalk, moving along the side of the old school building.

I make the trek across the leaf-covered walk, heading up to the stairs. I reach the double doors, painted black with tinted windows. I lift my hand to knock, and the door on the right opens, pushing out toward me.

"Hey," a surly girl says from behind the door, while staring at her phone. Her wavy black hair hangs down covering most of her face, and her oversized green army jacket rolls up to the bends in her arms, revealing beautiful almond colored skin. She walks past me and goes for the stairs. She sits and continues typing on her phone.

"Excuse me," I say. She groans a complaint, but her eyes never leave her phone. "I'm looking for Five. Is he here?"

"Yeah, out back…he's working on the overgrowth in the woods…" She pushes out with her right arm. "…all the way back, on the left."

"Thanks," I say, moving back down the stairs and heading toward the left side of the building. The girl doesn't even respond. I make my way around, passing a collection of HVAC units on top of concrete slabs next to the building. They hum rhythmically, but quietly, keeping the interior warm, I suppose.

"I am so glad, I chose heeled boots today," I say, moving across the leaf and damp grass covered ground. There are tons of kids out behind the school using the huge field. They play football, basketball, and a couple other games that I don't recognize. I wonder how many of them actually live here. I'm guessing not the girl in the purple hood, who looks my age…and who glares at me as if she could march over here and kill me at any minute. I wonder how far she can throw that javelin she's holding.

Deciding not to stick around and find out, I make my way to the woods. "Hello," I say, stepping through a small patch of bamboo, leading to fir trees. A small boy steps out, wearing gloves and a gray hoodie. He lifts large brown eyes to me, tilting his fuzz-covered head. "Hey…um…hi, is Five out here?" The boy gives me a big nod. "…um…"

"Xavier," Five says, stepping out from behind a fir tree, carrying a small collection of tree clippings. "No slacking off, lil' man. You have to pull your weight, too." Xavier nods again and points at me. "Aight, I tell you what…I'll take care of her…" He hefts the bundle higher. "…you take care of these."

Xavier shakes his head. "Okay," Five laughs, putting the bundle, that's bigger than Xavier by a lot, on the ground. He picks out several of the loose branches. "Make a cradle." Xavier makes a cradle of his arms. "Here you go." He places the sticks in the small boy's waiting arms. "Take those to the pile and come right back, okay?"

Xavier marches away. "And don't stop to play football. You're on punishment."

"Xavier?" I say, pointing after him.

"Good kid…just has some anger issues. He lost his aunt and uncle in a car accident a few months ago. They were his guardians. His mom's on some stuff, recouping in rehab." I nod. "No one's seen his father in years. I've been working with adoption agencies, trying to find someone to adopt him, you know?"

"Yeah. You're being you." He smirks and pulls his gloves off. I notice that he has a tattoo on the inside of his left forearm. It looks like a three-ridged lightning bolt with the point aimed at his wrist.

"So, what's up? You thought of some new questions you wanted to ask?"

"No, I wanted to talk to you about the…" I look around and lower my voice. "…explosion last night." He frowns and walks toward the school. "You know…the explosion downtown."

"I don't know what you're talking about Nicole."

"Oh, come on, you had to have heard it at least." He shakes his head. "Why would you lie about that?"

"That's a good question," he says as we march across the field.

I catch his arm, stop, and pull him around to me. "So, you're trying to tell me that the top three floors of a building go up…right after you left me…left me, right beside the building…and you didn't hear or see anything?"

He shrugs. "I don't know what to tell you."

"You could tell me that you might stop lying to me at some point." I storm off, marching away from him. He follows close on my heels.

"Lying? What've I lied about?"

I stop and turn to him, crossing my arms. "The explosion is probably the biggest one…but for starters, that whole sob story about growing up being a bully turned do-gooder…"

"…do-gooder…?"

"Yeah…and, uh, the philanthropic parts NOT being about you, and you bought this place…?" I shake my head. "I checked county records. This place was bought by the Andreus Arze Foundation ten years ago."

He fake smiles again and nods. "Oh, so, you got all the facts and I'm a liar now, right?"

"Yeah, pretty much."

His tongue parts his lips quickly, and he marches around me. Ugh, why is it that despite everything that I found out and that I know he's lying about the building explosion, I feel it in my gut that he's not lying about the rest?

"Five," I say, turning to follow him. He's already made it up the back steps...hand resting on one of the backdoor handles. I run up the stairs to meet him. "Just be honest with me...off the record. What happened?"

He pulls the door open and motions for me to go inside. I do with him right behind me. The place still looks like an elementary school on the inside. Vanilla-tinted cinderblock walls, linoleum floors, and the faint hint of Pine-sol takes me right back to the days of learning the alphabet and beginning math.

We reach the second crossway and stop. "So, both girls and boys live here?"

"Yeah, this is the dividing line..." He motions to his right. "...girls on this side..." Back to my right. "...and boys down here." I nod. "Unless you think I'm lying about that, too."

"That's not fair."

"No, what's not fair is you coming to my home and calling me a liar."

"Your...your home? You live here?"

"Yeah, I wanted to give the kids the sense of having a stable home so...I made myself an apartment down on the end."

"I understand that...what I don't understand is why you're holding back. What happened, Five? What are you so afraid to tell me?"

"Five," a deep velvet voice calls from the main entrance. Five groans and rolls his eyes. I turn and...it's those two guys from the picture. The shorter, brighter skinned guy's wearing a gray suit...and the other's wearing a black jacket and t-shirt. What are they doing here? Don't they know children live here? "We need to talk," the taller guy says.

I step back, moving closer to Five. "Five," I whisper. "Those guys..." He moans an affirmative noise. "...those guys were at your key ceremony and...they were there when the building blew up."

"They were?" I look at him. He's genuinely surprised this time.

"Who are they? Are they here to...you know, start trouble?"

He huffs a laugh. "Nah, um..." They stop right in front us.

"Five," the short guy starts, staring at me as if he could take a swing at me...or shoot me. "Who is this...woman?"

"Guys," Five starts. "I'd like you to meet Nicole Clark. She's the journalist writing the article about me for that magazine." He motions to me. "Nicole, I'd like you to meet my younger brothers..." He extends his hand to the taller guy with darker skin. "...this is Ezra..." Then the shorter one. "...and Andre." He leans in closer to whisper in my ear. "Andre's the baby."

I nod. I didn't notice before, but while they don't look much like each other, they both have similar features to Five. He and Ezra both have the broad foreheads and narrower nose bridges. Andre and Five share a skin tone and shape of their faces.

They all have deep brown eyes that seem warm, but something else, too. Five's eyes seem intense and focused. Ezra's seem confident, but somehow sad…as if he's missing someone. Andre's seem bright and always in motion…like the ocean.

All three of them have low cut hair and neatly trimmed goatees. Andre's hair is a few shades lighter than either of his brothers' hair is though.

I realize something and point at Andre. "Andreus…" Then move on to Ezra. "…Arze, as in Ezra backwards, Foundation." They nod.

"Yes," Andre says. "Five named the charity he started after us."

"Yep," Ezra adds, but somehow makes that one syllable sound as smooth as silk.

"So, you guys were downtown last night," Five says.

Andre and Ezra look at each other. "We…" Ezra starts.

"…were having dinner," Andre continues. "We'd taken AZ out to dinner because he'd done well on the SATs."

"Oh," Five says at the same time I think it.

"AZ?" I ask. They tip their heads to the young Latino boy, standing near the front doors. Has he been there this whole time? He wears a gray Bevelle High hoodie and stares out the door windows. He pulls out his phone, smiles, and quickly texts something.

"AZ," Andre calls. The boy looks at us and lowers his hood, revealing low, but not quite buzz cut, chestnut colored hair. He also reveals…is that a tattoo on his neck? A tattoo of a winged sandal?

"He's one of the kids here," Five says of the young Latino walking toward us. "He's a senior in high school. Varsity track athlete…" He runs track. That explains what the tattoo is, still doesn't cover why a high school senior has it. "…pretty smart too," Five continues. "He's got a full ride to go to any state school he wants, but he wants to stay close to home and work here after he graduates."

"Wow." Five nods.

Andre motions for AZ to leave. He smirks while turning back to the front door. "Listen, Five," Andre says, as if even he can't believe that's his brother's name. "We think we have a lead on…" His eyes dart to me. "…him…Ezra and I are going to hop a flight to New York and check it out."

"Let me know what you find out." Ezra and Andre nod at the same time and then, like it's a choreographed act, they both look at me. I nod. Ezra does it back, but Andre just turns and walks away. Ezra follows him.

"That was a little weird," I say. "Do they always talk in code like that?"

"Since we were kids. Andre's always been smart…probably a little too smart for his own good. Ezra's always been cocky…like he's got a secret that no one else knows, you know?"

I nod, turning back to Five, who's wearing a superior smirk on his face. "Don't give me that look. Okay, I used all my connections…trying to find out who was on the board of the Andreus Arze Foundation and couldn't…" I sigh. "…I got suspicious and took a shot. I'm sorry that I jumped to the wrong conclusion."

"Cool."

"Cool? That's it? You forgive me?"

"Forgive you? Nicole, we met yesterday. You don't know me, and I don't know you."

"Right," I say, looking down at the space between us.

"But let's change that."

"How?"

"Let me take you to dinner." I frown. "Arnie's downtown. Tomorrow night."

I swallow a lump. Okay, I don't know whether I should say 'yes,' because he's gorgeous, and I actually do like talking to him or if I should say 'no,' because I'm writing the article on him.

"Nicole?"

"Yes, but…only if I get to ask you a couple more questions for the article."

The corners of his mouth go down, and he nods. "Okay. Seems fair. Maybe give me a chance to prove I'm not a liar." I open my mouth to argue, but he turns me around and ushers me toward the front doors. "I'll see you tomorrow night, 7 o'clock at Arnie's."

"Wait, you don't have a car. Don't you want me to…?"

"I'll meet you there," he says, holding the door open. I nod and step outside. "Brandy?" I look at the girl still sitting on the steps texting away. "You're grounded…you know you're not supposed to have that."

She lifts two of the prettiest toffee-colored eyes I've ever seen with one of the frowniest frowns I've ever seen on top of them. She stands with a huff. "Ms. Pearl said I could have it back," she grumbles, while moving toward the doors.

"Well, Ms. Pearl didn't check with me," Five says as she slams her phone into his hand. She moves in past him, bumping him along the way. He clenches his jaw, shakes his head, and sighs. God, that reminds me of so many exchanges between my dad and me.

He takes a deep breath and comes back to me slightly calmer. "Arnie's at 7," he repeats and waves. I wave back and turn to make my way down the stairs. How exactly did I go from accusing him of possibly being involved in a building exploding to going on a date with him tomorrow night? I look back at the double doors.

"Yeah, Five…you might be a little too charismatic to be real."

****

Chapter 4: Spark

I'm wearing a skirt. Why am I wearing a skirt? And a short one at that. I look down. I hope it's not too short. 'Little black dress gets 'em every time,' Ronda told me when I told her about the conditions for the rest of the interview. Why'd I agree to dinner? Why didn't I negotiate for lunch? Why not coffee? Why is he already twenty minutes late, and I'm still here?

I groan again. Calm down, Nicole. It's not a date. It's an interview…with a gorgeous guy, who I could seriously see myself falling for. I shake my head. Stop it. Serious journalist…but I won't be on this story forever, so…

"Hey," Five says, walking up behind me. "Whoa, you look…" He looks me over again. "…whoa."

"Thanks." I take in his jeans, button-up, and leather jacket. "You…look like you normally do." He looks down at his outfit. "I don't mean that in a bad way, it's just…when you said Arnie's, I thought you wanted it to be a dressy thing. Like an actual date."

"Well, it is…but I always want you to be comfortable." He opens his jacket. "This is me comfortable. If you're not comfortable wearing a dress…" He checks my feet. "…and heels like that, then you don't have to wear them." I frown. I could've dressed casually. Ugh. "Don't sweat it," he says, pulling the door open. He motions for me to go in ahead of him.

I step into the dimly lit Italian restaurant, and he follows. "Good evening," the host says from his stand. "How can I…?" He looks past me at Five. "Ahem, sir, there's a strict dress-code at Arnie's. We have a reputation to uphold. All gentlemen are expected to wear a jacket."

"I am wearing a jacket," Five jokes, tugging on his leather coat.

I frown. "Five, we can go somewhere else if…"

"Why?" he asks, ignoring the host's sneer. "Is Arnie here? If he is, let him know that Five's here."

"Five?" the host says with a groan. "Right, like Arnie would know someone like you."

"Someone like him?" I snarl. "What's that supposed to mean?"

"Don't sweat it," Five says, casually.

I turn to him. "Clearly, that last shot wasn't just a crack at the way you're dressed," I whisper. "We should go somewhere else."

"But I love it here." I frown. He's been here before. Then why doesn't he know about the dress code…? I glare. …or about the jerk host? "It's the closest you can get to Greek food in this city."

"You like Greek food?"

"He loves Greek food," a super happy, older man says coming from the restaurant. His jet-black hair is slicked back with way too much product, and

I can smell his cologne already. His suit's nice though. Looks like Armani and tailored to fit his narrow frame well. He steps into the light, revealing perfect olive skin and large dark brown eyes.

"Arnie," Five growls with a low timber.

"FIVE!" Arnie returns, sounding even happier. They hug with Arnie patting Five's back several times. They separate, and Arnie taps Five's chest with the back of his hand. "Hey, can I get you your usual table?"

"Thanks. That'd be great, Arnie."

Arnie turns and notices the host glaring at Five. "Eh, is there a problem here?" Arnie poses. The host opens his mouth ready to cut loose with excuses.

"Nah, no problem," Five says, before he can. I glower at Five. He smirks and puts his arm around me. "Hey, Arnie…I'd like you to meet, Nicole Clark. Nicole, this is Arnold 'Arnie' Zanbaka."

"Hey, aren't you gorgeous," Arnie says, wrapping an arm around me.

"Thanks," I purr. "Nice to meet you."

"Pleasure's all mine." He takes two menus from the host. "This way please." Arnie shows us to a center table…intimate with a small candle lit at the center.

Five slips my jacket off and then pulls out a chair. He motions for me to sit. I do, and he pushes the chair and me in. How strong is he? It didn't even seem like he put any effort into it. He takes off his own jacket and passes them to Arnie as Arnie passes him the menus.

"This guy," Arnie says, leaning forward. "Forget about it. My nephew was being a pain in the ass to his teachers and my sister…got himself into more than a little trouble… couple of weeks at this guy's Group Home…and he comes back right as rain!" I scoff a laugh. "He's one of the best! Hey, I'll get you guys a glass of champagne, onna house!"

Arnie hurries away.

"I see why you didn't want to go anywhere. You get special treatment here."

"Nah, I really do just like the food here, plus I wanted to know how Anthony was doing. Turns out, 'he's as right as rain,'" he repeats, imitating Arnie's accent.

I laugh. "So, you said I could ask you anything…"

"Already?"

"Yep. Tell me what happened with that office building."

"From what I read in your article, the top three floors exploded… no one was in the building…but the top four floors are damaged, but salvageable thanks to the in-house sprinkler system."

"Thanks for parroting what I already knew because I wrote it." He laughs. "Five, you know what I mean. You heard that weird bird just like I did, except it made you run toward it."

"I went home," he says simply and leans back in his chair, staring at his menu.

I sigh and pick up mine. I thought Arnie's was a strictly Italian place but going over the menu…it's Mediterranean and Italian cuisine.

"Hi," a young blond-haired girl beams in her black apron and tie to match over a white blouse. She places a glass of champagne down next to Five and then one next to me. "I'm Holly, and I'll be your server tonight. Would you like something else to drink? Something from the bar, perhaps? Or would you like to hear our specials?"

"Tea," I say.

"Water…and we'll probably need a minute."

"Alright, I'll bring that right out."

"Thank you, Holly," Five says. Holly walks away.

I stare at the menu. Why is this so hard? Maybe, if he were just honest with me…I wouldn't feel so…awkward and angry.

He sighs and puts his menu down on the table. "I like you." I frown. "I've liked you since the moment I first saw you."

"Well, I barge in on you demanding an interview and…"

"No…that wasn't the first time I saw you." He takes a deep breath. "When I first stepped up to the podium, you were the only person I saw." I frown. "It was like the crowd was in black and white, and you were the only splash of color." He motions to me with both hands. "My eyes focused on you immediately."

I scoff. "I thought it was weird that one of my pics looked like you were looking directly at me."

"Only one?" he asks, leaning over his joined hands. I blush. "I'll make you a deal. I'll be completely honest with you, if you're completely honest with me."

"Okay."

"Now that means, you ask me a question, and I'll keep it 100…and then I'll ask a question, and you do the same. Deal?"

"Deal." He nods and then tips his head toward me. "Okay." I don't just want to jump into it with the building. I mean, he could answer the question without really answering it…but still be telling the truth. He sips his champagne. "Where did you head off to? You seemed like you were in a hurry after we got back to my car."

"I saw something going down, and I went to check it out."

"Something…?"

"My turn." I nod and sip my champagne. "Where'd you go to school?"

"Spelman for undergrad and Georgia State for my master's." He hums approvingly. "What was 'going down'?"

"Bad things." I open my mouth…but that's exactly what I figured he'd do. Answer the question without answering it. He's smart…he uses his disposition, his niceties, and even his slang to disarm people…and then sways them with how insightful he is. He smirks. It's as if he knows I'm trying to figure him out. Maybe, I should've gone direct…but specific. "Did you always want to be a journalist?"

"No. Not always. It was always between being a cop and a journalist."

"That's weird."

"Not really. I like to investigate things, get to the bottom of them. As a police detective or a journalist, I'd get plenty of both." He leans forward, as if I'm the only thing worth paying attention to in the world.

"I finally settled on journalist after researching my dad's side of the family and finding out that the police missed something in their investigation…my grandfather could've gone to jail for the rest of his life. A journalist found the missing piece of evidence and turned it over to the cops. He did a full write-up on it. If he hadn't, my grandfather would've never met my grandmother…gave her my dad…" I look at him. "…I would've never been born."

He sighs. "Hey, have we made up our minds?" Holly asks, placing my tea and Five's water on the table.

"I'll have the tortellini and roasted pork in white wine sauce," Five says.

"That sounds good, make it two…but could I have chicken instead of pork?"

Holly nods. "Alright. Those'll be right out," she says, claiming his menu, then mine.

"Your turn," Five says, leaning back with a relaxed posture.

"You got me talking," I admit. He smiles. "Alright. You said, 'bad things.' Care to elaborate?"

"Boom," he says in a low voice.

I tremble…my back feels tight. He admitted it…wait, did he admit to causing it or just that he went to check on it? "Do you know who…?"

"It's my turn," he cuts me off. I purse my lips and nod. "You mentioned your connection to your family being the reason you chose journalism…" His accent's changed. "…are you…close to them? Your family, I mean."

"My dad's side, yeah. My mom's side…" I shake my head. "…as far as I know there is no 'mom's side.' Probably why I like solving mysteries so much…because that's what she is to me. She got really sick when I was still young and...um..." I swallow a lump and try to do the same with the tears that still well in my eyes every time I think about mom.

"I'm sorry."

"S'okay." I sniff and check my eyes. "I barely remember her voice now." I nod. "My dad raised me alone, put me through school and everything. We went through a few bad patches, but..." I smile. "...now we're close. I talk to him all the time, at least once a day...usually." I laugh. "In fact, I called him before I came to the restaurant."

Five smiles. "Oh, that's good," he says with a nod. His eyes seem as sad as his brother's...Ezra's...

"What about you?" He frowns. "Are you close to your father?"

"No."

For a second, it feels like everything in the restaurant comes to a halt. It's like a scene out of a movie, where everything stops, even all conversation and background noise. The sound of silverware scrapping plates comes back and then light conversation. It's weird. It's as if his one word brought everything to a standstill.

"Here we go," Holly says, placing a plate in front of Five and then another of almost the same in front of me. "Need anything else? Parmesan? Refill on...oh, you haven't drunk much, huh?"

"We're fine," I say. "Thank you, Holly." She nods and walks away.

I unwrap my silverware, and he does the same...only that look hasn't left his face. What did I say? I bow my head and say a quick blessing. I open my eyes, and he's waiting for me to finish. I pick up my fork and collect some of the yielding, but firm tortellini. The chicken medallions are tender, but taste amazing...sweet, but just enough of a tang. The sauce is cheesy, but not overpowering of the other flavors. He has good taste in food...and he likes me, so his taste in women...

He chews his food slowly. That look remains. "Did you want to ask me another question?"

"No," he moans and continues eating. I think I might've lost him for the night.

We finish eating without any more conversation. I don't even want to ask him about the explosion anymore. In fact, I just wish I knew what to say to get that look off his face.

Holly comes back and clears our empty and nearly empty plates. "Will there be anything else?"

"Just the check," Five says.

"Mr. Zanbaka says it's on the house," Holly replies and passes Five a ticket.

"Then here," Five replies, exchanging it for a twenty. "This is for you then."

"Thank you, sir." He stands. "I hope you both have a great night."

"Thanks," Five says. He walks over to me and scoots my chair…and me back. I stand and pick up my clutch. Why is this so painful? I mean, he admitted that he likes me. I like him…interview or not, just a regular date should be going great after admitting that to each other.

We walk to the front, and he gives the coat check girl the ticket Holly gave him. She comes back with our coats, and Five helps me put mine on. He subtly slips a five into her tip jar and then pulls his jacket on as we walk past the host. He turns his nose up at us. I start to say something, but Five ushers me outside before I can.

"Why didn't you…?"

He shakes his head. "The way he treats me says more about his character than mine."

"There you go again."

He fakes a smile. "Well, I'll see you…"

"I'll give you a ride back to the Group Home."

"Nah, it's cool. I prefer walking."

"Then I'll walk with you."

"That doesn't make any…"

"I'll go with you and take a cab back." He stops walking and turns back to me. "Five, I like you, too…interview or not…whatever happened the other night…" I shake my head. "…I don't care."

"Okay…but I'll pay for the cab." I nod. He starts heading east, and I walk with him. He's still quiet, even though he doesn't look sad anymore.

We walk a few blocks in silence. It's cold out. Five slips his jacket off and puts it over my shoulders. "Before you say anything, I'm fine. I don't get cold." I nod and slide my arms down the sleeves. "You alright? The heels and all?"

"Fine. Five…are you?"

"Yeah, I'm good."

"Tell your face." He laughs. We continue walking, moving away from downtown and into the residential area.

"Nicole…"

"You can call me, Nikki…all my friends do."

"Nicole," he says again. I smirk. I'd smack him, but I actually don't mind when people call me by my first name. "Can I ask you something?"

I shrug. "Well, it was your turn."

"You're close to your dad…do you…" He puts his hands in his pockets, and his shoulder hunch. "…do you think he's…like proud of you?"

"Yeah. Don't get me wrong, he wishes I lived closer, but he tells me how proud he is of me all the time." He nods, and that expression returns all at once. Wait, same thing happened when he asked about my family, and I told him about my relationship with dad. Father issues…

"What about you?" He frowns. "It's my turn. How are things with you and your dad?"

"Which one?" he mumbles.

"Huh?"

"We…had our issues. He hated me…from the day I was born…" There it is again. It's as if his sadness…makes the world go quiet. Maybe it's just me. Maybe I feel his sadness in my heart. I take his hand and intertwine our fingers. There's a little bit of a shock…but it doesn't just touch my hand…it feels like it moves up my arm. It feels…

"Help…me…"

"What the hell?" I turn to the boarded-up house to our left. "Five, did you hear…?" He's already moving. Running toward the house, being as self-less as he always is apparently. I follow him up the single step and onto the porch. "How are we…?"

He kicks the door in without any hesitation or for that matter any discernable effort. He runs into the darkened house. "Five," I say, through gritted teeth. I fish my phone out of my clutch and turn on the flashlight, following him into the house.

The first room is a deep, but narrow living room. "Five?" I whisper. I hear something coming from the next room. I hit the light switch, and surprisingly the light comes on…until the bulb blows. "Damn!" I look around again. "Five?"

"Help…me…" that eerie little girl calls again. I shiver…and definitely not from the cold.

I head down the hall. "Five? GEEZ!" He steps out of a room on the left. "Don't do that! Did you find her?"

"I don't think there's a 'her' to find," he whispers. He crosses the hall, heading into the larger room there. I follow…and he throws a hand back to stop me. "Damn…I'm sorry. I should've told you to stay outside."

"What? Why?"

"Help…me…" comes from the other side of him.

"What is it?" I ask, shining my light on…on… "Is that a dog…?" I gasp, when it lumbers into the light. It looks like a big rat…shaved down…but with teeth like a shark…and its paws…they aren't paws at all. They look like hands…human hands with black cat-like claws at the ends…long and sharp.

It opens its mouth. "Help…me…"

"WHAT? I'm sorry…WHAT?"

"I'm sorry, Nicole…I'm so sorry." He looks at me. "Please don't tell anyone anything that you've seen…" He holds up his clenched fist. "…or that you're about to see…" He opens his hand and a spark appears. A tiny spark of electricity flickered across his palm. It does again and again. The electricity builds and flows between his fingers, like the tip of a Taser…casting a horrifying blue light across his face. "…but know that I'll protect you with my life."

****

Chapter 5: Others

I can't believe my eyes…I mean, I'm standing here, watching, and…

"Stay back, Nicole," Five growls. "I got you. It won't get by me."

…Five's using lightning…coming from his hand…to scare off some weird dog-hyena-looking thing with human hands for paws with long, sharp claws…that I swear sounded like a little girl calling for help.

The thing bares its teeth and stalks around him. The long hairs running along the back of its head and neck hang down over its face. Drool drips from its fangs and the tip of its long tongue drapes out of its mouth. It almost seems like the thing is smiling…on the verge of laughing even.

Five holds his hands together, as if he's holding a ball, and that frightening blue electric current moves between them. It sparks up the gaps between his fingers and then across to their opposite. His shirt ruffles as if the current creates its own wind. The smell of fresh ozone wafts over to me, and the crackle becomes louder. It doesn't scare the monster, but it makes me move back.

Five looks at me over his shoulder and smiles. "You said it felt like I was holding something back, well…" Electricity rips up his arm but manages not to burn his shirt. "…here's the real me."

He turns back to the creature, throws his hands out, and lightning flies at the dog thing. It runs right, avoiding it. The wall explodes behind it. The creature darts at us…no, it's coming after me. I stumble…stupid heels…and fall over. Its big sharp teeth glisten in the light from my phone. Five steps in front of me. The thing collides with him, wrapping its hand-paws around his arms. It tackles him. He turns…but it drives him into…no, through the wall behind me.

"Oh my God! Oh my God! Oh my God!" I scramble to my feet and break for the hall.

"Help me!" comes from the doorway in that same eerie little girl's voice. I stop and turn my phone to it…another one of those things peeks its head around the doorframe. Its mouth hangs open with its tongue dangling out. "Help me!" it repeats without moving its mouth.

Its big, beady black eyes search the room quickly. Its man hands smack the floor as it comes closer, slowly at first. It utters a hissing laugh and walks toward me, sharp pink-stained teeth catching the light. It's going to eat me.

"Help me!" I gasp and nearly fall again, because another one comes in behind the first one…or the second one… How many of them are there? Stop counting…and run. Kick these stupid heels off… I do. …and run. Run!

I turn the way I came and get three steps…the first one flies by me with a bolt of electricity propelling it. "GET DOWN!" Five yells, running toward me. I keep running toward him and baseball slide into second, moving between his legs.

Electricity whips around Five, moving out in waves. His arms cross over his chest, making an X, just before he throws them out again. He opens with both hands, frying the new hyena-dog things. They whimper before thudding against the wall. They fall, landing in humps of charred flesh. The smell hits my nose, and I force my dinner back down.

Five swallows a lump and looks around, keeping his hands open and ready to throw more lightning at anything else. He comes back to the first one.

"I think that's all of 'em." He offers me a hand. I push off and then crab walk away. "Nicole," he says, calmly. He renews the offer of his electricity-free hand. He leans forward, staring into my eyes. "I'd never hurt you; you have to believe that…now let me help you up."

I take his hand and let him pull me to my feet, but I can't stop breathing like coach just made me do wind sprints until I was ready to puke. "Are you alright?" He puts his hands on my hips and pats up and down my sides. "Did one of them bite you or anything?"

"No…no," I pant. Can't stop breathing faster. Hyperventilating, but somehow, knowing that you're hyperventilating doesn't help you stop. I guess that's why it's called a panic attack. If you had a choice, it'd be more of a panic decision. I'm rambling…in my own head…I'm rambling. "I'm fine…" I nod. "…I'm fine…I'm fine…" I shiver. "…I'm fine…"

He rubs up and down my arms, before wrapping his around me. "You are…you are. You're fine."

I nod as he gives me some separation. "I'm fine." I look up at him. "What was that thing? Those things? Where did they come from? How did they sound like a little girl? Why did they have human hands? Why…? Why…?" I feel dizzy. Forgot to breathe…or breathed too much…

"Nicole…?" He lets me go. Too bad. My legs feel like jelly. "…Nicole, you look like you're about to…"

"AH!" I spring forward…looking around with my hands up, ready to defend myself. "Wait, where…?" I'm on a bed…a small one. A twin, I think. I'm still wearing Five's jacket, but from my waist down is under a plain white sheet. I smell lots of antiseptic nothing…wait, no…it smells familiar. It smells like Pine-Sol. Vanilla-tinted brick walls…room's too big for one person, but that's how it's set up. I think I'm at…

"Knock, knock," is accompanied by a woman knocking on the open door. She's a black woman…very pretty, caramel colored skin, with long, curly jet-black hair. She smiles and her pretty, big brown eyes feel like warmth. "You're awake. That's good," she says, walking in. She pushes the sleeves up on her deep green cardigan and moves to the bedside. I move away. "I'm not going to hurt you. If we wanted to hurt you, we could've done it while you were asleep..." She bobs her head unevenly. "...or at least, restrained you."

I sigh. That's probably not as comforting as she thinks it is.

She places her blue latex glove covered hand over her heart. "My name is Pearl."

"Pearl? I've heard that name..."

"I'm Five's younger sister." My eyes get wide, and I gasp. "Still not going to hurt you," she says in a calming manner. "In fact, he sent me to check on you." My fists clench the bedsheets. She frowns. "If you're thinking about fighting me, you should know I've been taking Judo lessons since I was 12."

"Kickboxing and Muy Thai since I was 10," I answer.

"You should also know I'm a lot stronger and tougher than I look." She sits down on the edge of the bed. She takes out a small white oblong something. I try to move away again. She catches my wrist and shows me the... flashlight. "I'm just going to check your pupillary response." She holds my left eye open wide and shines the light in it. "Five says you took a couple of spills..." She does the same with my right eye. "...you might've hit your head..." She flashes the light from one to the other. "...okay, still good. I checked while you were asleep, but it never hurts to be sure." She slips the light into her cardigan pocket.

"So," she hums, reaching for my face. She takes me by the neck with her thumbs resting on my cheeks. The rest of her fingers probe the back of my head, where the skull meets the spine. "Five let you in on his big secret."

"Yeah." I look at her, looking at me as her examination continues. "Do...do you have a big secret?"

"We all have big secrets," she says, taking her hands away. She takes my left wrist with her right hand and looks at her watch. "Even you, I'm sure." She watches her watch for a few seconds, before lifting her eyes to me. "You know, for someone who's freaking completely out, your heart rate is astounding, even compared to most people's resting heart rate."

"I do a lot of cardio, too."

The corners of her mouth turn down. "Still got the sense of humor, too. That's good." She stands. "Like I said, my name's Pearl, and I'm Five's sister. I stay here at Olympus, and I'm in charge of the girls' dormitory. We have about eight girls staying here now, not counting me, my sister, Alijiah, or my sister, Ramona."

"Big family..."

She laughs. "Alijiah and Ramona aren't my sisters by blood, but they did set the rule that no boys are allowed on this side of the home and enforce it, in fact." I nod. "AZ's occasionally allowed to come over though."

I open my mouth to respond. "Yeah, AZ's the exception to that rule. He's kind of like our… messenger." She walks toward the door. "Your purse is on the nightstand." I turn to it instantly.

"And for the record…" She pulls her gloves off and stuffs them in the same pocket as the flashlight, pulling it out a second later. "…Five, Ezra, and Andre are my biological brothers…but I consider Alijiah, Ramona, Raymond, and AZ to be my siblings, too." She points the flashlight. "I'm considered a nurturer and healer…goes with the territory of being a doctor…" She sighs. "…but if you or anyone else threatens my family, blood or otherwise…" She snaps the top off the flashlight with an effortless flick of her thumb. "…I'll kill them," she finishes with a smile.

That one hit. It felt like she punched me in the stomach. Can't tell which was scary, the flashlight thing or that she said and did that with a smile.

"Oh, here you are," Pearl says. She motions to the girl from the porch. That surly teenager who ignored me and continued texting on her phone, her phone that Five took away. She frowns, glaring at me. "Brandy, would you please take Nicole over to the cross hallway?"

"Yeah, whatever," Brandy moans. "Come on."

I toss the covers back and grab my clutch. I put my legs over the side and check for my shoes. They're there, standing side by side. I slip my feet into them and stand. I pull my skirt down and follow Brandy down the hall.

"So, your name's Brandy, right?" She moans a positive response. "So, you've lived at this home for how long?" She doesn't respond. I look back to see if Pearl is behind us. She isn't. "So, do you know about Five's…"

"Hey, B," comes from the opposite direction. I look past Brandy. AZ stands in the center of the hallway dividing the girl's side from the boy's.

Brandy giggles and tucks her hair behind her left ear. "Hey, AZ," she says in a much warmer voice. "Sorry, I haven't been texting. Five took my phone again." I shiver. AZ noticed.

"Nah, I know. It's cool. I'll see if I can get him to give it back to you, but babe, you gotta stop cuttin' the fool in class."

"Yeah, well we all can't be stuck up popular girls like Chrissy Nations."

AZ steps forward and wraps an arm around Brandy. "And I told you," he whispers. "I'm not feelin' her like that…I'm only feelin' you like that." Brandy sighs and slides her arms under his. "Love you, girl."

"You better," she whispers. They separate. "Ms. Pearl wants you to take her to Five."

"I got her." Brandy points at him. "Not like that." He laughs, which causes her to laugh, too. They come together for a quick kiss. "Come on, this way." AZ turns to walk away. I follow him down the long hallway.

"You were there that night, weren't you?" I ask. He frowns, glancing over his shoulder. "The night that building exploded…I saw you talking to Ezra and Andre." He smiles a wickedly playful smile and faces front again. I notice the winged sandal tattoo on his neck again. It's incredibly detailed, especially for someone his age…and for one on the side of his neck.

"I know what I saw," Five says from the room at the end of the hall.

"EVEN IF THAT IS TRUE, YOU EXPOSED YOURSELF…ALL OF US!" Andre yells back. "DON'T YOU KNOW HOW DANGEROUS THAT IS?"

"Of course, I do," Five says. "I know better than any of you."

"BUT THAT DIDN'T STOP YOU, DID IT? YOU RISKED ALL OF US…EVERYTHING WE'VE BUILT…ALL OF YOUR AMBITIONS FOR ONE MORTAL…?" AZ looks at me with a concerned expression. "…ONE MORTAL, WHO YOU BARELY EVEN KNOW!"

"Ahem," AZ clears his throat, standing in the doorway. He motions for me to come closer. I step up and find Andre and Five standing across from each other, while Ezra leans against a desk on the opposite wall. "I brought her," AZ says in a humble voice.

I tremble again and try to keep my breathing steady. "Hey," Five says. "How are you?"

"WHAT DO YOU KNOW?" Andre snarls, marching toward me.

"AZ," Five says…and again…all other sound seems to cut out for a second. It feels like I went deaf. AZ steps between Andre and me.

Andre stops and glares at his brother. He motions to himself… "You're challenging me…" …and then me. "…for her…?"

Five steps forward and the lights flicker. "Nicole, please ignore Andre." His voice…it sounds deeper…more authoritative, but at the same time, it's stilted. He's not using slang or his southern drawl. "There you go," he says with a smirk. "Evaluating me…taking in everything I say and do." He steps forward. I step back. "You're safe here. I promise."

He takes another step forward. I extend a hand. "Five…" Deep breath. "…how did you do that…?" Inhale deeply. "…thing with your hands…and the electricity…and…?"

"And you expect her to keep our secret?" Andre asks. Five scowls and crosses his arms.

"Our…?" I gasp…and I can feel it. I'm starting to have another panic attack. Andre lifts his hand, aiming at me. I breathe harder and faster. Five lifts his left index finger, pointing at Andre. The lights flicker again.

"Relax," Andre says. "I'm not going to hurt her. Ezra, get her a chair." I wobble as a chair slides in behind me. I open my mouth to say, 'thank you,' but nothing comes out. Weird…my thoughts…are coming…slower…

"Andre, what are you…?"

"Just giving her a little something," Andre starts, but it sounds distorted. "…to help her rela-"

****

Chapter 6: Poseidon

"Aahh," I sit up…again…ready to fight my way out of…my own bed…? How did I get in my own bed? It's morning already. I pat my arms, still wearing Five's jacket. I guess I should be grateful no one's touching me unnecessarily, and if not for the whole, the guy I'm trying to date throwing electricity thing, I probably would be. Wait, am I still trying to date him? For all I know, he might not even be human.

I fling my legs over the edge of my bed…and my feet land on top of my shoes…again. Okay. Last night was insane, but I can rally. I can…Five throws lightning from his hands…and his younger brother can put me to sleep with his hands. No. That wasn't it. I felt something when he held his hand out to me. It felt like my heart slowed down. It was as if something made it beat slower. It made the blood flow slower…and I fell asleep from lack of oxygen to the brain…like drowning, but without water.

"Impossible," I moan, rubbing my forehead. Yeah, about as impossible as a man who can control lightning with his bare hands. I don't think I'm going to get past that one. I should go see him. He seemed open to an explanation and the fact that he doesn't want to hurt me is evident in my not deadness.

I take my hands away, open my eyes, and spot my keys and clutch on the nightstand. Good news, phone's in my clutch. Bad news, the battery's dead. I must've left the flashlight on. I put it on the charger and then slide out of Five's jacket. Whatever he is, why does he have to smell so damn good? I hurry to the bathroom and hop out of this little dress…with literal hops. I forgot how snug it is at the hips. I shower and blow-dry my hair. With it this short, it takes no time.

I return to the bedroom, thankful for super plush beige carpets. I pick an outfit that includes jeans and boots with a slight heel, in case I have to run. My phone buzzes a few times. I check it while pulling on my socks. Wow, only three texts from dad and a missed call.

I text him back, "Sorry, dad. Heading into work. Trying to save the midnight oil." I snicker at the goofy code he created. If sending it stops him from worrying anytime I respond with just a short text, then I'll do it every time though. The phone buzzes again before I can put it down. "Ok," is his response.

I sit at the edge of my bed to pull on my boots and the phone buzzes again, again, and then again. Someone's calling. Is it Five? Should I answer? Of course, I should. Don't be stupid.

"Hello?"

"Staff meeting in 20 minutes," Ronda says. "Where are you?"

"Ugh, sorry…I forgot."

"Well, I'll forget to pay you if you aren't here in 20 with an update ready on the Key to the City mystery man."

"Right," I moan, as the phone beeps three times. I grab a jacket and transfer the essentials from my clutch to its pockets. I pick up Five's jacket and hurry through my living room. Wish I had time to make coffee, but I guess I'll have to settle for the office swill.

I run downstairs, wondering where he put my car…right in front of the stairs. I never get this space. How did he…? I shake my head and climb in.

I blur through traffic, hoping my phone gets enough juice to at least last through the meeting. I pull up to the tiny office building housing *Georgia Now* on its fifth floor and hop out. I nearly clothesline myself with my seatbelt, but we'll ignore that, because I have exactly five minutes to make the staff meeting.

I hurry up the cracked, gum and cigarette butt-covered sidewalk, making a beeline for the glass double doors. Wait, who's that standing next to the doors in the long navy trench coat? He turns. I nearly swallow the gum, I'm not chewing. It's Andre. What's he doing here? Wait, I told Five where I work so he knows where I work which means…?

"Easy," he says, calmly with a hand extended. "I just wanna talk."

I back away and point at him. "Put your hand down!" I snap. He scoffs a laugh but does. He slips both hands into his coat pockets. "What are you doing here, Andre?"

"I could ask you the same thing."

"I work here; your turn."

"I just came to make sure you weren't going to tell anyone anything that you saw or that happened last night. My brother…" He makes a sweeping motion with his left hand. "…for some odd reason, seems to trust you. I can't afford to be that lax in judgment with people I don't know."

"How do you know I haven't told people already?" I swallow a lump and hope he doesn't call my bluff. "I mean, it's a predominately online magazine. I could've sent the article in overnight."

He laughs as if I just told him a joke. "Well, first of all, I've had Alijiah keeping an eye on your site, and Ramona keeping a watch on you. Nothing new was posted overnight…and you only just woke up thirty-five minutes ago."

"You were spying on me?"

"Checking up on you," he corrects. "Look…when my brother saved your life, he opened up a secret that's very dangerous for you to know. I just want to make sure that it's going to remain a secret."

"I could go in right now and…"

"Do what?" he asks without humor, but not in a concerned way either. "Tell your editor a fantastic story with no evidence…not even pictures?"

I swallow a lump. "There's the house with those weird creatures in it…and…and those burn marks Five left all over the walls. I could call the cops and have them investigate…"

"It's the damnedest thing. There was a fire last night…" My jaw drops. "…and an abandoned house burned down…with NOTHING in it. Luckily, the owner had it insured for triple its worth, so…"

Bluff, you officially have been called. "You guys are good at covering your tracks."

"We have to be. Your boss would think you're crazy. At the very least, she'd send you home for a few days. At most, she'll fire you."

"What did you do to me last night?"

"You were panicking. I helped you calm down."

"You drugged me?"

"Nothing that wasn't already in your system," he says with a calming hand moving forward. How can that be though? He did something to me. "Nicole Clark," he says forcefully, while stepping forward. "I need to know if you're going to say anything."

"You've already proven why I can't. Now, I'm going to be late for work." I try to step around him, and he catches my left wrist with his left hand.

He pulls me back around to face him. "I need to hear the words."

"Let go of me."

He draws my arm in closer to his chest…and I notice the tattoo on the back of his hand. It looks like the head of a fork, but with only three points…and what looks like triangles at the tips. "Say the words."

"I'll scream for help if you don't let go of me…right now," I say between gritted teeth.

He sighs but lets me go. I back away from him, heading toward the doors. He runs his left hand over his mouth and turns away. He storms off taking his phone out.

I hurry inside. I wonder whom he was calling. Five, maybe? The women he mentioned, Ramona and Alijiah. Wait, their sister Pearl mentioned them too. She says they live in the Group Home with her and Five.

Can't think about that now. I hurry across the lobby, showing security my ID badge. A quick (not really), musty (really, really) elevator ride up, and I'm at *Georgia Now*. I run past the cubicle farm heading toward the all glass meeting room, which looks like something right out of a television series, but Ronda doesn't see it.

"Nice of you to join us," Ronda says, as I slide into the last open chair, next to Steven. Great, Ronda's wearing her green wrap dress. That's her 'I had a bad date last night and need to feel good about myself' dress. She flips her shoulder length black hair that she clearly spent extra time on as well and smirks. "But you are just in time to give us an update on this mystery man…" She makes air quotes. "… 'Five.'"

"Um, well…" I seriously ponder, telling her everything that happened since I met Five…the explosion, the weird jackal attack, the lightning, and Andre. Staring down the table, all eyes on me, I realize that Andre was right. If I say anything, they'll have me locked up or at least, medicated and fired.

I nod. "…I have a lot of good information about him and some of his backstory, but I don't think it's enough to really give the readers a full picture of him. I should have it all in another day or two."

Ronda purses her lips and nods. Weird, I thought for sure she'd want to ream me out. I mean, this was supposed to be Steven's story, but Five picked me to interview him.

"As long as it's ready by print on Friday," Ronda says and scribbles a note on her legal pad. I nod. She lifts her eyes again. "Yes, Steven?"

Steven lowers his hand from its chest high position. "Look, I mean, I'm not one to harp, but this was my story…and if it were me, you'd already have it ready for a read through." Ronda frowns. Steven turns to me. "I mean, the way the guy was making moony eyes at you…did he answer your questions or just ask you out on a date?"

Ronda leans forward. "Steven, are you suggesting that Nicole…?"

"Ronda," I say calmly, while fighting the urge to punch Steven in his stupid nose. "What I have so far…" I start counting off on my fingers. "…Five has three younger siblings. In order of birth, he has a sister named Pearl, who is a doctor. He has a brother named Ezra, occupation unknown and a brother named Andre, whose occupation is also unknown, but he has the disposition of a boss or a money guy.

"Five runs the Mt. Olympus Group Home for troubled and abandoned children and teens with his sister Pearl and two other women, Ramona and Alijiah, who they consider family. All four of them live there, also. The women watch over the girls, and Five and his brothers watch over the boys, one of whom is a varsity athlete with a guaranteed full ride to the state school of his choice.

"The kids there are from diverse backgrounds and situations, but each one of them is expected to contribute to the facility's upkeep and cleaning through chores. Also, of course, regular school attendance is required as a part of their probation, and Five insists that each maintains a minimum 2.7 grade point average." I tap my pen on the table and glare at Steven, before going back to Ronda.

Her mouth comes down to a little asterisk, and then she makes the 'I'm impressed' face. I've only seen her make that face at Steven once…the other staff writers, three-four times max, but never at me.

"That's more than even the Mayor's office had in their press release about him," Ronda says. "…and they gave the guy a Key to the City." She nods and makes another note on her legal pad. "Keep at it. Get it to me in time for the print edition, but other than that, take all the time you need." I nod.

Ronda moves on to the next staff writer. I'm already a million miles away. Why didn't I say anything? Why didn't I say anything? I mean, at the very least, I could've said something weird was going on. There was something in the way he talked to me though. Something in the way that he talked to his brothers and AZ. It was as if he turned on an entirely different personality like a light switch.

"If no one has anything else," Ronda says, leaning back in her chair. "Alright. Get to it." She stands. "Good job, Nicole. You're probably the only person in this office who hates mysteries more than I do." I nod. "Go get to the bottom of this one."

"Right," I say, leaving the conference room. I head straight for my desk thinking about that symbol on the back of Andre's hand. I login and open a browser. "…but why a fork?" I mutter to myself. No, it wasn't a fork. It was a trident. Three tines make a trident, four for a fork. Thank you, *Big Bang Theory* reruns. *"Forks are for eating; tridents are for ruling the seven seas,"* as Sheldon explained. I frown. No way! It couldn't mean…

"Hey," Steven says, sitting on the corner of my desk.

"Hey," I say as a complaint without actually looking at him.

"You know, I wasn't trying to bust your chops or anything in there." I glare at him. "I was just trying to make sure you weren't falling for this guy's charms like the mayor did."

"So, that's what you were doing?" I ask and type P-O-S-E-I-D-O-N into the search bar.

"Yeah. You're my girl," he says, slicking his hair back. "I gotta look out for you."

"Or you could be acting like a pissy little snot because you feel like I stole your story." I lean back. "Could that be it?"

He grits his teeth. "Don't blame me when this guy turns out not to be what you expected." He stands and walks away.

"I won't," I mutter absently, leaning closer. "Poseidon (See also Neptune) Greek (Roman) God of the Sea…" I continue scrolling through. "…was believed to be able to control the sea and all manner of water." Blood's mostly made of water. "…was believed to have a short temper, unforgiving, unrelenting personality." That sounds like Andre.

I click on the symbol, and it redirects to a page with 12 symbols and Greek God names underneath. A thunderbolt…like the one Five has tattooed on his arm…for Zeus. A winged sandal…like the one on AZ's neck…for Hermes, messenger of the gods. I lean back. Pearl said that AZ was their messenger.

I lean forward again. Wait, did Zeus have two brothers? Yes, Poseidon and Hades…Andre and Ezra…Demeter and Hera…were his sisters…wait, Demeter was the Goddess of Grain, Agriculture and The Harvest, Growth, and Nourishment…that sounds like Pearl.

I log off. This is insane. It can't be true, but I saw it. I saw it with my own eyes. Five generated electricity…lightning…with his bare hands like Zeus hurling thunderbolts. I look back. I thought someone was… I sigh. Andre made me paranoid. Five…I have to ask him…but how do you ask someone if he's a Greek God?

****

Chapter 7: Gods

I can't believe I'm doing this. I knock on the front door. No one answers. I notice a doorbell painted the same black as the doorframe and push it. There's a buzz. The door opens shortly after. I recognize the little guy sticking his head out.

"Hey, Xavier, right?" He nods. "Do you remember me?" He nods again. "Is…Five here?" He shakes his head. "Oh. What about his brother?" He nods and motions for me to come in.

I follow him straight through the building, past the two hallways along the dividing line, to the doors on the backside. We reach the doors, and he points to them. "Out there?" He nods. "Aren't you coming?" He shakes his head and then makes a wiping motion. "You have to clean something?" He nods and runs off. Funny, Five made it seem like he has to stay on Xavier's case to get him to do his chores.

I push the doors open and find a bunch of boys lining up to play football or continue playing a game. AZ and Ezra stand on the sideline watching them. Not the brother I was hoping for, but then again, I didn't say which brother. I head down the stairs, moving toward the field. To the left, that older girl, Brandy, sits on the grass, watching a woman wearing a hood teaching the girls archery…while aiming at three targets…arrows at different locations around the bullseyes.

I approach Ezra and AZ, which seems to get the attention of the hooded woman. Wait, that's not a hood. It's a deep blue hijab, matching her long sleeve shirt perfectly. The front of her jet-black hair peeks out at the front.

"What are you doing here?" Ezra moans, drawing my attention to him.

I almost stumble but get it together. "I'm looking for Five. Is he here?"

"No," Ezra returns simply. He makes a shooing motion. "You can go now."

"Do you know where he is?"

"Wow," AZ moans with a whimsical expression. "She's persistent." He tugs at his hoodie, exposing the winged sandal tattoo on his neck again. His large brown eyes search my face. He leans over and whispers to Ezra, causing him to laugh.

"Do you know where he is or not?"

"His exact location right this second? No." Ezra crosses his arms. "Do I know where he went? Of course, but I'm not telling you." Ezra turns back to the boys, who left him behind on their march down field. "All I will say is that he's off with Andre trying to convince a friend to come home." He glares at me. "I'm sure he'll give you a call or something when he comes back."

"Not good enough."

He turns back to the game. "Too bad. Now, I suggest you leave before you irk me even more than you already have."

"I'd do it," AZ warns. "But that's just me."

I've had enough of being yanked around. "And by me, do you mean AZ, or do you mean Hermes?" AZ gasps and his entire body seems to vibrate and become blurry for half a second as if everything about him moved really fast.

Ezra looks at him and then glowers at me. "…or Hades?" Ezra's entire body seems to darken as if someone put a tinted window in front of him for a second. It's not just that, the dark circles under his eyes deepened and the shadow at his feet seemed to swell and then retreat.

"What did you say?" Ezra snarls, walking toward me. With every step, his shadow seems to seethe…expanding and contracting.

"I…I…"

He towers over me. "Did you just invoke my true name, mortal?"

"Look, I…" My mouth's as dry as a bone, which is funny because my palms are sweaty. I take a step back, and he watches me the way cats watch mice they're about to eat. "…I didn't…come to start any trouble…okay?" He steps forward, and his shadow seems to stretch out for me.

I turn to run, and AZ's already standing in front of me. I glance back at the spot where he stood just to make sure I'm not crazy. He wears a hard expression, but not nearly as menacing as Ezra's glare. He smiles suddenly and tips his head toward me.

I come back to Ezra, who reaches for me. A javelin lands in the space between his hand and me. I jump back, bumping into AZ. Ezra brings his hand in, clenching his fist. He turns to his right. "STAY OUT OF THIS, ALIJIAH!"

The girl in the hajib approaches, carrying another javelin. "I will stay out of it, if you do not hurt this one," she says, pointing at me. Her perfect peanut skin tone seems to glow, even against the harshness and shadows still coming from Ezra. In fact, I think it's getting worse. It looks like he's wearing a cape made entirely of shadows.

"You should really, back off," she says in a calm voice with focused eyes on Ezra. It looks like she's wearing a dress, but there are blue tights underneath it with comfortable athletic shoes adorning her feet.

Ezra steps closer to her, towering over her now. At least, it's not just me. "Are you challenging me, Alijiah?"

She sighs. "Of course not, Ezra." She motions to me. "But please keep in mind who has laid claim to this mortal and what that means." Ezra's eyes dart to me. He sighs, and the tension seems to leave him all at once. The shadows dissipate too. He looks around as if to verify that no one saw. Satisfied, he crosses his arms and turns his back on us.

"Thank you," Alijiah says. She comes back to me. "Alfredo, please take Nicole to Five's room and make sure she waits for him there."

I open my mouth to complain, but before I can, Ezra turns around again. Shadows creep over his shoulders and down his arms. "Are you insane? What if she...?"

Alijiah waves a phone in Ezra's face. "Here, you can hold on to this for safe keeping." Wait, that's not just any phone. I pat my pockets to be sure. That's my phone. Ezra takes it and slips it into his jacket pocket. I glare at Alijiah, and she points at the home with her javelin.

AZ puts an arm behind my back and ushers me toward the stairs. "Oh, and don't try to leave," Alijiah says. "I mean with AZ here; you won't get very far...and you'd be so lucky that he'd get to you before Ramona tracked you down." I look back over my shoulder. "That would not be pleasant."

I walk up the stairs and AZ opens the door. I slip inside, but not before stealing another glance at Ezra and Alijiah exchanging words. "Are they always like that?" I ask as the door closes behind us.

"Not nearly as much as Pearl and Ezra." He shakes his head. "Sometimes I think Five and Andre are the only ones he gets along with."

"Why?"

"He..." AZ crosses his arms and stares at the floor as we walk.

"When I first saw Ezra...up close...I thought he looked..." I shrug. "...I don't know. Sad?"

"That describes him alright."

We reach Five's door, and I turn to him. "So, be honest with me, Hermes." His face blurs and then his entire body...like everything on him just shook fast again.

He grits his teeth. "A...Z...," he growls.

"Sorry, AZ. So, are you guys really...you know...?"

"You know, I'm not gonna answer any of your questions without Five's okay, right?"

"Because he's the boss, right?"

"You got it."

"He's Zeus." He presses his lips into a line. "Right, right...not going to answer that." I nod. "Just one more question. Does Brandy know?"

His jaw clenches, and so do his fists.

"No, no...I didn't mean it as a threat. It's just; I saw how close you two are and..." I sigh. "I'm not saying, 'answer my questions or I'll tell her.' I just wanna know, so that I know who I can talk about this stuff around...if I'm gonna be around."

He swallows a lump. "She doesn't...in fact; none of the other kids here know anything."

"I won't say anything to her, I promise."

He nods. "I didn't get it, at first. Five's only known you a couple of days, and he likes you...like REALLY likes you." He smiles. "I see it now," he says, turning away. I smile and turn toward the interior of the room.

"Oh." I come back to AZ's head peaking around the doorframe. "...and Alijiah wasn't kidding about Ramona. If you try to escape, she will hunt you down, and it won't be pretty."

"I'll keep that in mind."

"Good. I'm gonna go and bring Five back ASAP, so...just sit tight." I nod. He vanishes...actually, vanishes.

"He's fast," I breathe. Okay. Cheek puffing sigh. Hold it together. No more hyperventilating until you pass out. Five is Zeus. When he gets here, I'll get him to explain...how he and the other Greek Gods are alive and well in Bevelle. Yes, because this all makes perfect sense.

I go over to Five's desk and sit in his little black swivel chair. I'm going to sit tight; I mean that's what they want me to do.

His room's so plain. It's clearly the biggest one I've seen, but that's the only thing it has going for it. Well, that and a dining room table with eight chairs around it. He also has a refrigerator and his own sink, dishwasher, and private bathroom. I lean to the right to get a better look. Surely, they wouldn't mind if I checked his room...just not leave it.

I stand and go over to the bathroom. I hit the light and...it's a perfectly normal, boring bathroom. Tub with a showerhead and shower curtain, toilet, sink...small closet...mirror with medicine cabinet...all white. I open the cabinet: pomade, toothbrush, toothpaste, floss, mouthwash, brush, Visine, and Tylenol. Completely normal, especially for a guy who deals with kids of varying ages all day. I'm looking at you, Tylenol. I close it and go back to his room.

The walls are all bare, and they're gray instead of vanilla like the rest of the building. His bed's king-sized at least and not a twin. It's a simple metal frame head and footboard though, painted the same gray as the walls...and floor. He has a couple of area rugs, but that's it. He could seriously use a woman's touch in here. Would I want to be that woman? Could I be? If he's really...?

"So," Five says, standing in the doorway. He looks like he just ran over my bike with my puppy under it. Wait, why have I been the one walking on eggshells? He's the one who kept all of this from me, including potential danger that I could've been in.

"Zeus," I say. His right-hand sparks with electricity. He shakes it off and clenches his hand into a fist. I take a step back.

He sighs but doesn't move forward or back. "Sorry." He shakes his hand again. "It's kind of an automatic reaction. Calling us by our old names is kind of like an accusation. Our bodies react whether we want them to or not."

"Like Ezra and the shadows when I called him, Hades?"

"Yeah, a little bit of the old king of the underworld creeping out of him."

"Or AZ with the blurring thing?"

"Fastest being on the planet. Our old names, spoken by a mortal, invokes our power."

"And by old names, you mean…"

"Yes, Nicole. We are the old gods of Olympus." I swallow a lump and focus on not hyperventilating…again. He reaches into his back pocket and retrieves…

"…my phone." He walks over slowly and offers it. I take it. "Thank you." He nods and backs away. "I get it…you're trying to let me know that you're not going to hurt me."

"I could never intentionally hurt you, Nicole, but I do hope you understand why I kept all this from you."

"Because it's insane?"

He laughs. "That too."

I turn around, grab his swivel chair, pull it out, and sit. I cross my arms and lean back. "Explain it to me then."

"Okay," he breathes. "Even I'm not sure of the specifics…" He walks to his left with his hands out as if he's carrying something. "…but when Zeus…I was at the end of my road…" His eyes go distant. "…I put myself and the other Olympians in a reincarnation loop."

"Reincarnation loop?"

"Yeah, I don't even actually remember how I did it; I just know that it was me."

"Why would you do that?"

"In case we were ever needed again. Say if the Titans came back from their exiles or if something else threatened mankind…we'd awaken in new bodies."

"Like pending war or terrorism?"

He scoffs a laugh. "Nah, mankind's always at the brink with those. This was definitely something else."

It's weird, I look at him, and I don't think god…hearing him use his neighborhood slang, he just sounds like Five. "So…what happened to the guy you're wearing?" He frowns. "I mean, if you reincarnated in that body, something had to happen to him, right? Are you controlling him? Suppressing him? Did he die?"

He laughs again and wipes his mouth. "Fair question. Nah. I'm still me. I'm Five and Zeus."

"How's that possible?"

"Andre once described it like this: Imagine there was a guy who lived to twenty-two years old. One day that guy bumped his head and got amnesia…all his first twenty-two years' worth of memories gone…" He snaps his fingers. "…just like that. Now, he's still as smart as he was and knows all the basics, so he goes on to create a new life for himself, starting from 22. One day, 20 years later, he gets his memories back from the first 22 years. He's still him from the last 20 years…but now he just has the memories of the first 22 years…" He pancakes one hand on the other. "…underneath those." He separates them. He extends both hands out to the sides, showing his palms. He brings them together. "He's the original him, but also the new him."

I nod. "Okay, that sets my mind at ease, a little…"

"Does it?"

"Maybe."

"Does it really?"

"I guess. So, what danger does the world or mankind face that made Zeus…"

"Five."

"…that made you come back?" I frown. "Wait, does it have something to do with that building exploding and those weird dog things with the little girl voices…"

"Crocotta," he says, shoving his hands deep into his pockets. "Yeah, nasty pack of scavenger creatures from ancient Greece. I thought I had all of them exterminated…" He shakes his head. "…but I guess, some of 'em survived."

"You mean, Zeus had them exterminated." There was no reaction that time. Because I didn't direct the name Zeus at him. "Zeus did it, not you." Still no reaction.

He looks at his hands to verify and smiles.

****

Chapter 8: Normal

"So, do you mind if I ask how it happened?" I ask as we round another corner. I thought he was just going to have us doing laps around the block, to get me away from the others. We've toured the entire neighborhood.

"It?"

"How'd you get your…Zeus's memories back?"

"I didn't," he says, hands deep in his pockets. "I've never not known who I was."

"How is that possible? I thought with the whole amnesia thing…?"

"Yeah, that explanation doesn't really track with me. Um…" He holds his hand up in a clawed, explanation way. "…from the day I was born, I knew I was Zeus." I gasp. He laughs without humor. "I know. Imagine being born…and knowing what you are…but because you're a baby, you have no way to tell people what you know, who you are, or anything."

"I'll bet that was frustrating."

He laughs, really laughs this time. "You have no idea," he says through his chuckles. I laugh. "My moms always did wonder how I was a faster learner than she heard most babies were.

"But, for the most part, I grew up like a normal kid. I tried to focus on that…growing up normal, hiding the part of me that was Zeus for as long as I could.

"After a while though, it didn't exactly feel like I was hiding it. Never had to think about that part of myself, so it faded into the background. I didn't even realize that I was becoming more and more Five and less and less Zeus." He sucks his teeth. "That one struck home when I was about 8 years old, and I saw this kid…scrawny, little guy getting picked on by six other kids. I wanted to do something, but I knew if I jumped in there was a chance that…well, you know…

"…but they started wailing on the kid, I mean, really just beating the crap out of him." He shrugs. "I don't know. I couldn't stand it. Next thing I know, I'm tossing kids off him like they're rag dolls, not as hard as I could, but still pretty hard." His lips press into a line. "Hard enough to break one kid's arm."

"Oh. Did anybody suspect…?"

"Nah, I mean, even my case worker just thought it was adrenaline or something, and I was a little bigger than they were, too. After a couple of days with the school counselor, the kid's parents, and the kid they were picking on's parents…no charges were filed, thankfully."

"Try to sound happier about that."

"It still eats me up, because I could've really hurt those kids."

"In case you missed it, they were hurting a kid..." He sighs. I grab his arm and pull him around to face me. I take either side of his face and make him look me in the eye. "...and on top of that, you were a little kid yourself. Yes, you might've had the memories of a...Zeus..." He smiles. "...but you were still a little boy." I give him a shake. "Okay?"

"Okay," he breathes, slipping his hands on top of mine. He takes another deep breath and stares into my eyes. "Thanks for that."

"Ahem...um..." I let him go. "No problem." I turn back the way we were walking and continue. "So, you said you stopped thinking like Zeus."

"Right. I'd stopped thinking like an Olympian. I started thinking like a kid...a kid who wanted to help a classmate on the playground. A god of Olympus wouldn't've given a thought to helping that kid. They fix big issues here and there maybe...but never micromanaged."

"You sound a little ashamed of that."

"I'm only ashamed that I couldn't see how different it was down here...for mortals..." He grits his teeth and releases a little groan. "...for humans...for people. From up there, it was easy to look down on people as if they were ants. Everything looked so small. Down here..." He nods and looks at me. "...you start getting a clearer picture of what's important." I smile and blush...a lot. I look away. "Like friends, family...protecting neighborhoods. Things like that."

"Family...?"

His face scrunches up just before he laughs. "Yeah."

"Yeah," I repeat with the same lighthearted tone. "I kind of get the feeling that your brothers and sister would do anything to protect you."

"They don't exactly agree with my new world view, but they don't mind going along...'cause they know I mean well."

I bob my head. "Ezra and Andre...have they always known what...? ...no, who they were? Did Pearl?"

"Pearl's always known. It was kind of like this secret between the two of us. Definitely, made growing up a lot less lonely.

"Ezra didn't awaken..." He turns to my slightly confused face. "...he didn't realize who he was until he was 13. With him being the God of the Underworld, it meant that communing with spirits was common. Honestly, a part of his mind probably shut all that off so that he wouldn't go crazy growing up."

"So, how did he...awaken?" He hedges. "If it's too personal, or you don't think he'd want me to..."

"No. It's just...we were walking home from school, and this cat was run over by a car, or at least, that's how it looked to me." He motions down to his feet. "I turned back to Ez, and he was looking down. I asked him what he was looking at and he said, 'the funny cat that that car almost hit.'" Five nods. "The cat's spirit kept going. It came over to Ezra and…when it touched him…" He opens his hand like an explosion. "…poof…instantly sent to the hereafter. It wasn't 'til he looked up and saw that cat still under the car's tire that he realized it."

"So, he really is Hades?" He frowns. "The mark on your arm, AZ's neck, and on the back of Andre's hand are how I guessed who you guys were. I REALLY guessed with Ezra."

His eyebrows arch and fall. "Ez didn't talk for almost three weeks after the cat thing, but there it was…he was Hades all over again."

"You knew?"

He shakes his head. "I can't tell for sure until someone awakens." He pushes out from himself. "I couldn't tell with Ezra if he was or not. With Pearl, I knew instantly."

"Andre?"

"Andre's literally always been too smart for his own good. I couldn't tell. I mean, sometimes I would get the impression that he was like me and Pearl, but others…" He makes a chopping motion, dividing his face in half. I love how expressively he is talking about his siblings. God or human, he loves them…really and truly loves them. "…he was shrewd. I mean, I'm still not 100 percent sure, but I think he knew the whole time.

"Eventually, he did tell me and Pearl that he knew…but only after he realized we knew who we were. He was ten when he told us and even told us why."

"Why? Was he as concerned about pretending to be normal as you and Pearl?"

"I doubt it. Even after he told us most of his reasoning…most of which, I didn't understand…I still never got the impression he worried about the mortals around us."

"Not like you, huh?"

"What do you mean?"

"You were worried about hurting those kids when you were a kid…did you ever get a handle on that? Are you able to fight 'mortals' without hurting them? And just how strong are you anyway?"

"Yeah, I did and very." I lean forward, staring at him, arms behind my back in full-on flirt mode. He laughs. "I haven't laughed this much in a long time," he says, sweeping a hand over his hair. I make a face, tongue hanging out of my mouth, and eyes crossing as he looks back at me. He laughs harder.

"Yeah," he admits still giggling. "It took a lot of work, but I got a handle on the physical strength, thanks to Pearl and Andre." He taps the center of his forehead. "They helped me put a mental block in here so that I can't access my full power."

"What if you need it?"

His eyes narrow. "I'd rather die than have to use it," he whispers.

"Whoa, don't you sound scary?"

He laughs again. "And don't you forget it." He smiles. Nice to know, I'm not the only one flirting at least. "As for the question…about how strong I am…"

"Yeah, because seriously, those hyena dog things…"

"Crocotta."

"Croquettas?"

He laughs. "Crocotta, nowadays people would call them a jackal mutation."

"I'll say. Whatever they're called, they were about the size of a lion or something. I know lions can weigh like 7 or 8 hundred pounds easy…and one of them tackled you and you're alright."

"I'll put it like this…even with the block in place…if I had planted my feet, I could've caught that thing with one hand…or a lion if I needed to."

"If you're that strong, then how'd it take you through a wall?"

"Physics. I can bench press a forklift, but I still weigh 190. It's weight, running into mine…without my muscles…" He pounds his fist into his other hand. "…boom."

"Or you could just be a wimp," I poke, while poking him in his stomach…that could double as a brick wall.

"Yeah, that sounds like me." He hits me with a flirty smile. "So, you're okay with all of this finally? No more hyperventilating?"

I shove him. "Why you bringing up old stuff?"

"Because I need you to be okay with all of this." I frown. We stop walking, and I turn to face him. "What?"

"Why do you 'need *me* to be okay with all of this?'"

He sighs. "Because, I wasn't lying when I said I like you, Nicole." My eyes probably look like two saucers, and my mouth is just hanging open. "I really do, and I want you in my life. If you're uncomfortable with this…any of it…I'll understand if you want to back away…from…" I shake my head. "…what?"

"You…barely know me."

"I want to know you." He caresses my cheek. "I want to know every part of your life that you care to share with me," he says in that stilted dialect and with a booming echo behind his voice. It sounds less like he was making a statement and more like levying an edict.

"Is this how you normally talk to girls?"

"No. You're the first person I've ever talked to like this." He reaches for and grabs my hands. "Is that alright?"

"Yeah." I nod. "…and I want to know every part of your life that you want to share with me, too."

"Okay."

"Liiiiiiiiiiiiiiiiiiiiike," I stretch out making it longer than one syllable. "Why…this?" His head tweaks. "Not that…" I hold our hands up. "…this isn't…hot." He smirks. I blush, because yeah, I just told the guy I like that I think he's hot. "Why is a Greek God, reincarnated as an African American man?"

He cups his chin. He starts walking again; I walk with him. "Honestly, I thought about that. I mean, I…Zeus had a choice of which body…Ez, Pearl, and Andre just came along for the ride." He nods. "He could've chosen anyone…any form…any sex…so, why this one?"

"What'd you come up with?"

"He knew it would affect him. No matter what situation he grew up in, he knew it'd affect the person he'd become. Looking down on mortals from Mt. Olympus, everything looked so small, so petty…their problems seemed hardly worth his notice. Down here, every problem seems bigger…more important. Up there, a thousand soldiers die in a battle and to him, it looked like pieces moving on a chessboard. Down here, even the death of one little old lady…" He taps his heart. "…you feel it. You know?"

"I know."

"And why black in America?" he continues. "…he needed a humbling experience."

"I like that."

"That Zeus needed to be humbled?"

"No, I like that…you recognize that you're not him anymore. You've been talking about him in the third person for a while now."

He frowns as if he didn't even realize it and honestly, I don't think he did.

"You were saying, humbling experience."

"Right," he says with a nod. "Think about it. If I'd been born in an affluent situation, it's a lot less likely that I would've gotten the perspective on the world that I did. I don't think I would've gotten this clear a vision on what needs to be done to try and fix it either." He takes a deep breath.

"And of course, there are places and people around the world that suffer more than a black man in America, but…" He nods. "…I get the feeling any of those places would've just made me harder…a harsher judge of humanity."

"I'm glad you chose here and this form…this normal life." I reach down and slip my fingers between his. I lean my head against his arm. "I'm glad that you chose to make the world a better place…" I smile. "…one bad neighborhood at a time." Not to mention, I'm glad he chose here, now, and this body for all the completely selfish reasons running through my head, but that's normal, right? Like telling someone, I'm so glad I found you.

****

Chapter 9: Stop

"So, should we turn back?" I ask, looking around the neighborhood that looks completely different in the fading daylight.

He nods. "Yeah, I just wanted to show you the new Community Center anyway."

"It was amazing…and the Andreus Arze Foundation funded it?"

"More or less. We managed to raise about a third of the funds and the rest came from the community, a couple of private donors, and a grant covered the rest."

"Letting the people do it for themselves." He points at me. "Nice." We continue walking and something that's been on my mind since he told me who he is…was comes up again. "Five, can I…ask you something?"

He frowns and purses his lips. "Wait, what have we been doing so far?"

"Oh, I see what the problem is. You think you're funny and because you were Zeus in a past life, no one's ever told you different."

He laughs. "You had a question, smart ass?"

"Yeah," I sigh, hoping that my voice comes down enough to indicate the change in tone for the conversation. He nods, and his face matches my voice. Good. "Your parents…"

"Cronus and Rhea…?"

"No. Your…human parents…your biological mother and father…" His eyes narrow. "…you know, the people who definitely didn't name you, 'Five.'"

"Them," he says, but his voice has weight behind it. It's not the same weight that seems to mute other sounds, but it's close. The rest of the world grows quieter as if it wants to hear his answer too. "My mom was a schoolteacher…her name was Reba…I thought it a little funny, Reba…Rhea." He shakes his head. "She used to teach at Fifth Street Elementary, before it closed down."

"What grade did she teach?"

"Kindergarten and then 3rd. The schools' superintendent said her talents were being 'wasted on finger painting and nap time,'" he says with a whimsical smile. "She didn't see it that way, but still…" I lean into the warmth he emits telling this story. He loves his mother so much.

He scoffs a laugh. "What?"

He shoves his hands deep into his pockets and hunches his shoulders. "She…she came home really excited when that happened. I was 4…and she'd just sent the babysitter home…and she couldn't wait to tell my dad, so she told me and Pearl." His eyes gaze straight ahead, but really, they're looking backward. "She didn't think we understood, but we did. I remember…" He takes his right hand out of his pocket and sweeps it outward. "...every word she said."

He flashes a huge smile, and his eyes fill with tears. "'You won't believe it,'" he says in a higher voice. "'The superintendent of schools came by today and gave me an award for my years of service and he personally said that he wanted me to teach the 3rd grade instead of kindergarten. What do you think of that?'"

He shakes his head. "Pearl and me, we clapped our hands and said 'yay!' She probably thought it was because we were matching her excitement...but we were proud of her. We were so proud," he reiterates in a lower voice. "Reba Godfrey," he breathes.

"Godfrey? So, that was your last name."

"No," he says simply. "That was her last name...our dad and our mom never married so..." He nods. I scrunch up my face. "What?"

"You know I want to know, right?"

"Yeah. I figured you would've done your research and found out Ez, Andre, or Pearl's last name, since they all still use it."

"Or you could just tell me."

"Where's the fun in that?" he laughs.

I do, too. "Fine. Whatever. So, does your mom still teach or is she retired?"

"Nah, she...uh..." Oh, his voice did that thudding thing, even the few birds around stopped chirping.

"I'm sorry. I didn't know." He waves his hands dismissively with his eyes closed. "May I ask when...?"

"It was about 5 years ago, right before I moved into the Home." He nods. "It was a...um...genetic defect...disorder or something like that. Pearl can explain it better." He motions to himself. "Of course, the four of us are immune because of...you know, but still." I nod. He sniffs and swipes his hand over his mouth quickly. "Oddly enough, it probably hit Andre or Ez worst out of all of us."

"What do you mean?"

He laughs humorlessly. "Andre was the baby, and she treated him like the baby. 'Her baby,' she'd call him right up to the end." I nod. "I think she got an idea of his superiority complex thing and used it to rein him in."

"Did it work?"

"Every time," he laughs. All humor drops away from his face. "But for Ez, it was painful because he was there when she passed...he watched her soul leave her body..." He motions out from himself. "...of course, being Hades, he actually saw her...she saw him for what he really was in that last second, he said, a few months later. Still hugged him though…then…poof she was gone."

I cover my mouth and nose with both hands. Doesn't stop the tears in my eyes though. He wipes a few away himself.

"Ez didn't talk for 3 months after that. He hated being Hades even more after that. He hated it so much that he…" He growls and turns away.

"Five…?"

"I'm alright," he says in that same growly voice. "…it's just…" He comes back. "…I've never really talked to anybody about this stuff. I mean, it's so hard…to balance the life of a mortal and be a god at the same time…and none of us carry that weight around with us like Ez does."

"You wish you could make it stop, don't you?" He frowns and looks away. "Not that you'd give up being you, but…you wish you could stop Ezra from being…him…from being Hades, don't you?"

"All that my brother's ever known, are the pains of this world," he says in that stilted voice. "And the one thing that used to make him forget those pains…is gone now."

"Your mom?"

He huffs a laugh. "Ez would kill me if he knew I was talking about him like this."

"How about your dad? Is he still…?"

He shakes his head. "Nah, pop took off just before Andre was born," he says in his original vernacular. "Honestly, even with my mind the way it was when I was a kid, I doubt I'd even recognize him if I passed him on the street now."

"I'm sorry."

"Don't be. When our mom turned her focus on us, he turned his to every other woman in the world. He eventually drank himself into another woman's bed, and we haven't seen him since."

"Still," I whisper, stepping closer. I tug at his shirt as I step into him more. He puts his arms around me, and I do the same. Why does he have to smell so damn good? And he's so warm. It's like hugging a muscly, teddy bear wrapped in an electric blanket.

"Thank you," he moans into my hair. "It's nice to get some of this stuff off my chest."

I take a step back and try not to stare at his chest, since he mentioned it. "No problem and don't worry. None of this is going public. In fact, I'll probably just kill the whole article about you."

The corners of his mouth turn down. "That's a real nice thought, but I'm pretty sure your boss would fire you in a New York minute if you came back empty handed after spending all this time with me."

"She wouldn't even need that long," I say absently, thinking about the staff writer who was escorted out of the building on my first day…and by escorted, I mean building security threw him out on the sidewalk while he hurled disparaging remarks about the Mexican bitch, who fired him. Never mind the fact that Ronda's clearly from Italian descent.

"Hello, Earth to Nicole."

I shake my head. "Sorry. I was just thinking about how long it'd take me to clear out my desk."

He laughs. "S'okay. Don't pack up your picture frames just yet. I appreciate the thought, but you should follow through on this story. Besides, it's about time it was told."

"Right. Well, not the reincarnated Greek Gods part, but the normal life, human being parts. Schoolteacher mother. Absentee father. That stuff."

"Cool," he says.

"I might even include the part about Andre being the baby," I joke, turning away from him. I start walking away and peer at him over my shoulder. "I mean, it'd be sooooo funny if for no other reason than to see the look on his face."

He catches up to me, chuckling. "Yeah, it'd be funny for the first couple of seconds…after that it'd probably be a lot more monsoon-like."

"What?" I laugh.

"When he gets pissed…just water everywhere…it's crazy."

"So, when he gets pissy…everything gets wet," I poke. He clenches his jaw, and his entire face becomes a little scrunched up mess as he tries not to laugh.

"Get 'em in now," he says with an amused voice. "We're only two blocks away from the home and I guarantee he's there with a million questions to ask you."

"Yeah," I breathe. "He kind of came to visit me at the magazine."

"He did?"

"No big deal," I say, putting, I hope, a calming hand on his chest. "He just wanted to make sure I wouldn't tell anybody about you guys." He nods. "And I'm sure if he has questions, they'll all be along the same line."

"Yeah, I guess, you're ri-"

A car, screeching to a halt beside us, cuts out all other sounds. Five extends his arms protectively and backs me away from it.

All four doors of the old school, yellow Impala open. A guy probably late teens or early twenties climbs out each of those doors. "See," front passenger says. "I told you it was him…"

The back-passenger guy pulls a gun from his belt. He cocks it and points it at Five. "Well, if it ain't Mr. Big Shot, mayor's boy himself."

"Call me paranoid," Five starts. "…but I think y'all got a problem with me." All but the trigger-happy leader laughs. He glares at them, and they stop laughing instantly.

I look back at the hedge, moving down a steep decline behind me. Not the best option for escape, but we could probably lose them long enough to make a break for it.

"My boss said your deal with the cops has made conducting business around here…difficult," the leader snarls.

"Oh, well, you should tell your boss I'm so sorry for trying to clean up the neighborhood and uplift the people." Five nods. "If your boss wants, he could open up a corner store…go legit…not have to hire kids like you."

"Kids?" the four complain almost at once. "I'm a man, bitch," the leader snarls. "Nah, he don't wanna open no damn store. He wants payback, bitch."

"Do you hear that?" the driver says, looking around.

"Shut up," front seat barks.

"Big G Twan wants you to come holla at him, bitch. So, he can thank you personally for ruining his business," the leader barks.

"Oh, Antwan King is your boss?" Five says. "Yeah, I went to high school with him. He was a couple of years ahead of me…plus he got held back a time or two. He had so much potential."

"I swear, I hear a big dog or something," the driver says, continuing to search the area.

"And I said, shut up," front seat moans with a shove.

"You sound like a bitch," leader-guy says. "Just like that little big-headed bitch behind you."

I scoff. "Big headed?"

"I wasn't gonna say," Five says. My jaw drops. "It's not big…it's…just full of wisdom and knowledge…" The three subordinates laugh again. I shove Five in the back.

All laughter stops as a growl rumbles through the group. "Okay, I know, y'all heard that," the driver says. They turn back to their car, and something lumbers out of the shadows on the other side, snarling the entire way. It steps forward into the yellow-orange glow of the streetlight, and it's…

"No way," Five moans. He takes another step back, pushing me with him.

"Is that…?" I start, still trying to verify what my eyes are seeing and make my brain get that they're really seeing it. "…is that a lion?"

"Yes," Five says. "…a very specific lion." The lion steps forward…and it's huge. It's the size of a bear…a big bear. Its paw comes down on the car's hood. The engine grumbles to a stop as the hood dents in on top of it.

"MY CAR!" the driver whines.

"SHOOT IT!" the leader barks.

"No, don't…" Five says, as they pull out their weapons. They open fire. A hail of bullets hit the lion…bullets that bounce off it with metallic ricocheting noises. They stop firing, realizing it has no effect. "…RUN!" Five yells.

"Nah," the leader barks, ejecting the mag and then reloading his gun. "We ain't goin' out like bitches." He points at the lion. "Shoot it again." The lion steps back, removing his paw from the hood. The car groans then wobbles to a balanced position…almost. The front left tire must have popped under its weight. The lion lifts its right paw and swats the car like a giant ball of string, sending it careening toward us.

I hear a crash and some yelling, but…muffled. I open my eyes. "Are you okay?" Five asks, staring into my eyes. I'm on my back, on the sidewalk. He's lying on top of me, protectively, supporting all his weight.

I nod as best I can. He stands and pulls me up with him. I look back and there's a gap in the hedge, but I can still see the overturned car's headlights. On the sidewalk, there's a splatter of blood and two of the guys, the other two might still be under the car. I swallow a lump and come back to the lion staring at us like two little mice.

"Nicole," Five says urgently. I nod, coming back…staring into his eyes. He cups my face, thumbs gently caressing my cheekbones. How can he be so strong, so forceful, and at the same time, so gentle and caring? "Are you with me? You're not going to…"

"I'm fine," I breathe and remarkably, it's true. "What do you need me to do?"

He nods. "I'd say run, but I doubt you would."

"Not unless you're running right beside me."

"Okay. Check on them, while I handle this thing. Call 911 too."

I take out my phone, while inching away from him. "How are you going to handle it?"

He takes a deep breath and draws his fists up toward his face, like a boxer. The streetlights flicker and dim, all at once. "Not sure," he says with that quieting sexy bass in his voice. Bright blue electricity crackles around his fists. "…I'm pretty sure I'll have to come up with a big Hail Mary play to stop it."

****

Chapter 10: Home

I kneel next to one of the guys on the sidewalk. Blood covers his face, so it's hard to tell which one. Judging by his clothes, it's the driver. He groans as I check him over. There's a gash on his forehead, but I think most of the blood there came from the car hitting him. He's also bleeding from his left arm. He's unconscious but breathing steadily. His sidewalk dwelling friend is conscious but writhing in pain, holding his head. I look to the hedge gap made by their yellow Impala. I can only hope that the other two are in as good a condition.

"911 emergency?" comes through my phone.

"Yes, hello…I'm at the corner of…um…"

"3rd Street and Palace," Five yells, placing himself between the circling lion and me.

"Thanks," I moan. "3rd Street and Palace in Bevelle…I just…" Crap, what am I going to say to her? I stand, glancing at the downed shrubs and small trees beyond the sidewalk. I can see the bottom of the Impala, and the headlights still showing through the brush. "…witnessed a car accident…" A little truth in the lie. "…there's an overturned Impala…two guys are on the sidewalk…bleeding…there were two more in the car… not sure where they are."

"Thank you, ma'am. Police and Ambulance are on the way. May I ask your…" I end the call. That's good enough. Just need to make sure help was on the way. I hope Five can handle the bulletproof lion before the police get here. I tear off the bottom half of the driver's shirt, try to make a tourniquet, and tie it tight around his arm.

A bright light and a crackle of electricity draws my attention back to Five and the lion. "Hargh," he bellows as he throws an electric jab at the lion with both fists. It hits, and the lion stumbles back as the sparks travel across its fur. It quickly shakes it off and rises again.

The lion darts forward, releasing a roar that sounds more like a car accident. It pounces. Five rolls out of the way. It leaves a dent in the concrete, where its paws landed…tearing up chunks when it goes to circle Five again.

"What is this thing? It's way too big to be a normal lion…and last I checked lions are tough, but not bulletproof."

"Right," Five says, moving to circle the thing. It looks at me. "HEY!" Five barks and throws a jolt at it that makes it cringe.

"You seemed to know it. You tried to warn them not to shoot it."

"It's the Nemean Lion."

"The who to what now?"

"The Nemean Lion, it was Heracles's first labor...this thing was kidnapping young, virginal girls..." No kidnapping for this girl. "...and the Nemean King wanted it killed..."

He holds his hands together. A steady current of electricity moves between them becoming increasingly intense. The lion plods toward him with its head low. Five throws his hands forward and hits it with a constant stream. He groans, but he seems to be pushing the lion back...or he was, until it planted its paws, burying its claws into the concrete, to hold its ground.

"Wait," I say as he closes one eye. "If I remember anything about Greek mythology, I know Heracles finished his Twelve Labors."

"He did," he groans, going down on one knee, but keeping the electricity flying.

"So, if he killed this thing, how is it here?"

"Not sure."

"But he killed it, right?"

"Nick...do you have a point?"

"Yeah, Sparky...how'd he kill it? Because I'm pretty sure that unlike you, Heracles couldn't control lightning."

Five lowers his hands, and the electricity stops. The Nemean Lion trembles and works to shake off the lightning's effects.

Five pushes himself up to his feet with some effort. "He strangled it," he says. I frown. He looks at me. "Heracles realized that the Nemean Lion's fur is stronger than any armor...even he couldn't pierce it because even the strongest iron shattered against it." He nods. "So, he strangled it with his bare hands."

"How?" I ask. "That thing's huge! There's no way he could've gotten his arms around it."

Five looks up at a telephone pole and then follows it to the next pole. "He improvised." He extends a hand toward each pole's top and throws a quick jolt. He separates a thick black cable from the poles.

The lion throws back its head and roars. "COME GET ME!" Five barks back. The lion charges, and Five runs at him. It jumps as Five does my baseball slide into second underneath.

He hops up and grabs the cable. The lion's on him again already. He darts to the right, letting one cable end drag while pulling the other end with him. He jumps over the lion's head and grabs the other end. He pulls on both ends at the same time and tugs the lion toward him, throwing it off balance. He runs at it, still pulling the cable, until he's able to jump on the lion's back.

He throws one cable end over the other, stands, and pulls as hard as he can on the X he created. The lion bucks and jumps, trying to throw him off. Five throws his head back, tugging harder on the cable. His eyes flash with an intense electric current. Electricity moves through the cable, causing it to spark the ends.

The lion's jumps and struggles lessen. It slows to a walk...before stumbling forward and falling flat on its stomach, tongue draped out. Five releases the cable and staggers down from the lion's back.

I run toward him.

"Stop!" he says, extending his hand.

"What? It's not dead yet?"

"Yeah, it is, but..." He moves to the lion's head. He lifts his right fist and takes a deep breath. His fist sparks with electricity, but it seems weak, diminished compared to what he normally does. He opens his fist, gives it a shake, and does it again. This time it crackles with power like normal.

"Five, what are you...?"

He pulls up on the lion's nose, holding its mouth open, and shoves his fist inside. "Hah," he growls, and the lion's body spasms and then...I turn my head as it explodes...or at least, I think that's what happened. I nearly lose my lunch when I see the proof that that's what happened...a big lump of smoldering flesh right next to me.

"Five?" He breathes like a sprinter and wobbles. "Why'd you do that?"

He looks at me. "What? Did you want the police to show up and find a giant lion with impenetrable fur, lying in the middle of the road?"

"Fair enough." He nods and walks over to a telephone pole. He kicks it, breaking it at about waist height. "What are you doing now?"

"You told 911 that it was an accident, right?" He walks toward me and wobbles again. "I'm making it look more like an..." He staggers forward. "...acci..." He falls, and I run up just in time to catch him. Mistake. He's heavy...too heavy. He gets his legs under him, just enough to stop us both from falling.

"Sorry," he moans, sounding exhausted. "That took a lot outta me..." He sighs. "...need to get back to the home...can't let...police...find me..." His eyes drift closed. "...too many... questions..."

I drape his arm over my shoulder. "Come on. My car is at the end of the block..." He looks at me. I take as much of his weight as I can and start walking...stumbling...nearly falling over.

"Why's...your car...?"

"I didn't know what to expect," I admit. "I thought for sure you guys might try to cover the whole thing up...I wanted to at least, give myself a chance to run away. I figured leaving my car on the back street would help that."

"Smart," he moans as we turn the corner. Sirens blare back the way we came.

"Come on," I groan. He leans against my car as I open the passenger side door. I lower him in and close it behind him. I take a deep breath. Wow, it feels like I just tried to fry a Nemean Lion. I move around the car as alternating blue and red lights, shine through the trees. I climb in, and he's already asleep, leaning against the door.

My phone buzzes as I start the car. "Hello," I snap, sounding angry, which considering…is better than sounding exhausted…or freaked out…or grossed out.

"Nicole, where are you?" Ronda asks.

"Um, I'm…in my car?"

"Where in your car?"

"I'm about a block away from the Olympus group home, why?" Ugh, why'd I tell her that? If she's following the police's newsfeed, she'll ask me to go back and cover the…

"I need what you have on the Key to the City story."

I look at Five, snoozing against my car door, head resting on the glass. "I…It's not finished…I need to…"

"I know that's why I said I need what you have. The owner is friends with the mayor, and both want a little more information on Five before it goes to print."

I sigh. "Ronda, what I have is on my laptop at home. I don't even have my tablet here to…"

"Go," Five says. I look at him and his half-closed eyes. "…I'll go with you…if you need to go…ho…" His head slumps. He's snoozing again as soon as it settles against the window. For half a second, I think about ignoring him, then I remember I don't want to face down Andre and Pearl with a semi-conscious Five on my arm.

"Okay, Ronda. Just give me ten minutes and I'll email you what I have."

"Thanks, you're saving my bacon this time." She ends the call, and I pull away quickly. I look in the rearview. The police are blocking off that entire section of the street. Good thing I pulled away when I did…don't want to answer questions about the most recent Key to the City recipient covered in blood, asleep in my passenger seat.

I hurry through downtown, occasionally checking on Five, wondering if the guys who just pulled guns on us are alright. Five must be rubbing off on me, because I'm also wondering if the police will figure out what that mess in the road is. Speaking of a mess, Five has Nemean Lion all over his pants and the bottom of his jacket and shirt. Definitely a good idea NOT to take him back to Olympus.

I pull up to my apartment…and of course, the guy with the ridiculously tricked out Jeep has the spot directly in front of the stairs. I pull in four spaces down and wonder how…

"…I'm up," Five growls. I fumble with my seatbelt and climb out. I run around the car just in time for him to open the door. He leans forward and nearly face-plants.

"Whoa," I breathe, kneeling to catch him.

"Sorry," he whispers and gets a grip on the doorframe.

"S'okay. I'm gonna need you to muster your strength to get up the stairs though."

He groans but stands for the most part. We limp up the stairs to my apartment. He leans against the door as I get my key in the lock. The door opens, and he stumbles forward. I breathe a sigh of relief when he lands on my couch, going over the armrest backward. I clench when I realize the blood and other assorted lion bits on his pants may not be dry. Let it go, just be glad you're both alive and safe.

I close the door. No time to worry about that anyway…Ronda was using her urgent voice. Amazing, in a night that includes a carload of guys pulling guns on us and an attack by a mythical creature, I'm more worried about disappointing my boss.

Five moans in his sleep and rolls over onto his side. I guess he's the reason I have a handle on this. I'm a little scared about how quickly I'm acclimating though. It feels weird, but like it fits…like it makes no sense, but perfect sense at the same time. Maybe, I'm compartmentalizing. That only raises the question, in exactly what compartment am I cramming this?

"And send," I say and then close my laptop. I laugh. Dad says mom used to do that when she'd send emails, too. As if how easy it is to email people amazed her.

I should probably get Five a blanket. I head for my bedroom while texting Ronda that the first half of the article is sent. In my bathroom… "Eeeeeeee!" I squeal. …I immediately yank all my underwear down from the shower rod and hide any and all things that might lead to an embarrassing conversation if Five needs to use it. I sigh and grab the soft, pale blue blanket from the closet's top shelf.

I check the bathroom one last time and then make sure my bedroom's not a complete mess on my way back to the living room…bed isn't made, but I could always tell him, I laid on it for a little while. Well, I'd tell him that if I could find him. I run over to the couch to make sure he didn't fall off. Nope. He left. Jerk. At least, he didn't stain my couch with lion's blood.

"Is that for me?"

"GEEZ!" I jump and then turn to him. "Don't do that!" He laughs. "Have I mentioned that you're not funny?"

"You might've said something about it."

"Well, remember it." He nods. I hold the blanket between us, wrapping both arms around it. "Are you alright?"

"Yeah, just needed to recharge my batteries…" He mimics a rim shot and says, "…ba-dum ping."

"Still not funny…" I shift the blanket to my left arm. I punch him in the stomach…which probably hurt my fist more than it hurt him. "…and you scared the hell out of me."

"Ouch, abusive much?"

"Shut up!" I snap and hit him again. "You passed out because of that block in your head, didn't you?"

His tongue sweeps across his lips quickly, and he stares at the floor. "Yeah."

"Why didn't you just break it or make an exception or something? You could've died." He stares at me…and it does funny things to my insides. "Just…don't die, okay?"

He takes my free hand and pulls it up to his mouth. He kisses it, and I feel a tingle move down my arm and across my shoulder. "I promise."

I nod. "You're sure, you're okay?" He nods this time. He's still staring at me, and it's still doing funny things to my insides. Different funny things. "Because if you're not…you can…" I swallow a lump of dry nothing, because my mouth is the Sahara. "…sleep…on…on the…" I motion behind me, tipping my head back, but my eyes dart down to those perfect lips of his. "…the…the…" I tremble as he pulls me closer. "…the couch…and…"

He slips his arm around me. He leans closer, bowing his head. I drop the blanket as his nose nuzzles against mine. "…and…um," I release in a breath from my mouth that won't seem to close.

"…you…could…" I put my arms over his shoulders as my head tips back. Our lips meet for a quick peck. "…you…could…" They come back together for another…and then his mouth opens a little on the third. I reciprocate. His warmth and those electric tingles move through me. He lifts me off the floor and turns so that he pins me against the wall.

Our tongues meet, and we part, just before coming together again. We roll and stumble through my bedroom door. I yank his jacket off and then do the same with mine. He snatches his shirt off and then does the same with mine. We come together again. His skin is on fire… and his tone chest and abs only add to my…eagerness…not to mention those arms. He holds my face and kisses me again as he walks backward toward my bed. I stumble over his boots and kick mine off. I start, undoing his belt as we fall onto the bed. I snatch it off and toss it aside…

****

Chapter 11: Mark

I roll over onto my side, taking my head off the pillow, resting on my left elbow. I take a deep breath and stare at him, staring up at his phone. His jaw clenches, and his eyes narrow. "What are you doing?" I reach for his phone, and he moves it away. "Texting your other girl?" I add, jokingly.

He looks at me as if I just said something crazy. Clearly, he didn't get the joke. "Why would I do that?" he asks sounding upset.

"I...I didn't mean anything-"

"I don't want anybody but you."

"You barely know me."

"Yeah, but here we are in bed together."

I bounce and pull myself up onto my knees. I lean over him. "It's not like we slept together."

"Well, we did sleep," he corrects. "We just didn't have sex."

"And whose fault is that?"

"You don't have condoms in your apartment. Whose fault is that?"

I snicker and give him a shove. "I don't sleep around like that...and whose fault is that?" I faux gasp. "Oh wait, that one's on my dad. Yeah, he taught me pretty early on that boys will say pretty much anything to get into your pants..." I shove him again. "...they'll even tell you they're a reincarnated Greek god."

He laughs and lays his phone on his chest. His left hand moves back behind his head, while the fingertips of his right-hand tickle my thigh. "I can wait for you, Nicole. I feel like I've waited my whole life to meet you."

"You barely know me," I repeat.

"I feel like I've known you forever." My heart thrums. It feels like that buzzing, tingling feeling I get whenever he touches me, just went through it.

I put my hand on his forearm and trace the lines of his muscles...moving across his thunderbolt. "This mark, do you all have one...? I saw AZ's and Andre's but..."

"Yeah, we do." He lifts his arm and looks at it. "Not all of them are as subtle as mine...and very few of them are as obvious as AZ's and Andre's." He shows it to me. "A thunderbolt has always been my symbol...trident for Andre...winged sandal for AZ..." He motions to his mark. "...Alijiah has an owl in the same place as my thunderbolt, except on her left arm...Athena's symbol. Pearl has two crossing bails of wheat..." He motions to just below his right collarbone. "...here."

"Do they appear when you awaken?"

He nods. "Yeah, but like I said, Andre hid his for a while.

"What about Ezra? What's his mark, and where is it?"

"It's his pitchfork with a circle between the prongs, and it's hidden in plain sight." He points to his forehead. "You can only see it when he's angry."

"Do the marks have any significance? You know, besides being your symbol." I run my fingers over his again, and a spark snaps. He laughs. "Not funny," I say before putting my fingers in my mouth.

"They're…a source of power…they're a connection to the truest version of the gods we once were." His tongue moves across his lower lip. He holds his left hand less than an inch away from his mark. It glows, but more than that…lightning travels from his arm to his hand.

"Wow," I breathe, staring at the soft blue glow, brightening my bedroom even more than the morning light. He closes his hand, and the gleam slowly fades from his mark. The light recedes.

"What?" he asks with a bit of a smirk.

"You're amazing," I whisper, staring into his eyes. "I mean, you can do these amazing things, and somehow you're still humble…still so self-sacrificing and just…"

He opens his arms. "Come 'ere." I lie down, and he wraps me up, letting my head rest on his chest.

I thought it was my imagination, but I feel warmth and energy coming from him. Every time we make skin-to-skin contact, there's this buzzing, electric, tingly sensation. It tickles my skin and makes me feel cheery all over. It doesn't hurt that his skin smells amazing, too.

He runs his index and middle fingers up and down my right arm and the same fingers on the opposite hand along my back. I purr like a fat, happy cat. "Can we just stay like this all day?" I lift my head so that I can look at him, looking at me. "I could call in, tell Ronda I'm sick, and you could…" I frown. "…do you even have a job?"

"You mean, besides being Director of the Mt. Olympus Group Home and Founder and Chairman of the Board of Directors for the Andreus Arze Foundation?" I make a face, because I completely forgot about the home not just being his home and his charity.

His phone buzzes. He groans and rolls his eyes as it vibrates again. "I'd love to, Nicole…really, I would, but I have to get back. I wanna check on the kids, make sure they're all okay. I also wanna check the neighborhood; make sure the Nemean Lion didn't do too much damage." His phone buzzes two more times quickly. "Besides," he lifts it and shows me the display. "Andre's already called me eight times since last night."

I nod and sit up. He climbs out of bed, and his boxer briefs hug EVERY inch of him. I blush and try to make myself look away. Yeah, that didn't work.

"Can I use your shower?" I point to the bathroom, straight ahead of him. "Thanks." He goes in and closes the door.

I climb off the bed and hurry over to the door. I knock. "Come in."

My hand is around the knob before I remember that he might be naked on the other side of this door…and if that happens…what will happen…because I know I wanted to last night, but that might've been adrenaline and all the other chemicals in my brain making me think…

"Nicole?"

"Oh, sorry…um…no, that's okay. I just wanted to tell you that since your clothes were covered with lion…stuff…I was going to try and find something for you to wear."

"Oh. I thought…well, I guess it would be too much temptation to ask you to join me in here, right?"

I look down at my skimpy tank and boy shorts and try hard not to think about tossing them and walking in. "Maybe," I say, not sounding like I even convinced myself that I don't want to. "I mean, aside from the whole water saving aspect of a co-ed shower." He laughs. "Um…" I scratch my head, trying to clear away all my imaginings of the boxer-covered parts. "…towels and washcloths are in the little closet behind the door."

"Okay," he says, just before starting the shower.

I go to my bedroom closet and start searching through…the left side. I sigh. Don't even think about it. I find an ash gray V-neck t-shirt that looks big enough to fit him and a pair of jeans. I lay them across the bottom of the bed and dig a pack of unopened boxers and tube socks out of the VERY back of the top left drawer. Don't think about it. Don't think about it. He didn't move out… "You kicked him out," I mutter to myself.

I walk out of my bedroom and go to the kitchen. I grab my remote so that I can watch the morning news, while making a pot of coffee.

"…though the incident was ruled a traffic accident caused by an as-yet unidentified animal…" I stare at the television. "…the contents of the overturned vehicle as well as the weapons found at the scene…weapons that police say had recently been fired…led to the arrest of three of the four passengers, once their injuries were determined to be non-life threatening. The fourth individual is still in critical condition. The police are withholding the men's names, pending further invest-"

I turn off the TV. They're alright. "I saved their lives…okay, so I called 911, but still…they pulled guns on us, and I still called for help after checking on them."

I take down two mugs and start making two cups of coffee. I add lots of cream and sugar to mine and… Crap, I have no idea how Five takes his or if he even drinks coffee. That's probably something you should know about a guy before you let him spend the night. I pour in a little of each for his and stir it.

I carry both cups to the bedroom, turn, and heel-kick the door. It sweeps in just as Five pulls the shirt down over those sick abs, which is okay because Derrick was so much smaller than him that I can still see every well-defined muscle through the shirt. I mean, I knew Five was big, but I didn't realize he was this toned, too.

"Is that for me?"

"Huh?" He tips his head toward me. "Oh, yeah." I offer him the slightly darker coffee. "I didn't know how you like it so, I just kind of took a shot."

"I'm sure it's fine." He takes a sip. "That is an interesting design." I frown. "The cups…"

I look at the little black cups in our hands, not even realizing which ones I grabbed. I examine the black cups with glazed silver glitter, giving them the appearance of a star-filled sky. "My dad gave me these. He said they belonged to my mom before they got married. They were her favorites." I hold my cup up and turn it so that the little 'stars' twinkle one by one.

"Yeah," he breathes. "Very pretty. Especially with that subtle moon in the background."

"Moon?" I examine my cup again…and I see the faint outline of a circle, but I've never noticed it before.

"So, where'd you find these…" He tugs on the t-shirt. "…snug-fitting clothes? …your dad's?"

"Ex." He nods and opens his mouth to ask a follow-up question. "…and no, I don't want to talk about it," I grumble. His face becomes stern, and he nods again.

"I'm gonna go take a shower," I complain. "…and then I'll give you a ride back to the home." Before he can respond, I hand him my half-empty mug and head for the bathroom, slamming the door behind me.

I start the shower and take a deep breath. The room refills with steam, before I finish undressing.

"That wasn't fair," I say as the water sweeps over my forehead and back into my hair. "It's not his fault. He didn't know and more importantly, he's not Derrick."

A knock comes from the door. I peek around the shower curtain… "Come…in…?" …glad that I decided not to go with the transparent one.

Five peeks his head from behind the door. "Hey…um…I can just walk back to the…"

"No, I'll…" I sigh. "…Five, I'll give you a ride back. Let me give you a ride back." He nods and steps back. "Five?" He comes right back. I extend my right arm around the curtain. "Come 'ere."

He frowns but complies and takes my hand.

"Derrick, that's my ex, and I lived together for almost three years. I thought we were going to get married, but it turns out that we were going in two different directions. His led to my former best friend's bed. I found out about the two of them back in April." He holds my hand a little tighter. "I know, you're not him…but still…I have all this stuff of his laying around to constantly remind me of what an idiot I was for those two and a half…" He cups my face and kisses me…all other thoughts leave my head, except maybe pulling this shower curtain further back.

We part, and my eyebrows arch on their own. "Thank you for telling me that." I nod. He gives me another quick peck and sweeps his thumb gently over my lower lip. "I'll be in the living room." I nod again, thoughts of a missing shower curtain still in my head. "Oh, yeah…your phone buzzed like three times in a row…someone's texting you."

"Damn," I moan. "What time is it?"

"Uh," he looks at his phone. "I got nine-fifteen."

"Late." Five ducks out of the bathroom, and I finish showering quickly…pretty sure I didn't actually wash my hair. I get dressed even faster and hurry out into the living room, still shaking out my damp hair. Five's standing by the door, holding my jacket, keys, and my favorite travel mug…something I couldn't seem to get Derrick to do for me for almost three years.

"Thanks," I say, before kissing him on the cheek. He helps me into my jacket, and I take my keys and mug. We reach my car. "Do you mind coming to work with me…for a…"

"You have bills to pay," he replies, opening my door.

"You're too amazing," I tell him, backing out of the space.

"No worries."

We reach the office in ten minutes…and I'm sure at some point, Five will be able to dig his fingernails out of the dash, and he'll find that invisible brake he kept trying to push.

"Do you wanna wait out here or…?"

"I'll come up with you."

I nod. We pass security, thankfully…it's fairly low so I get Five in with a "He's with me." We reach the fifth floor and start moving past the cubicle farm. "Okay, we can head out after staff meeting. My cubicle's the third one on the right," I say, motioning to it. "You can wait for me there."

"Sure," he says. "I'll just wait with the dark-haired woman and the pointy-nosed guy who came into Mack's with you."

"What?" I snap, coming back to him. He points. I stand on tiptoes and sure enough, Ronda and Steven are waiting in my cubicle. "Crap."

"So, that's no good?"

"Hard to say." I start moving toward my cubicle. Five follows. "The dark-haired woman's my boss, Ronda, and Steven's been a pain in the ass since you asked me to take over the story." Five nods but doesn't reply.

"Nicole," Ronda says, pleasantly. Okay, feeling less guarded. "There you are."

"Hi?" I say, trying to muster a smile.

"I was just telling Steven, how much the mayor loved your article so far. In fact, he loved it so much that we went ahead and put the first part online."

My jaw drops. "It-it…wasn't ready yet. I still had stuff that needed to go…"

"And," Ronda cuts me off, stepping out of my cubicle. "Is this the ever elusive Five?"

"Guilty as charged," Five says in that charming way that he says everything. He offers her his hand.

"Sorry," I moan. "Ronda, this is Five. Five, this is my boss and Editor-in-Chief of *Georgia Now*, Ronda George, and you already met, Steven Bender."

"Nice to meet you," he says, shaking Ronda's hand.

"Pleasure's all mine," Ronda says, checking Five over and making me kind of want to knock her around a little bit. "So, what's your real name? I'm sure it'll make the article that much more relatable if we can get your name."

"Five's fine," he replies. "I didn't really do this for notoriety or personal glory."

"So, you weren't just trying to leave your mark?" Ronda asks.

Five shakes his head. "I saw a need…something that was missing from my old neighborhood…from my old life…and I just wanted to fix it, so that no other kids had to grow up the way I did."

Ronda points her glasses at him. "That's good…" She nods. "…can I add that quote to the end of what we've posted online? It'll help explain away the name thing."

"Sure," Five says with a chuckle.

"Okay," she adds, tucking her hair back behind her ear. Is she flirting with Five? Seriously, just knock her around a little bit. "I'll leave you two to finish up the article." Steven groans and walks away.

Ronda steps out of my cubicle and catches my arm as she walks past. She pulls me a few feet away from Five. She stares at him for a moment, before turning to me. One perfectly manicured eyebrow goes up. "I need the rest of the article by noon…the mayor forwarded the governor what you had so far, and they're both going insane over it."

"Okay. I can finish it by then."

"Good." She peers at Five again. "And this may be a little unprofessional, but…" She tugs on my arm. "…yum." She walks away.

"Tell me about it," I whisper, staring at him as she leaves.

****

Chapter 12: Visitors

"Would you mind swinging by that back street?" I frown. "I just wanna see what kind of damage the lion did." I nod and make the turn, moving past the home. At the end of the block, the police blocked the next street, except for local traffic as the sign suggests. "Turn around and park at the curb." Five looks at me with a heartbreaking expression. "Please."

I turn around and park not too far from where we were last night. Five's already out of the car before I can shift into park. I climb out and go to the back, popping the trunk. I open it and pull his leather jacket out. "Five," I say, running to catch up to him. He looks at me. "I know you don't feel the cold, but…" He nods and takes the coat from me. I know he doesn't need me to, but I help him into it.

"Thank you," he says, adjusting the collar.

He ducks under yellow police tape and moves down the sidewalk, the cracked and splintered sidewalk. In the street, you can see skid marks where the car slid before hitting the curb and flipping over. They pulled the car out of the trees lining the sidewalk and the telephone pole's gone. Five checks the neighborhood, noting everything. He puts his hands on his head, releasing a cheek-puffing sigh.

"Five." He looks at me, fingers still intertwined. "This isn't your fault."

"I was here. That's why it came after me."

"How do you know it wasn't after me?" He scoffs and shakes his head. At least, that got him to lower his arms. "Hey. Those guys in the car. They were after you…would you blame you being here on that? Or is it just bad luck? Lion? Thugs? What are the odds that both would find you at the same time?"

"You don't have to make this okay, Nicole."

"Not trying to." I tug on his jacket. "Just trying to make sure you're going to be."

"'Preciate it."

"Five! Five! Five!" a group of kids comes running up through the trees. "Did you see? Did you see?" a little girl says still trying to catch her breath.

"A car flipped over…it smooshed the trees," a little boy says.

"Knocked over the telephone pole too," another boy says.

"I know," Five says, flawlessly switching on his kid-friendly voice. "Apparently, those bad guys were here to do bad things…but they forgot one thing…" He holds a finger up, wrapping the twelve children around it. "…that even deer don't like drug dealers…and that's why one ran out in front of them."

He points that finger at them. "Even the deer are looking out for you guys. You remember that next time you think about doing something bad…" He points two fingers at his eyes then points them at the children. "…even the deer are watching."

"That's not true," a boy whines from the back of the crowd.

"Yes, it is," I say. "Why do you think Santa uses 'rein'-deer?" Gasps fill the crowd.

Five laughs. "Alright, y'all go play…or do your homework if your teacher gave you some."

"It's Friday," the first girl says as the crowd starts filtering back down the hill.

"What does that have to do with anything?" Five asks. "If you got homework, wouldn't it be better to knock it out and not worry about it all weekend long?" She ponders his suggestion, while backing away. "Hey, Tamika…" The girl stops. "…y'all are coming to the book reading at the home Wednesday night, right?"

"Who's reading?" a little boy asks from the top of the hill.

Five laughs. "Not Andre."

"We'll be there," Tamika says and gives a quick wave, before her and the boy disappear down the hill.

I laugh. "I thought it was just me."

He puts an arm over my shoulders and guides me back toward the corner. I look back at the torn-up street. I can't even imagine how strong and tough that lion was and the fact that Five beat him…at a fraction of his actual strength. I shake my head.

We cut across the field, heading toward the home's back door. Alijiah and the surly girl in the green army jacket meet us. What was her name again?

"Brandy? Alijiah?"

Brandy huffs and largely ignores Five. Alijiah holds the door open and ushers the smaller girls by us. She looks at Five. "Hey," she says. "Taking the girls out for a little archery practice. Patience has a competition coming up and…Ramona's out doing…" She shrugs and shakes her head. "…whatever it is that Ramonas do."

"Probably trying to convince her brother to move in," Five suggests.

"Another old dude?" Brandy complains, storming down the stairs.

"Brandy's in a mood. I gotta go," Alijiah says, pulling her sleeves up to her forearms.

"Al," Five says. She stops at the bottom step. "Is everything alright?" She nods. "The boys…?"

"Out with AZ doing some neighborhood cleaning…" She tips her head toward the field. "…so that they wouldn't get into areas that they shouldn't be in." Five frowns. "Don't worry," she whispers. "Even Pearl's not mad…Andre is, of course."

"Of course. Is he here?"

"Nope," she says with a smile. "You two have the place all to yourselves. Bye." She waves.

"Hey, we…" I start, but Alijiah's already halfway across the field. I sigh.

"You okay?"

"Yeah," I say, walking through the door, he's holding.

"I saw your face, looking over the spot of the…" He makes air quotes. "'…accident.'" We move down the hall to his room. "I get it, okay? This is a lot to take in…reincarnated mythical gods…something's almost killed you. Twice." We walk into his room, and he pulls off his jacket. He lays it across the sofa and frowns. He turns so that we face each other. "…if you wanna walk away, I…"

"Stop it. I told you last night, I'm not walking away from this…I…"

"Wouldn't let her walk too far," a man's voice says. "…if I were you."

"No damn way," Five grumbles, staring out his open door.

"Who?"

A man steps out from around the corner. He moves through the dimly lit hallway slowly, purposefully. He steps into the light. A white guy with tan skin, jet-black hair, and steel blue eyes. He walks in with his arms behind his back, draped in a dark trench coat. In fact, he's wearing all black like Johnny Cash, minus the shades. He's hot, but in an obvious chiseled jaw, dimpled chin way.

"Never know what or who might try to kill her next. Hello, Zeus." He stops a few feet away. "No. Wait." He points at Five. "That's not your name anymore, is it?" Five swallows a lump, but his worried expression doesn't change. "How've you liked the presents I've sent you so far Qu…"

"How did you escape, Perses?"

"You know him?"

"Perses, Titan of Destruction."

"At your service," Perses says with a bow.

"I thought the Titans were giants."

"That's just what they wanted people to think." Five's fists clench so tight that his knuckles turn pale.

"Bingo," Perses says with a wink. "And to answer your question, a friend let me out."

"You don't have any friends." Perses smirks. "What do you want, Perses?"

"Oh, be fair. You never answered my question." Five's jaw becomes granite hard, and his eyes narrow. "Did you like the presents I've sent you so far?" He smirks, but Five is seething. "Come on. I resurrected the Nemean Lion. That had to impress you. I mean, I found a living pack of Crocotta, just for you." Perses nods, looking proud of himself. "And the chimera..." He puts his fingertips to his mouth and kisses them with a 'mwah' sound. "...stroke of genius."

"Chimera?"

Five looks at me. "That office building explosion."

I nod. "You sent those things after me?"

"He sent 'em after me."

Perses walks over, and Five's back tenses more. Perses looks at me. "He's right. I sent them after him." He smiles with a big, over exaggerated nod. A thud sounds, and it takes me a second to catch what just happened. Perses punched Five in the face. "BOOM!" he bellows and bounces like an excited boxer pre-fight. He stares at Five, who's still reeling from the hit.

Five stands up straight and wipes a speck of blood from the corner of his mouth. Five's eyes dart to me and so do Perses's. "It's true!" Perses sings. He holds his fist in front of his mouth. "Oh, oh, oh..." He chuckles. "...you really do care about the mortals now."

"What do you mean?"

"This one...the king of kings...THE god of gods...Zeus almighty never cared about mortals before. They were playthings to him...an amusement at best, something to pass judgment on at worst."

Five averts his eyes trying his best not to look at me. "What does that have to do with you hitting him?"

Perses points at me. "I see why you've let her keep you company, Zeus. She is a brave mortal..." He glares at me. "...to speak to a god in such a way."

"Well, god or man, you seem like a normal jackass to me."

Perses scowls and marches toward me. I step back as he reaches for me. Five catches his wrist, and their eyes meet, electricity passing between Five's. "Don't."

Perses snatches his hand away and steps back. "Oh, so there is a line. You won't defend yourself, but you'll defend these..." He looks at me. "...mortals." He puts his hand under his chin as if thinking it over. "Or is it this mortal, in particular?" Five's jaw tenses again. Perses steps back and tips his head to the left. "Do you hear that brother? He cares for this very specific mortal."

Another man appears from around the corner. This one is a black man. He has a low afro and a thick, full beard. His big brown eyes seem sullen, morose even. He shoves his hands into his jean pockets, ruffling the dark gray button up he wears.

"Prometheus?" Five says, sounding even sadder.

"MY BROTHER IN ARMS!" Perses says as if he just revealed 'a brand-new car!'

Fives looks to Perses then comes back to Prometheus. "How…how did you escape?"

"A mortal," Prometheus says in a weathered, but charming voice. "A mortal man was excavating in Greece…he uncovered my catch. Your bird fled," he snarls.

"When?" Five asks.

"Twenty-eight years ago…" Five swallows a lump. "…I have roamed this mudball, observing these…" He points at me. "…perversions of mankind."

"What do you mean?"

He glares at me. "You were never meant to be this. I gave man fire…I gave them counsel…wisdom. I nurtured them, while Zeus and his Olympians mocked man's struggles. And then…he gave them you."

"He gave men, women? What's wrong with that?"

"I didn't create women any more than he created men," Five says. "I nurtured equal wisdom in women at the request of Demeter, Artemis, and Athena."

"Yes and look at the state of the world now."

"I have been looking at it," Five says. "For the same twenty-eight years, you have."

Prometheus snarls and grabs Five by the shirt, slamming him against the wall. "Did you spend millennia before it having your innards pecked out by that devoted eagle of yours?" He shakes him. "Well, did you?" He punches Five in the face and then does it again and again.

"Stop it!" I step forward.

Perses steps in front of me, wagging a finger in my face. "Tsk, tsk, tsk."

Prometheus throws Five to the floor and kicks him in the stomach. He points down at him. "I will teardown everything your hubris has built and then I will return and teardown everything you hold dear." He points at me without looking. "And I'll start with her."

"No, you won't," Andre says behind me. He and Ezra walk in confidently. Ezra glares at Perses, while Andre's focus stays with Prometheus. "Perses…Prometheus, I don't know how either of you got out of your respective cages, but if either of you wishes to continue your existence on this plain, I suggest you withdraw. Now."

"You wouldn't dare," Perses says. "Not so close to Zeus's pet."

"Don't ever think we're as soft as our younger brother," Ezra says. "If not for wanting to keep her alive, we wouldn't have given you this much warning."

Prometheus turns and walks toward me. Andre steps in front of him and puts a hand on his chest. "Are you challenging us, Titan?" There's a creak and then a deep, stuttering groan from the sprinklers overhead. The pipes rattle and vibrate.

Prometheus knocks Andre's hand away. "What if I am?" Andre takes two steps back at the same time Prometheus does.

Andre holds his left hand about waist-high and puts his right hand on top of it. He looks at me. "Nicole, if you value your life…" He comes back to Prometheus. "…try not…to move too much."

I stare at Five. "Wasn't planning to."

Prometheus pulls a long straight sword with a rectangular guard…out of his sleeve. There's no way that thing fit up his sleeve.

Andre pulls a trident…out of the back of his hand…how did he do that…? I mean, it looks like it's made of water, but still. He twirls it around, sending water in every direction and… Whoa! …it definitely doesn't look like water anymore. The head looks like it's made of gold, and the shaft looks like polished steel.

Prometheus extends his empty hand in front him, his fingers spreading wide, and in his other hand, near his head, points his sword's tip at Andre's heart.

Ezra crosses his arms and closes his eyes. "You might wanna take a step or two back though, Nicole…" His head tilts toward me, and his eyes open slowly. "…if you really don't want to die, that is." I swallow a lump and do what he says.

Prometheus darts forward, before I can finish my second step. Andre spins on his heel and twirls his trident before taking a baseball swing. They clash, and the pipes above rattle…and so does the floor.

Andre finishes his swing and pushes Prometheus off, he comes right back though. Andre twirls his trident in a blur of motion and several metal-on-metal clangs sound as Prometheus jabs at him repeatedly.

Andre stabs upward, catching the sword between two trident tines. He flicks his wrist, the trident spins, and the sword flies away. Andre lunges at Prometheus with the three tips forward. Prometheus pulls another sword out of his other sleeve and forces the weapon down. They meet shoulder to shoulder, weapons still scraping against one another with a teeth-chattering, metallic whine. They glare at each other.

"So, being trapped in a human shell hasn't slowed you down, Poseidon."

"The name's Andre…and you're still as weak as always, mortal lover." Prometheus grits his teeth. They separate and collide again and again. I take another step back moving away from the thunder of metal hitting metal. My heel splashes. I look down. Water covers the floor.

Andre pushes Prometheus off again and takes a stance…with his trident head pointed down and out in front of him. He glares with his mouth turned up into a smirk. Prometheus slides to a stop with a slosh of water. He notices the puddle covering the entire floor. He looks up and sees the sprinklers all trickling a few drops at a time.

"Finally noticed that, did you? Huh, peasant?" Andre says. His trident's head glows with a soft green light that looks like seafoam washing over it. "This is the end for you." The water around Andre ripples outward in expanding circles. It ripples in a few other spots around the room, too.

Prometheus looks around, making a mental note of the other ripples. He comes back to Andre and pulls another sword out of his sleeve. "Titan of Forethought, indeed," Ezra moans in that same stilted tone that Five uses.

"Brother," Perses says. He edges around Ezra and walks over to Prometheus. He puts a hand on his chest. He looks at Andre over his shoulder. "Later." Perses slinks out of the room. Prometheus backs out with his swords still up to defend himself. They move down the hall and vanish around the corner again.

"Are-are they gone?"

"Yes," Ezra says, slipping his hands into his coat pockets. "You can drop the barrier, Andre."

"Barrier?"

Ezra nods. "Andre put a wall of water around the room as soon as we realized what was happening. If not, the whole home would've come running to see what the noise was." He steps forward and his shoes splash. He looks down at the floor. "If you've ruined his throw rugs, he's going to be upset with you, brother."

Andre raises his trident above his head in his left hand. The water flows up into the sprinkler heads. After about ten seconds, the floor's as dry as a bone. He releases his trident and it falls into a puddle, clinging to his left hand. It reabsorbs back into the mark on the back. He smirks, before turning to face Ezra.

I run over to Five and kneel beside him. "Five, Five, are you alright?" He sits up as if nothing had happened. His face is a bloody mess, and his clothes are stained, but other than that, nothing seems to be wrong with him. He sits with his knees up and his arms resting on them, staring off into nothing.

"Five?" His eyes dart to me. "Are…are you…?" Before I can even finish the question, I throw my arms around him. He sighs and slips his arm behind my back, but he's not really hugging me. I let go and sit back. He's staring at Andre, which is fair, because Andre's glaring at him.

"Thank you," Five grumbles.

"Whatever," Andre growls, storming out. "I'm going to get Ramona and check on Alijiah and the girls. Ezra, would you go find AZ and check on the boys."

"Sure," Ezra says with a shrug. They leave the room.

"He saved your life," I say. Five looks at me curiously. "Isn't that why you thanked him, because Prometheus and Perses were going to kill you?"

He shakes his head and stares at the floor. "I thanked him for saving you."

"What…? Why?"

His head bows further, and he looks even sadder. He shivers. "Because I couldn't."

****

Chapter 13: Weapons

"Are you alright?" I ask Five for the sixth or seventh time…I don't know.

I lost count, because even when he says, "Yeah, I'm fine," it feels like he's lying and not just because it sounds like someone shot his puppy.

"Are you sure?"

"Yeah."

"You're an idiot that's what you are," Andre snaps as he paces by us for the eighth or ninth time. Ezra leans against the backrest of Five's sofa. He crosses his arms with a smirk. It's so weird, just a few minutes ago, they were being gods…talking to other gods…and that insane fight, which I'm sure shook the entire building…and call me crazy, but I feel like even with that, they were holding back.

Now, they're standing around talking as any three brothers would. Except these three brothers are gods, which makes the way they talk to each other that much more amazing.

"Please tell me why you didn't kill both of those idiots. You could've reduced them both to burning craters with a thought." Five's jaw clenches. I reach across his simple Ikea dining table and grab his hand. His eyes meet mine. The way he's looking at me… "And please don't tell me you couldn't because of your seal…because I'm the one who helped you make it, brother." Andre leans over Five. "So, please tell me why…"

"You know why!" Five snaps, sounding furious for half of a second. He sighs and glares at his brother, moving just his eyes.

"Inexcusable!" Andre growls.

Ezra chuckles and looks away.

"He couldn't've," I say, making their eyes land on me. "When he fought that lion, he…"

"Held back like an idiot," Ezra brags. "Our brother put a limit on how much of his power he can access at a time…only a fraction of a fraction of his true power." Wow, all three of them can do that, code switching back and forth between a southern drawl and that stilted, stuffy way off talking seamlessly.

"So, you know that he couldn't've…"

"He can exceed that limit anytime he wants," Andre says. "He chose not to."

I look at him. "So, it's true?" He turns away. "Wh-why would you do that? You could've been hurt and…"

"I would've destroyed you."

"What?"

He rubs his finger on the table as if trying to wipe away an invisible spot. "Have you heard the story of Dionysus?" I take my hand away and sit back, arms crossed over my stomach. "I'll take that as a 'yes.'" He nods. "Well, since you know that his mother, Semele, was mortal…you know what happened when I revealed myself to her."

"She died," I mutter.

"She was incinerated," Andre snarls.

Five's head sinks further. "He incinerated her?"

Ezra lifts his right hand while his left stays near the bend of his right arm. "As gods we're beings of pure power and no one…not Cronus…not Uranus before him…is as physically powerful as Zeus was. In fact, if he'd cut lose with even a tenth of his real power, he'd have probably destroyed the entire building…if not half the city." I look at Five, both his fists clenched tight on the table. "He was so powerful that mortals burned to ash or turn to stone in his presence…" Ezra crosses his arms again. "…because his power was so great," he ends as if mocking Five.

It hit too. Five's shoulders tense up that much more. "It won't happen to you," he whispers. "I won't let it." I stand, walk over, and kneel in front of him. He stares into my eyes. "I won't."

"And I appreciate the thought…but what would've happened to me if Prometheus had killed you or if Andre and Ezra hadn't shown up." His jaw clenches all over again. "Exactly. They probably could've killed me with a flick of their wrists." I reach up and caress his cheek. "Protect me…by protecting yourself."

He nods. I wrap my arms around him. "I don't know why you care about me so much," I whisper. "…and I don't care. I don't want anything to happen to you…so…" I nod. "…don't let anyone use me as a weapon against you. I already get the idea the stakes are too high. So, if there's anything I can do to help you…help you stop them, I will." He nods against my shoulder.

"I would've risked it," he says. "If Perses had…if either of them attacked you, but I took a shot, bet that they wouldn't because they were here for me."

"They could've killed you in your weakened state," Andre warns. He touches his chest. "The gods inside of us may be immortal, but the bodies we're in now are basically as mortal as this woman. Don't forget that."

"I won't," Five says.

"Why did they come here?" I ask. They look at me again. "I mean, if they knew there was a chance, you'd kill them…why'd they risk it?" Five frowns and looks at Andre, who's wearing a similar expression. "I mean, I know Prometheus kind of hates women, so it's not like I'd go visit his house, so…"

"She does have a point," Ezra says. "Even going so far as to challenge us…three on two…when any one of us could've killed them."

"That was out of anger," Five says. "He lost control of himself." Andre seems unconvinced. "Brother, when have you known Prometheus not to have thought things out ten moves in advance?"

"True," Ezra and Andre admit at the same time.

"And on top of that," Five continues. "Perses WAS in control…he was calm…"

"Yeah," Ezra hums. "Usually when a fight breaks out, he'd go as wild as Ares."

Andre slips his hands into his jacket pockets and turns toward the door. "I'm going to do some research." He pauses in the doorway. "You said, Prometheus told you a mortal was the key to his escape." Five nods. "There can't have been that many new excavations in the last 30 years in Greece. Hopefully, this same incident was replicated with Perses." He walks out. "Try not to get yourself killed while I'm gone, brother."

"On the good news front," Ezra says, standing. He shows us his phone. "We convinced him to come home…well, new home," he jokes. It's weird. Even with Ezra joking and being all light-hearted and everything, he still seems sad. No, sad isn't the word. He seems miserable…like my dad when he'd try to put on a brave face after mom passed. "I'm gonna go let him in and then I have some business to take care of elsewhere."

He backs out of the room and points at us. "You two don't do anything I wouldn't do." He turns and walks away.

I come back to Five, who's arms are still wrapped around me. "You okay?"

"No. You?"

I put my arms around him again. "Getting there." We sit here, holding each other, and his warmth washing over me, those amazing tingles running through me.

"Ahem," comes in a deep cottage cheesy, thick voice. Five lets go of me enough to turn. "I hate to interrupt," a tall man with a thick black beard says from the doorway. He removes his black hat, and the curly strands of hair hanging from his temples become frighteningly pronounced. He places his bag down and holds his hat over his heart. He peers at us over the tiny rectangular glasses, positioned at the tip of his nose. "…but may I come in?"

"Of course," Five breathes. He stands and pulls me to my feet with him.

"Thank you," the man says in a thick, New York accent with a hint of Yiddish pushing it. "I was wondering if you remembered me. I've only seen you the one time, but your brothers have come to see me so much that my family even knows them by name."

"Yes, I remember you, Mordechai," Five says, offering him a hand. They shake. "Mordechai Feinstein, it's my pleasure to welcome you to Olympus."

"Well, I'm not sure if I'll be staying long, but..." He nods. "...I definitely wanted to come and see it with my own eyes..." He sighs. "...and I saw Prometheus and Perses on their way out." Five groans and bows his head. "And you, miss...well, I'm not supposed to fraternize with women on the Shabbat, but the sun only just went down and for you, I'll make an exception."

"Sorry," Five says. "Mordechai Feinstein, this is Nicole Clark. Nicole, this is Mordechai." I offer my hand, but he just nods. Five leans into me. "Mordechai's Orthodox Jewish...he's not even supposed to talk to you today, I think shaking your hand might be a step too far." I nod.

"So, are you...um..." I look at Five before coming back to him.

"Oh, that..." He nods and pushes his right sleeve up. "I was born Mordechai Feinstein, son of Jeda and Marsha...but you may know me better as..." He shows off his mark, which looks like a hammer crossing a giant clamp over an anvil surrounded by flames. "...Hephaestus, Olympian god of Fire and Weapons Maker of the gods."

"Wow," I breathe. "Did you just awaken?"

He laughs, while replacing his sleeve. "No, no. I've known who I was for the last 10 years...made finding a wife very difficult, you know?"

"How do you mean? Were you worried you'd hurt her or something?"

"Did you really just read up on me?" Five asks.

"Yeah, pretty much."

He scoffs. "Hephaestus was married to Aphrodite, Olympian goddess of Love and Desire and honest to goodness force of nature," he says coming back to Mordechai. "...hence she was the most beautiful being ever to walk the earth."

"Kind of hard to choose a wife, when you've got that image of your ex running around your head...especially considering how it ended."

"She cheated on him." He nods, and I know that nod too well. I saw that nod in the mirror every day for three months whenever I needed to leave the house. That's the nod of someone who's been betrayed by someone they gave their everything to and tries to muster the strength to face the day. Time for a subject change.

"So, what finally made you decide to come for a visit?"

"Ah!" Mordechai picks up his doctor's bag and moves over to the dining table. He puts it down and turns to us. "For the last 10 years, I've been going insane with the metalwork. I've been creating weapons nonstop like a madman. It was like a compulsion, I couldn't stop myself, but..." He holds a finger up to me. "...I was determined to stay out of any brewing war, just like I did last time."

I nod.

"Wait," Five says. He puts his hand over his face and swipes down his chin with a moan. "Please tell me that Andre and Ezra didn't force you to come down."

"No, no," Mordechai says, waving his hat at us. He tosses it on the table just past his bag and opens the purse-like top. "Like I said, I started crafting weapons like a man possessed…nothing major, a knife here…an axe or hammer there…but…" He holds up both pointer fingers before reaching into the bag with both hands. "…when my weapons started being more specific, I knew my time on the sidelines was running out.

"It started with this…" He places a U-shaped object with five strings moving up from the bottom of the U to a bar crossing it at the top. "…it's a lyre, but that's not what struck me as odd about it." He lifts it higher and moves his thumb along the base. It flashes gold and spreads until it looks like…

"A bow?" I ask.

He nods. "The symbol of Apollo becomes his and his sister's weapon of choice."

"Raymond and Ramona," Five chuckles.

Mordechai moves his thumb the opposite direction, and the bow becomes a lyre again. He places it on the table next to his bag. "Before I knew it, I'd crafted Poseidon's trident and Hades' pitchfork and Helm of Darkness…"

"I saw," Five says.

"So, that really was HIS trident?" I ask. "…like it was really, really Poseidon's trident?"

"Yes," Mordechai says. "I fashioned it with my own two hands." He nods and peers into his bag again as if the weight of the world were inside of it. "It's when I crafted the final piece of the Spear of Triam that I knew I had to come down here and give it to you myself."

Five frowns with a husky sigh and crosses his arms. He looks down, and his forehead wrinkles. It's a worse expression on his face than when Perses first walked in.

"The Spear of Triam?" I ask.

"Aye," Mordechai says, scratching his beard. "The Spear of Triam…the only weapon capable of defeating Cronus…even if only temporarily."

"I thought you…I mean, Zeus was the strongest god."

"Strongest, maybe," Mordechai says. "…but when it comes to durability, no one could touch old Cronus. He healed nearly instantly, and he was almost as powerful as Zeus." He nods and reaches into his bag. "It's because of that… that I had to bring you this." He pulls out a clear orb about the size of a softball. It's weird, but a storm cloud seems to float inside… I gasp. …a storm cloud that generates its own lightning making the sphere flash.

Mordechai steps closer to Five and kneels. "My liege."

"Don't do that, old friend," Five says, pulling Mordechai back to his feet. He opens his hand, and Mordechai gives him the glass softball.

"What is that?" I ask Five with squinting eyes, half expecting it to flash again.

"This," Five says and wraps his fingers around it. He squeezes, and the glass cracks. I feel a tug on the back of my jacket. Mordechai pulls me closer. The glass shatters, and a blinding flash of pale blue light erupts. I close my eyes and turn away. Mordechai holds his hand over his eyes. The light subsides quickly…as quickly as a lightning strike.

I come back to Five, and he's holding what looks like a spear…the tip of it looks like the lightning bolt etched onto his arm only…the whole thing is made of pale blue light. A spark of electricity runs the length of it, causing it to glow brighter for a second. The smell of fresh oxygen cuts through the air, and the room feels cooler but buzzes and hums. The lights flicker.

"This," Five picks up again. "…is my thunderbolt."

****

Chapter 14: Fight

"…aaaannnnnddddd," I drag out while banging out the last few words on my latest assignment. "…where he'll study Business Law." I smirk, God of Commerce. Little parts of their old personalities find their way into their modern lives. "…done," I say aloud. I hit save and start doing a quick scan for typos or my usual, the occasional repeated word.

"I saw a typo," Steven says, sitting on my desk.

"Liar," I growl, scrolling down the article.

"Alfredo Zapata, Star Sprinter of Bevelle High," Steven reads. He scoffs. "You really plan on milking this hood stories thing." I glare at him. "What?"

"Ronda gave me two follow-up stories on Five and the Mt. Olympus Group Home. One was on the home itself, and the other was supposed to focus on an individual success story. I chose AZ, because he's kind of an awesome kid." …who's also the reincarnation of the Greek god Hermes, but he doesn't have to know that part.

"And I'm guessing that you've been going to the home a lot to get the full story…" He nods. "…on this kid."

"Well, that and other reasons."

He laughs without humor. "So, you've been seeing that Five guy for the last few weeks."

I figured that was the real reason he came to hang around my desk. It's true. He doesn't have to know that either though. I sigh. I've been with Five every day for the last three weeks. Partly because we're…a thing. Ugh, we haven't really said what we are yet. I mean, we haven't slept together yet…only slept in the same bed together. That one's still on him… I almost actually groan. …because every night…it's like the slow torture of overwhelming sexual tension.

The other reason…well, what I think is the other reason is that he wants to keep me safe. It's been three weeks since Perses and Prometheus came to the home. Pearl and Alijiah said they put up wards, whatever that means, so that they'd know if any other Titans came to the school.

"Earth to Nicole," Steven says, leaning closer…wrinkling his already wrinkled gray suit.

I just look at him and smile, while writing Ronda and Evelyn an email to let them know my newest article's in the cloud.

"I gotta say," Steven continues, shaking his head. "I don't like that guy…and I definitely don't trust him." I frown but continue typing. "He seems like he's hiding something if you ask me."

"Well, you don't have to like him. You're not the one dating him." I look up at him. "I'll like him enough for the both of us."

"So, you two ARE dating?"

"I don't really see how that's any of your business." I hit "Send." and start shutting down my computer.

He scoffs a laugh and shakes his head at my announcement that I sent an email. "Nicole, it's my business because I care about you."

"Steven, you've made it more than abundantly clear that you only care about getting into my bed…correction, my pants." I shake my head. "You don't need a bed." He opens his mouth to refute the claim. "Which is exactly what you've been trying to do since I was an intern."

"Can you blame me? I mean, have you seen you?"

"Yeah and if you hadn't tried to do it with every single intern to come through here, I might actually be flattered."

"…but it's different with you."

"You told Amber Tyson the same thing when I told you I had a boyfriend." I take my jacket from the back of my chair.

"…I mean it. I've never felt this way about a woman before."

"Taylor Hartford, the next intern pool."

"…it's special with you, because I'm not usually into black girls, but you're so gorgeous."

"Little racist," I suggest. "…and you said the same thing to Keisha Pope the year after that." I grab my bag…that is actually another overnight bag, since Five only lets me go home to grab a change of clothes…usually with Ramona trailing me, even though I've never actually seen her. That reminds me, I seriously need to do a few loads of laundry.

"Look," he continues, holding a hand up in front of me. "I get it. He grew up in the hood and now he's making something of himself…the tall, dark, mysterious stranger…"

I sigh again and focus on not kneeing him in the nuts. "You know, Steven, I might actually give you a shot if you were a little more like Five."

"…black?" he asks with a nod. "From the ghetto?"

I scoff and step around him. "No. Selfless. Self-sacrificing. Earnest. A nice guy who's hard working."

"I don't work hard?"

"You used to…" I step closer. "…back when I was searching for an internship, and I saw that you guys had a few open slots…I did my research. I read as many of *Georgia Now's* archived articles as I could. Most of my favorites were yours. You were so insightful, so warm with your writing. You gave every story a sense of humanity that I thought was amazing…" I purse my lips and shrug. "…now, I don't know what happened to you between then and now, but I think you should look into it."

He bows his head and stares at the floor. I walk away.

The elevator doors slide open, and I move across the lobby. "Have a good night, Ernie," I say to his ever-present smile behind the security desk.

"My son's still available," he says with a warm voice and those graying eyebrows turning up.

"Yeah, but Ernie," I say, turning so that I can keep him in sight, while walking backward. "If I dated your son, that would mean you and I could never be together." He laughs and waves me off.

I step outside and…that's weird… I look around. For the last three weeks, every time I've left work, Five or AZ has been here waiting on me.

I walk down the sidewalk, fishing my car keys out of my bag. Weirder, there's a girl sitting on the hood of my car. She's a pretty, little white girl, bright blue eyes. Her long strawberry blond hair hangs around her head and down her back in big dangly curls.

I march toward her. Regardless of how nice her heeled boots are (yeah, I'm suffering a little shoe envy), I wish she didn't have one of them propped up on my front bumper. She groans, probably because her skinny jeans are too tight. I do love the black leather riding jacket she's wearing though.

She looks up and notices me. One perfectly manicured eyebrow goes up. She bounds off my hood. I hope she didn't scratch my paint job. "Are you her?" she asks with a decidedly Midwestern accent and a point.

"That depends on what you mean by 'her.'"

"Are you, or are you not, Nicole Clark?" she says with aggravation peppering her voice and an expression to match.

"That depends on who's asking."

"God," she groans, rolling her eyes before pinching the bridge of her nose. "You're just as annoying as Andre said you were." She motions to herself. "I'm Ramona."

"Ramona?" I cross my arms, because this girl does not match my expectations. She's not nearly as scary as they make her out to be. "Prove it."

She nods with the corners of her mouth going down. "Okay. That's smart…I'll give you that." She pushes her left sleeve up, revealing a mark on the inside of her wrist…no, there are two of them. The one closer to her hand is in the shape of a bow and arrow with the arrowhead pointing toward her palm. Below that…well, further up her arm is a circle with outward facing crescents on either side.

"Artemis," I whisper.

She frowns. "So, that part's true, too…" I frown as she lowers her sleeve. "…that you're able to say our names without forcing a reaction." I nod.

"Alright," she says, turning away. "I'll follow you as far as the Home, but after that…" She nods, causing her bouncy hair to bob up and down. "…let Five know that I'm going to visit Raymond."

"Okay." She goes two cars down and throws her leg over a forest green motorcycle. I climb into my car as she puts her matching green helmet on. She keeps her word and follows me through downtown and to the home. I park out front, and she zips by me without even a glance back.

I grab my bag and hurry up the front steps. I get ready to push the call button, and Brandy opens the door. "Hey," I say.

"Hey," she moans, sounding annoyed, as usual. "If you're looking for Five, him, AZ, and that Jewish guy are out in the back woods."

"Thanks, Brandy." She nods and hurries down the steps. I take my bag down to Five's room and drop it just inside the door. I come back and wave to Xavier and another boy as they run past me, heading toward the yard.

I cross the field and head for the woods. I wonder if AZ and Mordechai are helping Five clear some more of the overgrowth back here. Last time I was out this way I don't remember it being that bad. I make my way through the bamboo and around the fir trees. A loud clack fills the air and then another one.

"Five?" No response, but a lot more clacks. I start running toward the clearing. The trees separate and…Five swings at AZ with a bamboo staff, and AZ avoids it easily. They exchange a couple of quick clack-inducing attacks. AZ stumbles back. Five's so much stronger than he is, but AZ's faster. Five's got skill-advantage too which is probably what's helping him make up for the difference in their speeds.

I groan, because that reminds me that I've missed almost a month of kickboxing classes.

"Hold," a tank-top wearing Five says, holding up a hand to AZ. They lower their bamboo staffs. Five walks over and cups my face. "Hey, you."

"Hey," I purr, just before he kisses me. I have to take a deep breath every time he does, or I'd probably have died by now. We part. "Sweaty," I moan to his smiling face.

"Sorry."

"It's alright. Gotta keep those skills up." He nods. "Hey, AZ," I say with a wave. He nods. "Mordechai." He smiles from behind his anvil that's almost the size of my car. How does he move that huge thing around? Speaking of moving things around. I come back to Five. "Sparky, where's um…your thunderbolt? I didn't see it in your room."

"Oh that, I…"

"I came up with something new," Mordechai says. "I figured that we couldn't always carry our weapons around…not in this modern age, you know?" I nod. "So, I found a way to seal the weapons into our marks."

"Like Andre's trident?" I ask. They both nod.

Five stabs his bamboo stick into the ground, leaving it standing up. He holds his left hand up to the thunderbolt on his arm. Electricity passes between his hand and the mark, like it did that morning we were in bed together…and I just made myself a little horny.

The mark glows, and he puts his hand on it. He pulls his hand back, and his thunderbolt flashes back into the world. He twirls it like the bamboo, hand moving over hand. It glows pale blue, and tiny sparks of electricity move along the shaft. That did not help with the horniness.

"Whoa," I breathe. He smirks.

"That's nothing," AZ says. He stabs his bamboo into the ground and then touches the mark on his neck. His feet seem to blur without him moving, and the same happens to his head and right hand. He comes completely back into focus, and he's wearing winged sandals in place of his shoes. He has a staff that looks like the medical symbol, two snakes climbing a winged scepter. The wings look more like axe blades though. He also has a silver plate helmet on his head with silver wings moving backward.

"Cool."

He vanishes. "I know, right?" he says from behind me. I laugh. He does too. "So, how'd the article turn out?"

"You'll have to tell me. It should go up online first thing in the morning. It'll also be in the print version tomorrow afternoon." He nods. Hard to believe he didn't even want to do it. I wonder what changed his mind.

"Mordechai," I say, turning to him. "How did you…?" He heaves a giant pair of tweezers over his left shoulder…and a blacksmith's hammer over his right. A chain connects them at the bottom of their handles.

He tips his head forward and smiles. I nod. "Okay, Mordechai. Yours are cool, too."

"That's all I'm saying," he moans with a shrug. We laugh…until a black shadow sweeps in around us. Five and AZ look around with annoyed expressions. Mordechai raises one eyebrow and tips his head to the left and then the right.

"Ezra plays too much," I say, although, it's more as if I'm hoping. These shadows seem paler than his do, but somehow more menacing.

"Ezra and Andre are on a trip, checking on another awakening," AZ says.

"How did I know you were going to say something like that?"

The darkness surrounds us and starts to bubble up as if it were drawing shadows together to make itself taller. It creates a circular fence between the rest of the world and us but lets the sun's light shine down from the top. We're in our own little arena. I hope we won't have to fight like gladiators.

I step back and AZ's still there. He puts a comforting hand on my shoulder. "Don't worry," he whispers. "Five would never let anything happen to you." I nod.

A part of the shadow falls making a doorway. A woman stands in the portal, wearing a leather jacket. "...Ramona?" I mutter. It can't be. Plus, this woman's hair is dark...so dark that it looks purple. She steps through, and sunlight hits her. Her perfect olive tinted skin seems to glow gently. She lifts dark eyes, glaring at Mordechai, then AZ, before settling on Five. "Friend of yours?"

"Styx, what are you doing here?" Five asks.

"Styx? Like the River?"

"The river was named after the goddess," AZ says.

"Styx," Five says. "Titaness of the Underworld River Styx..." He swallows a lump. "...and Personification of Hatred." The expression on her face could've told me that. "She's literally the bridge between life and death..." He looks at me. "...Ezra may hold dominion over the dead...but she holds the keys to the kingdom."

"Where is she?" Styx says.

"Styx," Five says. "Calm...do-"

"NO!" She trembles. She's furious. "I let you trick me...you and your brother, convinced me to turn on my own people...to fight for your benefit and when I couldn't convince my husband… she killed him…"

"Athena did what she had to," AZ says. "Your husband was fully prepared to kill you...and anyone else that…"

"SHUT...UP...!" She throws her left hand out to her side. Some of the darkness peels away, flowing across the ground like water. "I'm sick of waiting...sick of waiting for someone...anyone to return...sick of waiting to see my husband again...sick of waiting on Prometheus and Perses to put their plan in motion..." She lifts just her eyes to us. "...but mostly, Zeus..." Electricity ripples along his thunderbolt and then up his arm. "...I'm sick of waiting on you to pass judgment on her…"

"You know I won't do that."

"What are they talking about?" I whisper to AZ.

"War between us and the Titans, the Titanomachy. Styx sided with us against her own people...her husband, Pallas, Titan of Warfare...not so much. Athena killed him...but since he never actually declared a side…"

"It wasn't a righteous kill?" He nods.

"I gave you a chance, Zeus..." Another bout of electricity, this time rippling along his entire body. "...don't ever say I didn't." She lifts her left hand above her head. "Come forth."

The darkness along the ground moans and groans. Slowly, pale white blobs appear in it. The blobs round out and rise from the darkness. "Sk-sk-skulls…?"

"Styx, you didn't," Mordechai says, angrily.

"What did she do?" I ask as the skulls…and their skeletal bodies pull themselves out of the dark water. Most are in the shapes of human skeletons, holding… Keep down your lunch, girl. …spines like swords. The others look like dogs, maybe wolves, and big, jungle cat skeletons.

"These poor souls," Mordechai says, pushing his glasses further up on his nose. "These poor souls are border dwellers. Souls that got lost between this life and the next…" Mordechai glares at Styx. "…easy prey for the river goddess."

"This is gonna turn into a fight, isn't it?"

"Tear them apart!" Styx snarls.

****

Chapter 15: Betrayal

The skeletons circle us. There's a disturbing clinking, creaky rattle every time they move. AZ lifts his axe, staff thing. Five twirls his thunderbolt like a staff.

I pull Five's bamboo staff from the ground. I'd back up a bit, but we're surrounded. Mordechai taps his anvil with the hammer, and it bursts into flames. The fire swirls then vanishes into his right sleeve. He twirls his hammer, which looks more like a sledgehammer now, around. He extends his arms drawing the chain tight between the clamp and hammer.

"You're gonna fight in that?" I ask Mordechai, taking in his long black coat and slacks.

"Why not? As good as anything to fight in, right?" I nod and extend my bamboo. "I don't think you'd do much good against these things with that. They may look like normal bones, but I promise you they're denser and stronger." I nod. He smiles. "…but hold on to it if it makes you feel better."

"I will."

"AZ," Five says with that sound-dampening boom. "Thin the herd a little, would you?"

AZ smirks and twirls his axe-staff thing around. He takes a sprinter's stance. "Go," I breathe. He flashes a toothy smile just before he vanishes. A skeleton's feet lift off the ground with its left femur smashed. Another one spins like a top with a demolished shoulder. One falls in half to my right, bending sternum over pelvis. One of the animal things' head explodes.

I come back to Styx, and her eyes dart around following the random dispatching of her monsters. She grits her teeth before coming back to Five, whose eyes are closed. He opens them slowly. "You!" she growls. "Fight your own battles!"

"Fair enough," he says in stilted voice. "But I promise you won't like how this ends."

Okay, I'm a little scared. He doesn't sound anything like himself, stilted booming voice or southern drawl. He twirls his thunderbolt and as soon as it stops spinning, he jumps up. He comes down in the center of a skeleton mob. He hits one and… Yipes. …it didn't shatter. It exploded into bone dust.

He hits another one, and the same thing happens. He twirls it again and takes out three with the same amount of effort as just spinning it. He stops with the thunderbolt running the length of his right arm, the jagged tip just beyond his hand.

"You're mortal now," Styx complains. She pulls out a knife that looks like a sickle…only not as curved…and the blade looks black. She points it at Five. "You shouldn't be this strong."

Five points with his free hand. "Why don't you fight your own battles, Styx?" Lightning crackles at the tip of his thunderbolt. "Or are you still afraid of me?"

"Five!" I snap, before I can stop myself. Why's he taunting her? This is completely different from anything I know about him...but not Zeus. In fact, the more he experiences from his past, the more Zeus-like he's become.

He half turns to me with sorrow in his eyes, as if he wants to apologize. That look melts into one of horror. "NICOLE!"

"NICOLE!" AZ shouts almost at the same time to my left. A shadow looms over me. I turn to...a skeleton...but definitely not human. This one looks like a bear, standing on its hind legs. At least, it has the height, teeth, and claws for it.

I stumble and fall. It comes down...with something around its neck! It's Mordechai's clamp. "I got it," he says. He uses his clamp and pushes it downward onto what might've been its stomach. "You're a big one, aren't you? Well, bye-bye." He brings his hammer down, crushing its head.

I stand. "Thanks, Mordechai."

"My friends call me, Morty."

"Thanks, Morty." He smiles...until the ground rumbles. "What's she doing no-?" I cut out, realizing that it's not Styx doing this. It's Five.

Electricity flows over Five's muscles and down his thunderbolt. He's seething. Lightning crackles and flies off, tearing up parts of the ground around him and the smell of fresh ozone cuts through the air. Everything goes gloomy as dark, ominous clouds fill the sky.

"You," he growls in a boom that sounds like thunder. He lifts his thunderbolt like a javelin and aims at Styx.

Her teeth gnash together, and she takes several steps back. Her eyes bulge, and her arms move forward defensively. She's afraid...no, she's terrified. She really thought Five was just a mortal with Zeus inside, not the reincarnation of the Greek god.

"Get him!" she shrieks. Several of the remaining skeletons rush him all at once. A sphere of electricity surrounds him like a plasma globe. The skeletons explode instantly.

Styx swallows a lump and trembles violently. I see why the other gods were all afraid of his wrath. He's going to kill her... "Five," I yell over the boom of thunder. Arms wrap me up. "What are you...?"

"Getting you away," AZ snarls before doing exactly that. I look back to where I was just in time to see a stray lightning bolt strike there. "...before you get faded."

He lets go of me. "Thanks." He nods. We turn back to Five, who didn't even notice. That must've been what happened to Dionysus's mom. The ambient power that ripples away from him must have killed her. I clutch my heart. "Is he…going to…?"

"I think so," AZ whispers.

"Can you stop him?"

"I don't think we could even get close to him," Mordechai says.

A portion of the darkness moves away from Styx's wall and darts toward Five. I open my mouth to warn him, but before I can it wraps around both his arms, his shoulders, legs, waist, and even his neck. She has him…is he going to d…

"That's quite enough of that," Andre says. "Brother."

He and Ezra come down in the space between Five and Styx. Ezra has his hand extended toward Five.

"What're…you…doing?" Five growls.

"Stopping you from making a mistake," Ezra warns. Mistake? Styx attacked him…I don't want her to die, but to say he's making a mistake by killing her?

Five looks past them at Styx. She takes a step back. Five throws his head back, and his arms move in close to his body with his fists, thunderbolt and all, clenched and raised. Lightning comes down striking him directly… I squint but try to keep my eyes on Five though. …the darkness vanishes around him.

The boom comes less than a second later and drowns out everything. My ears ring. Stay with Five… he draws back and throws his thunderbolt as more shadows wrap around his arms and legs.

Andre steps forward and deflects the thunderbolt with his trident, driving it into the ground, wedged between two tines. Five yells something and Andre barks something else right back, still forcing the thunderbolt down as if it might try to escape. I almost caught the end of that one.

Five lifts his right hand, toward his thunderbolt that still seems to be driving itself into the ground. His clenched fist separates, his fingers spreading wide. The thunderbolt explodes into a million, little, pale blue stars as Five's hand clenches into a fist. He opens his hand, and it reforms there, all on its own. He twirls it around, cutting the shadows away from himself.

AZ steps forward. "ANDRE! EZRA! Have you two betrayed us for the Titans?"

Ezra glowers at AZ. "Don't be absurd!"

Andre raises his trident as Five runs at him. They clash… and this time the ground definitely shakes. Andre grits his teeth, struggling to drive Five's thunderbolt into the ground. He lifts his eyes to Five. "This…isn't…the plan…it's not our fault…you got so upset, because…she threatened…your mortal…" I frown. I've heard Five laid claim to me, but does that mean he thinks I'm his property or something? Five puts his hand on Andre's chest and gives him a shove. Andre stumbles back.

Five inhales deeply through his nose and stands up straight. He points his thunderbolt at Andre. "Explain yourself now, brother," he says in his booming voice. "Or I'll come at you as if I intend to kill you." His eyes dart to Styx. "You're next."

"I'm sorry, brother," Andre says. "But I can't let you mess up my plans. I need you to think through this. Styx has been on the outside this whole time…not in Tartarus…not in your reincarnation cycle…out in the world this whole time." What is Andre getting at?

"Time's up," Five says, still in his booming voice. Is he really going to…? He spins his thunderbolt and lifts it behind him with his free hand out front. He kind of puts me in the mind of Prometheus just before he and Andre fought. Andre takes a stance with the tip of his trident aimed at the ground out in front of him. He glares at his brother.

"Ezra," I say. He crosses his arms and scowls. "Please don't let them…"

Five vanishes before I can finish, leaving a little spark of electricity where he was. Andre's eyes bulge. He spins and swings his trident outward… hard. His trident hits Five's thunderbolt…and it looks like a flash of lightning and has the boom of thunder.

Andre takes a few steps back, before coming back at Five. They both vanish. Thunder sounds to my right coupled with a spray of water…it smells like seawater. It repeats to my left and then several times directly in front of me.

Ezra stands perfectly still with his arms crossed and his eyes closed. Styx follows the insanity with just her eyes. She backs away slowly. "DON'T…" Ezra booms, pointing a black trident at her…no, not a trident at all. It only has two tines, like a pitchfork missing its middle teeth. "…MOVE!" Styx trembles, but not out of fear. It's as if she can't move.

Five and a clearly winded Andre come to a rest between us. Andre extends his trident defensively. Five stands up straight and marches toward his brother, thunderbolt in hand. I tremble…it's as if I can feel his anger from here. "Five," I sob. "…you can't…" He stops in his tracks.

"No one can beat you with your thunderbolt," Andre snarls. The hard edge returns to Five's expression instantly. "You know that."

Five lifts his thunderbolt, holding it horizontally. "True." He squeezes until it breaks in half and explodes into little stars again, flittering away on the wind. He throws the portion in his hand away like a handful of powdery, glowing stardust. He takes a boxer's stance. "I'll take you apart with my bare hands…like I used to when you sassed ma too much."

Ezra lowers his arm, and his staff falls into dust and disappears. I gasp as Styx darts by Ezra and a still struggling Andre.

"FIVE!" He forms a new thunderbolt…too late…I scream as Styx moves past him with a spray of blood. She turns, throwing a few more blood droplets off her blade. Five falls to his knees, dropping his thunderbolt, clutching his left side. His thunderbolt clangs as it hits the ground…and the electricity drains away. It looks like a silver staff with a sharp, jagged lightning Z of a tip. "Five," I moan.

Andre lifts his eyes. Styx snickers. She marches over to Five and raises her sickle above her head. "Goodbye, Zeus."

She brings her arm forward… "FIVE!" I shriek. …Styx stops and jumps back. Ezra takes the spot directly in front of Five and Andre in front of him.

"Don't push your luck," Andre growls. "We may have stopped our brother from killing you…but that doesn't mean we won't kill you to stop you."

Styx smirks and lifts her sickle near her face. "It doesn't matter. The deed is done." She laughs maniacally and slices the air with her weapon. The darkness converges on her. AZ rushes forward and wraps his arms around the shadows. It falls apart, like leaves in a breeze. AZ's arms empty quickly.

"Is she…gone?" AZ looks down at his arms and nods. His helmet, staff, and sandals blur and then vanish. I run to Five's side. "Five? Are you…?" He grits his teeth and leans into me. I drop the bamboo and wrap my arms around him. His eyes close and his body goes limp. "Five? Five?"

"I figured as much," Ezra says over my shoulder. I put my hand on his chest and shove him away as hard as I can…which doesn't amount to much, but he steps back. "What's your problem?"

"You're my problem! He got cut because of you!"

"He's not just cut," Mordechai says. "I think he's been poisoned."

"Poisoned?"

"A specific poison," Ezra says. "It's distilled from the waters of the River Styx…" He frowns. "…I…Hades used it to punish particularly wearisome denizens of Tartarus…but…they're already dead…"

"What do you mean?" I shout.

Ezra steps closer and holds his hand over the bloody spot covering Five's left side. A purple light surrounds the injury. Black smoke rises from the gash, and Five groans. "His wound is poisoned with death itself." He steps back. "If we don't cure him soon…he'll…" I tremble and hold him tighter.

"Let's get him inside," Andre says. I pick up Five's powerless thunderbolt and swing it at Andre as hard as I can. He catches it by the shaft. "He's my brother…let me help him."

I tremble again, but AZ's hand on my shoulder eases some of the tension. "I'll get him back to his room."

I nod and come back to Andre with a glare. "When we get back to Olympus, you better have a damn good explanation."

****

I switch the rag over Five's forehead for a drier one and replace the ice pack. I wonder if I should change his shirt again. He's already sweating through this one. He sweated through his sheets, too. We may have to move him to the couch to replace those. He groans, and that tension vein springs up in his neck again. I dab another rag along his lips and wipe his neck. I toss it in the pan with the others. "What can I do to help?" I whisper.

"Nothing," Ezra says, leaning casually against the doorframe. I glare at him and cup Five's right hand in both of mine. "I'm serious. There's nothing you can do for him."

"We should take him to the hospital. There has to be some kind of medicine or something and…"

"And they'd be lost," Andre says, sitting at the dining table.

"You don't know that."

"I know that hospitals' staff are trained to treat illnesses and maladies that they can recognize and diagnose…" He rests his head on his fist. "…not magic."

"Magic?"

"Not exactly," Ezra says. "The water from the River Styx is the essence of death itself. It's been used to ferry souls from this world to the next since time began." He looks at Five. "Basically, by imbuing her blade with a poison derived from it, Styx has created a bridge between this world and the next. Little by little, that poison is syphoning his life away…preparing him for the underworld."

I tremble. "He can't die." A tear splashes against my hand. I clench his tighter. "He can't."

"We won't let him," Andre says.

"We need Raymond."

"Raymond? Ramona's…um…boyfriend?"

"Boyfriend?" Ezra says. "No. Raymond is Ramona's twin brother."

"Twin brother…" She's the reincarnation of Artemis, so that makes him… "…Apollo, the Sun god?"

"Not just sun," Andre says, rising to his feet. "He's also the god of Music…and Healing. If he combines his abilities with Pearl's…they should be able to save him."

I stand up causing my chair to scrape the floor. "THEN GO GET HIM!" Andre's eyes bulge and dart to Ezra. I stab at Andre with an accusing finger as he comes back. "This is your fault…if you'd have just let him go after Styx…instead of distracting him…he wouldn't be in this mess."

Andre frowns. "You don't understand what's happening here. We're working with forces beyond your comprehen-"

I stomp over to Andre and slap his stupid face. He stares at me as if he's not sure what just happened. "Don't you dare patronize me. I don't need to comprehend the specifics of god issues…to know that when your brother is fighting for his life, you don't get in his way…you don't leave him vulnerable…and you do not let someone attack him. And most of all, if any of those things do happen…you do whatever it takes to help him get back on his feet. Is that clear?" He glares at me. I jab at him again. "Is…that…clear?"

For half a second, I think he might attack me, but then I remember I'm angrier than he is. I point to the door. "Go!" He turns and walks away. Ezra watches Andre walk out. "You too!"

Ezra laughs. "Starting to see why Five likes you so much." I scowl. I point at the door again and mouth, 'go!' "We'll hurry…I give his mortal body another 48 hours on the outside." He follows Andre.

Five groans, and I run to the bed's far side. I sit and grab his hand…his trembling, clammy hand. Still, I hold it tight.

"Five? Five, are you okay?" He grits his teeth, practically frothing. I stifle brand new tears. I must be strong for him now. Keep your voice steady. "Do you need something to drink? Another ice pack?" His eyes open to tiny slivers, only barely showing his dilated brown eyes…searching… "Five?"

He finds me. "I…knew it," he growls. "…ugh…" His back arches, and he writhes in pain.

"You knew it? Knew what?"

His fingers…his icy, damp fingers wrap around mine. "I…knew it…" He swallows a lump. "…the first time…I saw you…"

"On the courthouse steps?" I ask with a laugh.

He moans and shakes his head. "Before…saw you…running…"

"Running…?"

"Woman…dropped her wallet…ran after…her…"

"…two blocks to give it back to her." He nods. "That was a half hour before the key ceremony."

"…the way she…thanked you…her daughter…loved you…instantly…" He inhales a deep, wheezing gasp. "…me…too…"

"You love me?" His body relaxes all at once. His fingers stop gripping mine. All tension leaves his face. "Five?" His chest rises and falls, erratically…but the alternative…I shudder.

I stand and lean over him. "You know what?" I whisper. I kiss him and then wipe some of the sweat away from that little dimple below his nose. "…I might love you, too."

"Knock, knock," Alijiah says from the doorway. I sit back and wipe away my tears. "Hate to interrupt."

"No, it's fine." I motion for her to come in. "Please."

She walks in and moves to the opposite side of the bed. She stares at him and trembles. "Oh," she moans. "I didn't expect to react like that."

"Why not? You care about him."

"I do…in so many ways…"

"Oh, you…" I motion to Five.

"No, no," she moans. She makes an outward swiping motion with her arms, before delivering a definitive, "No." She points at Five. "Zeus." She points to herself. "Athena." Between them. "…father and daughter."

"Oh. Wait, that didn't seem to matter much in mythology."

"Yeah," she says. "Don't even get me started on that." I laugh, and she does too. "It's hard, you know? Being what we are…the memories of ourselves as gods constantly mixing with our current lives."

"I've thought about that. I can't imagine it, but I've thought about it."

She takes Five's other hand. "Whatever you think of Andre and Ezra, they're completely loyal to Five…a lot more loyal than Poseidon and Hades would ever be to Zeus." I frown. "I trust them. If they stopped Five from killing Styx, I'm sure they had a good reason."

"No reason could justify this." I shake my head. "Andre probably put you up to this. Got you to come in and calm down the hysterical woman."

"No, he really didn't." She scoffs. "And if he were ever that condescending to me, I'd punch him right in his smug face." I laugh. Her smile comes down to a gentler expression. "You're wrong about him though. I think of them as my brothers…and I like us better this way. And while I think of them as brothers, I'm loyal to Five above all others."

"Well, yeah…he was your dad."

She smiles. "He rescued me. Not Zeus rescued Athena; I mean…Five rescued me." She shakes her head. "I was attacked by an angry mob in my hometown. It was right after a group of terrorists attacked several cities around the world…hurt hundreds of people…some…died. It was awful.

"I hadn't even awakened as a goddess yet, so I was scared out of my mind. The mob surrounded me, and they were yelling things and throw rocks and whatever else they could find…and then…" Her entire demeanor changes. Her smile becomes as bright as sunshine, and her eyes sparkle. "…it all just stopped."

She sighs and looks at Five. "He intervened. He tried to talk them down, but it was a mob and you know how mobs can be."

"Not really, thank God."

She smiles. "Well, they were horrible and refused to listen to reason. Five ended up knocking a few of them out before they finally dispersed. He took me to the hospital, stayed with me until my parents arrived. A few days later, I awakened as Athena…and he was right there again. It was as if he knew. I recognized him for who he really was right away…the man who saved me and Zeus."

She caresses Five's hand. "I moved here to be close to him and never looked back." I nod. "I thank Allah every day that he found me."

"Allah?"

She looks at me. "Yes. I still have my faith. Does that surprise you? Scare you a little?"

"Definitely doesn't scare me. I have a few cousins that are Muslim," I add under my breath. "They're a little militant, but I know people that follow the faith aren't bad people because of it." She nods. "It's just…you know that this is Zeus…and you were, Athena…"

"Ah." She nods. "You're wondering how I can be both a Muslim and a Greek god."

"Kind of big question mark on that one."

"When I first awakened, it nearly destroyed me. I mean, coming to grips with what I was as opposed to who I am. It was a nightmare. Five sat me down one day and asked me why I couldn't be both. I didn't really have an answer for him."

She bobs her head unevenly. "So, I turned the question on him. I asked him how I could be both, knowing absolutely that one is true and only having faith to go on for the other. He smiled, staring out the window. He told me that while he was Zeus, there were gods before him and that there would most likely be gods after him. For all he knew, there was a greater power out there, guiding him…teaching him just like the mortals. He told me that he'd heard other mythologies, studied other religions, and he saw nothing in our shared past that would refute the existence of Allah, the Messiah, or any other religion's belief.

"That's why they call it faith," she repeats with a tone of reverence in her voice. "Because you don't know through evidence…you know from faith… you believe…you pray…and you seek guidance." She bends down and kisses the back of his hand. "It was the happiest I'd been in a long time and to this day, even I don't fully understand why. I mean, he never answered the question, but somehow it filled my heart with joy."

I laugh silently. "He does that, doesn't he?"

"Yes." She stares at me, and her smile changes slightly. "I'm glad he found you, Nicole."

"Wha-why?"

"Because you make him…better. He was already an impressive man, but now he has you. He can share his human dreams with you…someone to push him in his endeavors." She caresses his cheek. "But at the same time…" She nods. "…from what AZ told me, you bring out the vengeful god in him, too. He needs that. He needs to be both the charming diplomat and the conquering king if he's going to reach his goals." She stands, reaches across Five and taps the bottom of my chin. "And I couldn't imagine a more fitting queen to take this journey with him."

"Thank you."

She bows her head. "I'll leave you two alone, okay? Pearl's already started dinner for the kids. When she's done, I'll bring you something back and some soup for Five."

"I'd appreciate that, thanks." She nods and walks away.

I lean closer to Five. "She loves you so much," I whisper. "You can hear it in her voice. See it in the way she looks at you." I play with his fingers, so cool to the touch. "I can understand why." I trace the vein moving up his forearm, going toward his mark. I stare at him, while tracing the mark's outline with my pointer finger.

"Ow," a spark shocked my finger. I jump back and put my finger in my mouth. "Hmm," I moan, sucking my static plagued digit. "It's never done that before…" I stare at him again and slowly move my hand back toward his mark. "…not when he wasn't awake and doing it on purpose." It sparks again, but this time it doesn't hurt. I don't think it hurt last time so much as just scared me.

I move my hand close again, hovering over his mark. It sparks. Steady electric current moves between my hand and it. Weird. Electric tingles climb my arm. It moves across my bicep, circles my shoulder and then dances along my collarbone. My skin prickles as if a thousand tiny feathers sway across it. It carries a sort of numbing, relaxing feeling that somehow tickles at the same time.

It travels through my chest before, oddly enough, it feels as if it's nudging my heart. I touch my chest. It feels, amazing, but so weird at the same time. I scoff a laugh. "Maybe it's your way of tattooing your name across my heart." I take my hand away, and the electricity ceases.

Five stirs…his eyes remain closed, but his head shifts from one side to the other. "Nicole," he whispers. "Nicole."

"I'm here." I caress his cheek. "I'm here." His tension eases. He drifts back to sleep. I didn't know that actually worked outside of movies. "He really loves me." I climb onto the bed with him and rest my head on his chest. He wraps me up, holding me close. His hand grips my shoulder, and he pulls me even closer. "Rest, babe. I'm here, and I'm not going anywhere. I just found you, I don't know what I'd do if I lost you just as fast." I close my eyes and drift slowly off to sleep.

I moan. It's too bright...and...my neck's stiff. Why's my neck...? I sit up...on Five's couch. I fell asleep on the bed. Why am I? I turn and there's a guy leaning over Five in a dark green hoodie. I jump to my feet...my sock covered feet. I come back to captain hoodie. "Who are you?"

He peers over his shoulder with part of his ear-length blond hair hanging over his soft brown eyes. His chiseled jaw tenses and then relaxes. He turns back to Five.

I run over to him and notice a pale-yellow glow coming from his hands... hovering over Five's wound. "WHAT ARE YOU DOING?" He looks at me again, but still doesn't answer. "WHAT ARE YOU DOING?"

I grab him by the hoodie and pull as hard as I can. He doesn't budge. "STOP IT!" I start hitting him... I don't know if he's a god, human, or what, but I can't stop myself. I keep pounding on him with closed fists. He takes it without complaint or reaction...he stays focused on Five.

"What are you doing?" I take a step back, preparing to kick him in the head. Someone wraps me up and pulls me back. "Who...?" I look back. "ANDRE! What are YOU doing? Who is that? Let go of me!"

"Man, you're noisy first thing in the morning."

"Morning, already...?"

"Sunday morning in fact."

"I slept for two days?"

"If I promise to answer your questions, will you calm down?" I frown but nod. He lowers me to the floor and lets me go. "Alright. First..." He points. "...that's Raymond. He's healing Five's wound."

"He could've just said that instead of letting me hit him."

"Actually no, he couldn't. Ray's mute."

"Mute? But he's a reincarnated god," I say. Raymond glares. "No offense." He shakes his head and turns back to Five. "I thought you said he needed to work with Pearl to heal Five."

"They did...all night in fact. It's why I moved you to the sofa, to give them room." I nod. "You slept for two days, because feeding Five intravenously proved ineffective since it was life energy he needed. So, we set you up with a drip, and Pearl tethered your life energies together."

"She...? How?"

He shrugs. "She said it was pretty easy though...something about your life energies converging or something. So, she set you up with the I.V. drip and then the two of them went to work."

I slide my sleeve up to my elbow and sure enough, there's a bandage and little piece of tape just below the bend. "So, I got the energy from the I.V...."

"...and Five got it directly from you." He bows. "My brother is alive thanks to you."

I shake my head while replacing my sleeve. "Couldn't any of you have...?"

He shakes his head. "Pearl tried with me...and Ezra...and even herself... but none of us were compatible." He shrugs again. "Said it was kind of like being matching blood types for organ donation...except on a spiritual energy level."

He frowns and looks at Raymond. He laughs. "Exactly."

"Exactly what?"

"Ray made a joke about donating pants...and how you could probably fit into his sister's skinny jeans, but he definitely couldn't." He waves his hand. "You had to hear him tell it."

"Hear him tell...? How exactly did you hear the mute tell a joke?"

Andre leans in close and puts his hand next to his mouth as if he's about to whisper a secret. "Ray's mute...not deaf."

"Sorry," I whisper. Ray shrugs. He half turns to me, keeping his left hand over Five's wound, and his right extended toward me. "What?"

"He wants to link with you, so that you can 'hear' him, too." I look at Andre, and he motions toward Raymond. "Go on. He sets up a telepathic link so that he can talk to you directly."

"Telepathic? Telepathy isn't real."

"Well, as someone said recently...'he's a reincarnated god.' Nature compensated for his human body's inability to speak."

I scoff at Andre's impersonation and step forward. Ray taps the center of my forehead. *Hello,* he sings in my head. Wow, it's weird. His voice is pleasant, but he doesn't have a Midwestern accent like his sister. *I know. Weird, isn't it?* You heard that? *What part of telepathic link wasn't clear?* I glower at him.

He smirks into a soundless laugh. *Don't worry, everyone sounds like their narrating their own life in their head... and sorry for not answering you earlier, but I couldn't. I must establish the connection before I can communicate.*

"Do you have to...?"

No, once it's established, I can reconnect anytime, and I can let as many people or as few as one person hear me at a time. It does get harder to connect with multiple people over long distances though.

I open my mouth.

Yes. It's still pretty cool.

"That actually even annoys me," Andre says.

Ray scowls and pokes his tongue out at Andre then looks at me. *Ray? I like that.*

Five coughs. "Five?" I run to the other side of the bed. His eyes flutter and then open slowly. "Five?" I whisper.

"Nicole?" he whispers back.

"I'm so glad, you're…" He springs forward and wraps his arms around me.

"You're safe." He trembles. "I had so many nightmares about you dy…dy…" He shakes again and holds me tighter. "…damn you, Nyx…"

"I'm fine…I'm fine." Why does he blame Styx for his nightmares? We part. My eyes dart to his lips. I lean forward to kiss him and pause. He kisses me. I moan because it's so good, and I missed it so much. I press my forehead to his. "Five…you said…"

He shakes his head. "Just let me enjoy this…enjoy being here with you for a little while longer."

"I…" My eyes dart to the left, and I notice Ray and Andre already left. *You're welcome. Have fun.* I hate to agree with Andre, but that does get kind of annoying.

Five lays back, and I rest my head on his chest. He caresses my right shoulder and that electric tingle moves to my heart. I don't know what that is or even if he's doing it on purpose, but why do I love it so much?

****

Chapter 17: Recovery

"So, in summary," Ronda says, leaning back. "I'd like you all to congratulate Nicole on being nominated for the Georgia Press Association's top prize in the category of Lifestyle Coverage." The entire table of staff writers applauds. "And I'd like to announce her promotion from Junior Copy Writer to Staff Writer." They applaud again...except Steven. "We're having an office set up for you, and you'll be able to move in on Monday."

I laugh through a "wow." I shake my head. "I had no idea. I mean, when I filed that story about AZ...I mean, Alfredo, I had no idea it would get this much traction."

"Traction?" Steven growls. "More like a snowball down a hill."

"What?"

"Steven?" Ronda growls.

"Let's not forget that this was my story to start with. If not for her shaking her ass in Five's face, she wouldn't..."

"Steven, you are not helping yourself in any way, and I suggest you shut your mouth right now!" Ronda warns, pointing her glasses. He huffs and sits back in his chair. "If there are no other announcements or story ideas...?" Ronda looks around the table at all the faces still in shock over Steven's outburst. "Meeting adjourned." Everyone rises except Ronda. "Nicole, stay for a minute. I need to talk to you."

Steven leans close to my ear. "She's probably going to tell you you'll have a private bathroom in your office and that your golden toilet has a seat warmer built-in." I glare after him, before coming back to Ronda, who's doing the same.

"Come closer." I move to the seat next to her. "Woman to woman, is there any merit to Steven's claim? I mean, I know Five asked you to dinner for..."

"Of course not," I snarl. "I didn't ask to take over the Key to the City story...Five did...and he only did that after Steven basically called him a thug with something to hide."

She nods and nibbles her glasses' earpiece. "I just had to make sure, considering that you've admitted to dating Five for the last month and a half." I nod. "That being said, would you like to file a sexual harassment claim against Steven?" I frown. "For insinuating that you seduced Five to steal his story, and I'm sure he's hit on you more than a few times."

"Only every day since I started, but it's nothing I can't handle. Besides, I honestly feel like something happened to him right before I got my internship here."

Ronda sighs and cups her hands. "His wife cheated on him and then left him." I gasp. "You didn't know?"

"No one really talks about it, and any time I tried to talk to him on any kind of personal level, he flirts and makes me shut down." I sigh. "No wonder."

"That's still no excuse for his behavior, especially lately." Ronda rubs her eyes with her glasses dangling from the same hand. "Of course, if no one lodges a complaint there's only so much I can do about it."

I stand up. "Let me talk to him. Remind him that once upon a time he was my internship's site supervisor…and not that terrible a guy."

She sighs. "Alright, but if he keeps up this unprofessional behavior, I will do something about it. Even if it's just giving him crap assignments from now on."

"Okay."

I walk out and head straight to Steven's office, which is empty. The door's wide open, so I step in. I was hoping I just didn't see him. I touch the baseball bat, signed by Dave Justice, sitting on top of his desk. The signed team roster from the '91 Braves. The three baseballs he mounted underneath it, signed by three pitchers whose names I don't remember and can't read because they look like a doctor's prescription.

His random bits of baseball memorabilia give him a sense of home that he probably lost after his wife…I wonder if that's what it really is. Is he just having this much trouble recovering from his divorce?

I make my way back to my cubicle. I wonder what I'll put in my office to make it home like. Probably a framed copy of that selfie I snapped of Five and me. Despite his complaint, at the time, he loved it. Pictures of mom…dad…another one of my boyfriend… I huff a laugh. Five's my…

"You can't make your whole career on Five, you know," Steven criticizes behind me.

I sigh and grab my jacket. "…and I'm not trying to…right now, I'm trying to get my former mentor out of the funk he's been in for the last few years…" He frowns. "…and figure out a way to get Five to actually wear a suit for once…for this Georgia Press Association event."

"Well, what do you expect when everyone…"

"…everyone is not your wife." The look on his face is heartbreaking, but this is probably why he hasn't recovered. No one's just been honest with him. "Not everyone's going to leave you if you put your trust in them…if you put a little faith in them." I put one arm around his neck. "Even though you've been a jerk to me lately, I still consider you a friend."

He trembles. "Shut up! What do you know…?" I step back, and he has tears in his eyes.

"I know that I'm one phone call away if you ever need to talk." He bows his head and walks away.

I slip my jacket on as my phone starts buzzing. I didn't think he'd take me up on that offer this soon. "Hello?"

"Nicole?" Ramona answers.

"What's going on? Is Five okay?"

"Crap," she groans. "I was just about to ask you if you'd seen him. I figured he was with you since he didn't tell anyone where he was going."

"He should be resting."

"That's my point, idiot!" I growl. "No, she hasn't seen him either."

"Who's that? I didn't hear…"

"Who do you think, idiot?"

Pardon my sister's personality. It's just how she gets when she's worried about someone and right now, we're seriously worried about Five.

Have you tried to call him?

No. Why would we ever think of calling him? We decided, instead to panic and call his girlfriend first.

No, I mean, did YOU try to call him?

Oh. Unfortunately, he's the only person capable of blocking me out any time he sees fit. Sorry…my sister and I kind of worry the same way.

I nod. No worries…about you or Ramona. I'm on my way. I'll call Five, too. We'll find him.

Thanks.

"What are you smiling about?" Ramona rumbles.

"I gotta go, Ramona. Bye." I end the call before she can clap back. I hurry to my car and drive like a mad, horn-abusing woman.

Ray?

I'm here.

I'm about to turn into the neighborhood now and…I see him!

Where?

He's walking, about six blocks away from Olympus.

Which direction is he heading?

Um, East, I think.

He's heading toward the high school. It must be about one of the kids. I'd know if it were AZ, so…

Brandy?

That's what I'm thinking.

Let Ramona and everyone else know, I'm going to pick him up.

Will do.

I huff a laugh. I like Ray. He's so easy going.

Awww, I like you, too.

RAY!

Ow, mind yelling…Ray, signing off.

I laugh to myself again as I pull up next to Five. "Where do you think you're going, mister?"

He frowns. "I got a call from the school. I have to go pick up Brandy."

"And how exactly are you going to do that without a car?" I park at the curb. I climb out…nearly clotheslining myself with the seatbelt…march around the car and stand in front of him. He stops with a huff. "And when you're supposed to be recovering from injuries and a near-fatal poisoning?"

He looks over my head and sighs. "I'm fine." I punch him in the stomach. He flinches but doesn't budge otherwise. "Hey…abusive, much?"

"You scared the hell out of me. So, don't you dare stand there and act like it was nothing." I hit him again, before I can stop myself. "Not with me."

He wraps an arm around me and holds me close. "I'm sorry. I didn't mean to make it seem like nothing," he says in stilted voice, complete with boom. He takes a deep breath and then steps back. "But I'm fine. Really."

"Okay. Then I'll give you a ride to Brandy's school."

"Nah, it's fine. I can walk it…"

"I'm sorry. Did it sound like the choice was left up to you?"

He frowns. "You're bossy lately."

"Well, when my boyfriend almost dies on me, I have a right to be!"

"Boyfriend?" I cover my mouth. We've never actually talked about possessive pronouns before. We've spent almost every day together since we met. I have no idea how he… "Well, I guess if my girlfriend says get in the car…" My jaw drops, and I stare at him. "…I have to get in the car." He smirks and steals a quick peck before walking around the front. "You coming?"

I snap out of it and run to the driver side. He holds the door for me and closes it after me. He climbs in, and we head five more blocks down the road to the high school.

I park across from the main entrance in the area designated "Visitor & Faculty/Staff Parking." Five climbs out. "If you want…you can wait here…" I shake my head and follow him up the steep, concrete gray stairs, leading to the deep green double doors at the front entrance. We walk in, and he heads, through corridors that look suspiciously like the ones at Mt. Olympus, except with lockers, straight for the main office.

He slides his hands into his jacket pockets and goes straight for the counter, tinted in alternating shades of gold, silver, and black. He leans forward a little. "Hey, Lynn," he says to the silver haired woman behind it. She smiles warmly and walks over to meet him.

I stick to the doorway. Brandy slouches in a chair to my left, arms crossed over her stomach…and an almost as surly-looking girl with a mess of pulled hair sits across from me, leaning forward eagerly. Her left foot bangs out an arrhythmic beat.

Five points at Brandy with his thumb, without looking at her. "What'd she do this time?"

"Fighting."

"Again?"

"SHE STARTED IT!" Brandy barks.

"AND I'LL END IT TOO, BITCH!" the other girl snarls, jumping out of her chair.

"QUIET. BOTH OF YOU!" the woman snaps, shutting them both up instantly. The other girl falls back into her chair. Her eager lean remains, but she bows her head.

Five sighs and leans with his back against the counter. He stares at Brandy. She crosses her arms and averts her eyes, trying to look anywhere but at him. She's actually pouting. Man, they really do remind me of my dad and me. Five tilts his head back. "Lynn," he starts in a lower voice. "...about Brandy's...situation..."

"Don't worry," she whispers. "We haven't called her probation officer, and the school's enforcement officer promised that no charges will be filed."

Five sighs in relief. "Thank you so much."

Lynn pats Five on the back. "Go easy on her. She's still having a hard time."

Five stands. "I know." He walks over to Brandy and points to the door. "Go. Red Prius, out front." Brandy stands in a huff and walks past him.

"Next time, I'll pull out that fake ass hair of yours, bitch!" the surly mahogany skinned girl rumbles.

"BITCH, my hair's real!" Brandy snaps, stepping back into the room. "...not like that nappy ass bird's nest you got up..."

Five steps in front of Brandy, cutting her off. He holds one finger up... "Car." ...and then aims it at the door. "Now." His voice mutes all sound. Brandy retreats...and turns away quickly.

"That's right, bitch!" the surly girl says. "You better listen to yo' daddy and..." Five glares at the girl. Her mouth snaps shut, and she sits back.

Five comes back to me and tips his head forward as he passes. I follow him outside. Brandy leans against my car, arms crossing over her stomach again. I know that posture as surely as I know the look on her face. She's already regretting the inevitable fight she's going to have with Five.

She lifts her eyes and scowls as soon as she sees him. Yep, too well. Five opens the door and pulls my seat forward. He tilts his head to the gap, and Brandy falls into my tiny backseat.

What happens next is the most awkward ride in the short six months since I bought this car. I check the rearview. Brandy stares at Five and then lowers her eyes when she catches me staring at her. He stares out the window with his fist at his mouth. I almost laugh…thankfully, I don't. My dad told me when he did that it was because he was worried. 'Maybe, that would've been the time I'd said something inadvertently that I couldn't take back.'

My dad always made raising a teenager seem like a balancing act on a very thin rope. I should admit…in hindsight, I thought of myself as more of a minefield. One wrong step and kaboom step right into an argument… I catch Brandy in the rearview again. …even when I knew I was in the wrong.

We pull up to the front of the Home. Five climbs out and Brandy's behind him. I climb out in a hurry because she's already making a beeline for the front doors, and Five is on her heels. "Wait," Five snaps. Brandy sighs and turns to face him, arms crossed over her stomach. "What happened?"

"She said some slick sh-"

"Language," he snaps before she can finish.

Brandy huffs. "She called my momma an old white hoe and that her and my old drug dealer, spic daddy deserved to die."

Five takes a step back, wipes his mouth, and comes back to her. "And does that make any of that true?"

"She shouldn't've said it. I don't care if it's true or not. I'm not gonna let anybody talk about my momma like that."

"Brandy, you can't keep going off every time someone says something about your mom."

"You always say that…it's not about my mom, it's about…"

"Your mom and all the hurt feelings that you won't express because…"

"So, you just know everything just like always, right, Five? You're just gonna tell me how I feel! Never mind how I actually, really feel, right?"

Five growls. "Brandy, I'm trying to help you, but I can't help you if you keep knockin' my hand away every time I reach for you!"

"I DIDN'T ASK FOR YOUR HELP!"

"FINE. YOU'RE GROUNDED!"

"GREAT!" She fishes her phone out of her pocket and slams it into his waiting hand. "TWO WEEKS AGAIN?"

"NO, LET'S MAKE IT THREE!"

"Fine!" she rumbles, stomping up the stairs.

"Fine!" Five replies putting her phone in his pocket.

"FINE!" she barks back, before slamming the door behind her.

Five trembles. He walks up the stairs and stops at the top one. I move to his side. "Go talk to her." He looks at me. "Actually, talk to her…not yell." I stare at the doors with him. "Trust me. It's what she wants more than she knows."

He sighs and turns around. He sits on the top step. "I wouldn't know where to start."

"Reminding her that you care about her is as good a place as any."

He sighs. I sit next to him and lean my head against his shoulder. "I'm scared," he whispers.

"You're…?"

"…scared." He nods. "Brandy scares the hell out of me. I don't think I could worry about her more if she were my own daughter."

"I see that."

"…but the thing is, she's also what scares me about the world as a whole. Humans seem so willing to inflict their pain on the world…to make others suffer because they have…"

"Misery loves company." He looks at me. "Which is even more reason that you should go talk to her."

"…I'm not sure if the things I have planned to do in my lifetime will actually help humanity see that constant fighting isn't the answer…I want people to see that holding on to pettiness and feelings of resentment will only lead to ruin."

"Are the humans an allegory for us, brother?" Andre asks from the door. He walks over and stands beside Five, staring out over the front yard. "…in the same way that Brandy is an allegory for all of humanity?"

"Yes. No. Maybe," Five says. He holds his left hand in his right and bows his head. I slip my left hand between and intertwine our fingers.

"What does he mean?" I whisper.

"Towards the end," Andre says. "…the historians got it wrong…mythology." He crosses his arms. "We, Olympians began to turn on each other. The Titans were beaten, the Primordials were a story of old…we had no battles to fight anymore. So, we turned on each other. People started losing faith in us…"

He shakes his head. "Hades and Zeus, brothers fought like the bitterest of enemies." I gasp. "It's probably why Ezra's so passive now."

"She reminds me so much of…," Five says, but trails off before finishing.

Andre smirks and tilts his head to the left. "I can see that."

"Who, Ezra?"

"No," Five says. "Ares. Brandy reminds me so much of Ares. So, much potential in them…wasted…"

"Well," I start. "Ares's potential might've been wasted, but…Brandy's in there…right now." Five purses his lips and nods.

"Besides, Ares was led astray by Hades," Andre says. "In the end, the only person capable of stopping Ares's rampage was Athena...they fought for months...constantly, without breaks, food, drink, or sleep. They fought until they joined with the land. Athena could've beaten Ares...but I think she was just tired of the fight."

Five tilts his head skyward. "The rest of us were soon to follow. We were the downfall of us."

****

"Well, I hate to leave you two when you're on such a cheery subject." I kiss Five on the cheek. "But since you two seem to be as thick as thieves again, I'm gonna go inside and leave you to talk." Five watches me all the way to the door. I turn to him, make a talking sock puppet move with my right hand, and then point to Andre. He nods.

I go inside and turn left instead of right. I look back and AZ's standing at his doorframe, staring at the girls' side. What's he doing here? Shouldn't he be in school? He holds up three fingers and points to the left. Does he know that I'm…? I make my way to the third door on the left and peak in.

"What are you a stalker?" Brandy grumbles, sitting on her bed. "Or did Five send you to make me say, 'thanks for the ride home.'"

"I'm pretty sure Five has no idea I'm even here." She frowns. "I just want to talk. Can I come in?" She pulls her knees up to her chest and nods. "Thank you."

"Whatever," she mumbles.

"I don't understand you, Brandy." She scoffs and turns away. "I mean, you seem smart, clever, and passionate, even if a little misguided. So, why do you waste your time fighting idiots that mouth off at you pointlessly?"

"You know what, you can go now."

"Nope." I sit in the chair at her desk…that are both just like Five's. I wonder if that was her choice or his.

"Gah, you're so annoying."

"I've heard that."

"Well, allow me to verify the rumors. It's true."

I laugh. She even sounds like me. "I didn't realize you were funny, too." She bows her head. "And so pretty."

Her head lifts, and her eyebrows tweak. "You…you think I'm pretty?"

"Yes. And all that other stuff too." She smiles a little but wipes it away quickly. "Five's right though. He's extending a hand to you, and you just keep smacking it away and that is not smart."

"You don't even know me."

"Fair enough." I stand and walk toward her. "May I?" She shakes her head. I arch my eyebrows and give her my best puppy dog eyes. She groans and scooches over to her left. I sit on the edge of her bed facing her.

"So annoying," she murmurs.

"You're right, Brandy. I don't know you…but I wasn't trying to help either. Well, not help you." I stare out her window. "I'm here to help Five, because he does know you…and he thinks the world of you."

"He's got a funny way of showing it." I smile. "What's so funny?"

"Brandy, does Five yell at you a lot?"

"What?"

"Like when he reprimands you…not abusively or anything…just he gets angry and raises his voice?"

"Reprimands? Who talks like that?" I lean forward. "Fine. Yeah, okay? He yells all the time…" She lowers her voice. "…when I get in trouble." She comes back up. "But I yell right back and before I know it, we're arguing. Not talking, just screaming at each other."

"Yeah." I tilt my head back. "After my mom died, my dad and I got into screaming matches all the time…and over the stupidest stuff. Like one time, I left my homework at home, and the teacher wrote me up…and I yelled at him because he…" I make air quotes. "'…let me forget it.'" I shake my head.

"Wow, petty much?" I snicker, thinking about what Five said earlier. She frowns.

"Okay. I'll take that one. It was pretty petty…I had my own pretty petty party constantly going on back then." I sigh. "In fact, it wasn't until my third year of undergrad that I realized why we'd always argue."

"Why?" she moans, leaning forward…like looking in a mirror.

"I yelled, because I was hurt, and I didn't know any other way to express it. I'd lost my mom…who was like my best friend and I did NOT handle it well. My emotions were all over the place and that's not even considering that I was a teenager.

"My dad was a different story though. He yelled because he was worried about me. He could tell that I was in pain…suffering, but he had no idea how to help me."

"He couldn't just kiss your booboo and make it better anymore," she mutters, staring at her left hand held in her right.

"Yeah. Exactly." I shake my head. "I didn't realize until I was 21 that it wasn't his fault that he didn't know how to 'fix me' or that that scared the hell out of him. It was my fault that I didn't let him in though." She lifts tear-filled eyes to me. "We missed out on so many good times together, because we just didn't know how to talk to each other anymore."

"So, your dad argued and got upset with you because he worried…because he loved you?"

"…so much. If not, I'm pretty sure he'd have let me run wild and not gave a damn about my future."

"D-do you think…?" She sniffs and wipes away a tear quickly. Her eyes dart up to stop subsequent tears from falling. "…do you think Five cares about me…? And that's why we yell at each other?"

I put my hand on both of hers. "I know he does." She nods, and more tears fall anyway. "Brandy, he may not be your father, but I promise you, he cares about you more than enough to fit the bill." She shudders, and more tears fall away. "Brandy?"

"I love him too," she sobs. She lifts her head. "Sometimes, it's just so hard to talk to him…like I want to tell him all this stuff going through my head, but I can't."

"I know. And it's okay." I move closer to her. "You'll be able to one day…and then the two of you will be closer than ever."

She wraps her arms around my waist and rests her forehead just above my collarbone. She shivers, and tears fall against my collarbone. "Why can't that be today?" she moans.

I put my arms around her, my left-hand pats her back, and I stroke her hair with my right. "That's a good question and the truth is…well, only the two of you can answer it…together." She leans back and looks at me. "Aww, look at you." I take some tissues out of my pocket and give them to her.

She sits back and wipes her face. She sniffs and smiles. "Your last name's Clark, right? You're the woman who wrote the article about Five?"

"Yeah."

She nods. "You must really care about Five, too." I frown. "Not in the same way, just…you like him…like, like him like him…maybe, even love him a little bit."

I giggle awkwardly and shuffle. "What makes you say that?" Wish I'd asked that without the nervous laughter continuing.

She laughs this time. "I don't know. I mean, to start with, you're here talking to me for him…" I purse my lips and nod. She wipes her nose. "…but more than that, I read your article. You're a good writer…"

"Thank you."

"…and it was basically a love letter to Five."

"Whhhhhaaaaaaattttt?" I stretch out.

"It was in the way you wrote it. At first…" She makes a chopping motion. "…like in the first half, it was just a bunch of facts and boring stuff."

"Really?"

"Well written boring stuff," she adds with arched eyebrows. I nod. "…but about halfway through, the way you wrote it changed. It went from 'he did this' and 'he did that' to 'he inspired' and 'he led.'" She smiles. "It was pretty obvious from the start of the article to finishing it…" She points at me. "…you caught feelings."

"I did no- Is it that obvious?" She nods. "Yeah. I did. Bad," I moan like a depressed sheep. She giggles. I love to hear her laugh. It's so much warmer than most peoples' laughter is. It's the laugh of someone, who's gone through hell and come out the other side…like Five's and Ezra's.

"That's a perfect example of what I mean," I say. "The fact that you read that article and picked up on that right away, tells me that you're just as smart and insightful as I think you are."

"Clever. You said smart and clever."

"And a little bit of a smart ass." She laughs. "It's okay, having biting, sarcastic wit is a sign of intelligence." She nods. I pat her tissue-filled hand. "Think about the stuff I told you…and if you want to talk to Five, I promise he'll listen. I'm gonna go back outside…make sure he and Andre aren't duking it out on the lawn."

"What?"

"Fighting."

"Oh. Why?"

"They had an argument recently about a woman…"

"You?"

"No," I groan in a deeper voice. "Ha. No. I did not leave any room for confusion." She giggles. "I'll see you later."

"Hey," Brandy says as I reach the door. "If um, I need to talk to somebody… some time… um, could that somebody, be you?" I pause to think it over. "I mean, I'm not sure if I'm there yet with Five. None of the other girls here are as old as I am and…" She shakes her head. "…I can't really relate to Pearl, Alijiah, and Ramona." She rolls her eyes. "Especially not Ramona."

I nod and slip one of my cards out of my back pocket. "Here." She takes it. "My cell's on the back…" She flips it over as I move back to the door. "…and I'll see about getting your sentence reduced."

She smiles. "So, you're a lawyer and a writer now?"

"Jack of all trades," I say, stepping around her doorframe…and nearly running into "…Five?" I whisper and peer back at Brandy's door. "What are you…?" He bounds off the wall and tips his head to the right. I follow him down to the cross hallway. "Were you eavesdropping?"

"Yeah," he admits, solemnly. "Thanks…for talking to her. You're better at talking to her about this stuff than me."

"No. It's just…some things you need to hear from someone who's been through it and not from someone in the thick of it with you."

"Either way, thank you."

"Anytime."

"I know," his voice takes on an amused ring. "Especially since you caught feelings for me." I gasp and cover my mouth and nose with both hands. He covers his mouth with one hand imitating me.

"No," I moan from behind my hands. I shake my head and stalk away from him.

He follows close on my heels. "It's okay."

"No."

"It's okay."

"No." I turn to him. "Don't look at me and no." He smiles. "I was perfectly okay letting you think that you caught feelings first." I lower my hands, staring into those big brown eyes of his. I sigh. "Five...I..."

"Interesting." I gasp for a completely different reason this time.

"Prometheus," Five snarls, left hand dangerously close to his thunderbolt mark. "How'd you get in here? Why are you here?"

Prometheus steps out from around the corner, near the back doors, in a...hmm, I guess I'd call it a hat in hands kind of way. It's sadder than Five did when I figured all this out, but the guilt is definitely there. "I've been here a while," he says. "It took some time to get through Demeter's barrier undetected, but once I did, I figured I should stay a while longer."

Electricity moves between Five's arm and his hand. "Wait," I say, putting my hand on his. "Prometheus, are you okay?"

He looks at me. "I'm confused."

"It's called common human decency," Five says. "Most humans have it. Nicole clearly has too much."

"Not that," Prometheus says. He motions down the hall. Five grits his teeth. "I...overheard your entire conversation with that mortal...and you were so insightful. The way you related your life to hers, was brilliant in its simplicity."

"Thanks?"

"I never intended for you to become this."

"What do you mean?"

"He's talking about when he stole fire for human beings," Five says. "It wasn't actual 'fire.' Fire was an allegory..."

"Nice use of the word."

"Thank you. ...for enlightenment and wisdom. When he stole 'fire' from me and gave it to mankind, he stole knowledge and gave it to men."

"Men?" I turn back to Prometheus. "Let me guess, just men."

"I didn't know their potential," he mutters. "I had no idea they could become...this. That they could aspire to...more." He motions down the hall. "That mortal girl..."

"Brandy," I correct him. "Her name is Brandy."

"...Brandy...I can hear it..." He moves his hand next to his right ear. His hand claws as if gripping something. He turns it like a knob. "...I can hear her mind working...calculating...planning..." He looks at me. "...you inspired her."

"Now, do you understand?" Five asks in his booming, stilted voice. "Do you understand why I came down on you as harshly as I did? I had every intention of dispersing that wisdom to mankind, but I wanted to do it for all of mankind…men and women alike."

Prometheus bows his head. "The punishment was so harsh…"

Five steps forward, but I hold his hand…keeping him near me. "If you truly think so," Five continues. "…go back…read a history book…read up on how women suffered because they were thought of as less than men…how they still suffer." Prometheus lifts sorrowful eyes to me. Five wraps an arm around me and holds me close. "I wanted my sisters and my daughters to be thought of as more than testaments to domesticity."

"AND WE WERE," Alijiah rumbles, just before extending a silver spear tip over Prometheus shoulder.

"You said it," AZ says, bringing his staff a breath away from Prometheus's neck from the other side.

Prometheus doesn't raise a finger to defend himself. His eyes move languidly to AZ. "Well, if it isn't Zeus's errand boy." AZ grits his teeth and presses his staff forward until the wing rests against Prometheus's neck. A tiny trickle of blood flows from the point of contact.

"Stop," Five barks. AZ and Alijiah look at him. "Prometheus, if you promise to go in peace and never return here, I'll let you leave without incident."

"You what?" AZ snarls. "I heard him mention Brandy on more than one occasion…"

"He got through Pearl's barrier," Alijiah adds. "If we let him go, what's to say he won't tell the other Titans how he did it."

"Nothing." I hope Five has a more convincing follow-up than that.

"If I go," Prometheus says. "If you grant me safe passage, I vow on my power as a Titan that I will not harm anyone here, nor will I return without permission."

"What about the others?" Alijiah growls.

"I won't tell them either," he says, staring into her eyes. They both come back to Five. He tips his head toward the front door. Alijiah lowers her spear and AZ takes away his staff. Prometheus turns and walks away. He stops. "Five, you should know that Perses intends to resurrect his parents and his brothers…" He pushes the door open. "…not just his family, all of the Titans in fact. He wants to open a portal between this plain and Tartarus." Prometheus vanishes, and the door swings closed behind him.

"Am I crazy?" I start. "Or did he just say Perses intends to open Hell?"

"Pretty much," AZ groans. "Pretty much."

****

Chapter 19: Doubt

"For the sixth time," I whisper to Five. "…I'm fine. After the Nemean Lion, I don't think anything will faze me anymore."

He laughs softly and leans his forehead against mine. "I don't doubt it." I laugh…and turn so that I can kiss him on his cheek. He kisses me on my cheek. He nuzzles his nose against mine. I feel his warm breath against my lower lip. It smells like cinnamon…and electric sex…he HAS to know how much I want him. "You act like you wanna kiss me or something."

I nibble my lower lip. "Or something," I breathe. He kisses me, and I lose the cafeteria around us. I drape my arms over his shoulders, and he puts his hands on my hips. We kiss again, and his tongue meets mine. Amazing electric tingles, dance along my lips…my tongue…and my hips and I…

"AHEM," AZ moans. Alijiah, Pearl, Raymond, and AZ stand in the doorway.

I tried to warn you that we were coming, Ray says. *But apparently, you can't hear me when he…well…has your attention.* I cover my mouth and adjust awkwardly. *Don't be embarrassed…Five's ridiculously hot.* Ray, are you…?

"Children eat here," Pearl snarls. They walk in and join us at this small cafeteria table. I mouth a quick 'sorry' to Pearl. She shakes her head.

The six-little colorful round seats attached to the miniature circular tables are kinda hard on my butt but aren't too uncomfortable. Pearl sits on the other side of Five. Alijiah sits in the opposite seat and Ray sits beside me.

"Tell her what he said," Alijiah demands.

Five sighs. "I don't believe him. There's no way Perses could've found a way into Tartarus without Ezra knowing about it."

"Brother," Pearl moans. "…as I've said, Ezra may be the King of the Underworld, but he's not the gatekeeper…" She swipes out from herself. "…Styx is."

"Yeah," AZ says. "But I know how powerful she is…and there's no way he can use Styx to bring back all of the Titans." He shakes his head. "If anything, she might be able to pull one Titan back across the river at a time. And even then, she'd need years to recharge."

"She's had years," Alijiah says. "Millennia, actually."

"Then why now?" Five says. "Why bring back Perses now? And as far as I could tell, Prometheus came back years ago. He seems the most…um…" He looks at me.

"…acclimated?"

"…yeah, acclimated to this time…other than Styx."

"He said he'd been walking the earth for 28 years," I say. "Just like you. I think his return triggered yours…all of yours really."

"Which means Perses came after," Pearl suggests.

"What about Mordechai?" AZ says. "I mean, so far, all of us have been younger than Five. What's with Mordechai?"

"Um," I interject. "I think his beard and…" I close one eye to remember the word. "…pe'ot…might have you confused." AZ's head tilts in a questioning manner. I put my index fingers to my temples and make little circles coming down. AZ frowns, but nods.

Pearl leans forward. "Mordechai is only 27. He'll be 28 in a month."

"Really?" AZ chirps. I nod along with Pearl. "He looks so much older."

"Speaking of which," Five says. "He should be a part of this conversation."

"I'll go get him," I say, standing up.

"I can get him," AZ says. "And I'll be back in a fla-"

"It's okay." I motion for him to sit down. "I want to…plus, long day at my desk. I need to stretch my legs." AZ nods, and I turn toward the cafeteria doors.

"What I don't understand," Alijiah rumbles, in as much as a rumble as her pleasant voice can muster. "Why did you let Prometheus go? We had him."

I pause at the double doors, wanting to hear the answer, too.

"Because," Five says, sounding weary. "I saw it in his eyes. Doubt. It was a tiny hint of doubt in what he was doing…his reason for hating me…all of us." Five crosses his arms and nods. "It's that same doubt I saw in his eyes when Zeus argued with him. Like maybe he's repentant." Five looks at me. "Like he wants to be a better person than he used to be." I smile and walk out.

I think Andre was right about Five. He sees allegories…makes connections to everything in life. It's probably why he goes about things the way he does. He's a small fish in a big pond, but he knows his ripples can reach far and wide. I nearly laugh, considering that he's Zeus which means technically he's a huge fish in a big pond.

I make my way to the back hallway…and its only resident so far. I hear a metal on metal clang and start running. I don't know why. If he's under attack by another god, there isn't a damn thing I can do to help him. One more clang sounds. I reach his doorway and… Mordechai brings his hammer down on a glowing piece of metal. Clang.

"Nicole, dear?"

"Sorry," I say. "I didn't mean to intrude. I just heard the noise and thought…I don't know what I thought…" I shake my head. "…sorry."

"It's alright." He holds the glowing piece of metal up to his face, the white-hot light reflecting off his glasses and highlighting his reddish cheeks. I hold my breath, because I can only imagine how hot that is. He inhales deeply, sucking air in through his mouth. The metal's glow fades quickly. He twists his clamp to get a look at it from either side. "Perfect," he declares. He taps his anvil with his hammer, and it vanishes in a puff of fire.

He lays his hammer down and takes the short sword blade from his clamp. He works to fit it into a grip and guard.

"Who's that piece for?"

He huffs a laugh, while fitting rivets into the hilt. He goes over to a wall… How did I not notice that when I first came in? …filled with weapons. There are shields, spears, axes, swords, daggers, something that looks like a spiked brass knuckle, a few maces, and a bow with silver arrows next to it.

Mordechai finds a place for the short sword and hangs it. "Sadly, this…all of it, is for Ares."

"Ares needs that many weapons?"

"God of Chaotic War," Mordechai says, picking up a Trojan helmet with a large reddish-orange brush moving down the center and a tail hanging off the back. He puts it on top of his dresser and ruffles the brush.

He picks his coat up from the bed and slips it on over his black vest and white button up. "Ares tends to use whatever's handy and is a master of all weapons." I nod. "Speaking of weapons," he continues, walking over to his dresser again. He touches his clamp and hammer, and both burn to nothing without burning anything else. He takes a box from his top dresser drawer. It's big enough to hold a watch, but not quite big enough for say, a cup.

He walks over to me. "Have you ever heard about the dagger made of Stygian iron?"

"Of course, I haven't," I say in a lighthearted manner.

He laughs. "Well, it is said that a dagger made of Stygian iron…that's iron dipped in the River Styx…was dipped again after being forged." I stare at the box in his hand. Does he have it in there? "This dagger was believed to be so powerful that it could actually kill a god."

I gasp. "So, there's a weapon that could kill gods…that anyone can use?"

He chuckles again. "I doubt it. Superstitious nonsense, of course."

"Says the reincarnated god of Fire."

That one made him belly laugh. "True. True. The Stygian Dagger, though…it couldn't kill a god, but it could cause some serious damage…especially to demigods." I frown. "Heracles and the other half-god, half-mortals." I nod.

"So, you have it?"

"No." He takes one hand away from the box and shows me his palm in an explaining manner. "But when I awakened a few years back, I searched for it. I tracked it down to a collector in New York. He valued it highly. It just so happens that with my restored memories, I knew how to find a weapon he'd value more."

He nods. "A not-so-even trade later, and I had the dagger."

"But I thought you said you didn't have it."

"I don't. Well…" He opens the box... "…not anymore." …revealing two rings. One looks like blackened metal surrounding platinum trim, and the other matches it, only made of gold…but they're not…I don't know how I know, but I do. They look like wedding rings, simple bands…with the dark metal on the outside and platinum and gold on the inside.

"Morty, if you're asking me to marry you, you should know Five won't be happy…plus my dad would kill me if I converted to Orthodox Jewish."

He laughs. "No, no…but…" He takes the gold ring. "…these are for you." He slips it onto my right middle finger, and it fits perfectly. "I melted the dagger down…" He shifts the box to his other hand and claims the other ring. "…and forged these two rings out of it." He places the platinum ring on my left middle finger.

"Now, while they can't defeat a god…they can repel a god and temporarily nullify their powers." He nods. "Trust me, I tested them."

"I don't doubt it." I look at my fists. "And I really don't want to know how you did that. Nullify? So, with these rings on…"

"When you punch a god…it'll be just like you're punching a mortal. Also, you'll probably be able to slay monsters and other 'mythical' beasts." I nod. "Raymond says you have a pretty vicious punch so…"

"Well, my dad did insist on me taking kickboxing classes since I was a kid so…" I nod and hold my right fist higher. "Thanks for this."

"You're very welcome. Thanks for the visit…"

"Oh, right…the reason I came. Five's meeting with the others in the cafeteria, and he wanted you to join."

He nods, grabs his hat, and motions toward the door. "Who am I to keep a god waiting?"

"A god yourself," I say, slipping his hat out of his hands. I place it on his head and straighten it. He smiles and follows me into the hall.

I look down at the beautiful, perfectly crafted rings on my middle fingers. I lift the platinum ring on my left hand and notice the lightning bolt etched long ways across it. I check the gold one and sure enough, it has the same lightning bolt.

"Morty, can I ask you something?"

"You just did." He smirks and tips his hat forward.

"Why the lightning bolts? Is it because Five's 'laid claim' to me?"

"Of course."

"Of course," I repeat sounding unconvinced. "What does that mean…laid claim to me? Is it like I'm a pet…or…" My mood drops. "…or like I'm his property or something?" Mordechai laughs. "It's not funny."

"Your misinterpretation is." I frown. "When we were gods, we would lay claim on mortals to signify they were important to us. They were favored…not to be possessed or used…but to be treated as the most precious example of humanity…a god-like example on earth."

"Me?"

He nods. "It's his way of saying he loves you." I take a deep breath that catches in my throat. "Gods have been willing to kill other gods…give up being gods themselves to protect their claimed mortals."

He loves me. *I could verify for you.* YOU MOST CERTAINLY WILL NOT! *Ow, ow, ow…mind yelling!* Then stop intruding! *Sorry, Five was wondering what was taking so long.*

Mordechai and I walk into the cafeteria. Ezra, Andre, and Ramona have come in. Ezra sits at the table with the others, but Ramona and Andre stand, Ramona behind her brother, hands on his shoulders.

"Are you alright?" Five asks. I nod. His eyes move to Mordechai. "What were you two talking about?"

"What? Nothing. Why?"

He points at my face. "Because you're blushing."

I touch my cheeks. "I…" I nibble my lower lip. "…just heard something good about you."

"Yeah?"

"Yeah."

His eyes dart to Mordechai and back to me. "Oh." He takes my right hand and holds it up to his face, examining the gold ring. "So, you made them?" Mordechai nods. "What about the other piece?"

Mordechai shrugs. "I'll have to find a few more pieces of Stygian iron for those."

"Alright," Five says and returns to his seat, pulling me down beside him. Five turns to Andre, and all eyes follow his.

Andre sighs with his hands behind his back. He opens his eyes slowly. "First, let me say this…" He looks at Five. "…I know you never asked me about it other than when it originally happened, but I didn't betray you when we fought Styx.

"It took me a little while to put all the pieces together, especially since pretty much all our former lives are considered mythology."

"So, no evil Titan plans section in the library?" I suggest.

Andre smirks. "Not so much. It took some time to figure out what Perses's endgame is. I won't lie, finding out that Styx was working with Perses and Prometheus gave me a solid lead.

"Also, I knew that if you'd killed her that would've made Perses step up his plan and proceed faster, quieter. I'm sorry that I didn't explain that…but it was pretty hard to get a word out when you're being attacked by the most powerful Olympian EVER…"

"AHEM," Ezra says, making the entire cafeteria vibrate.

Andre sighs. "I'm sorry, Five. I shouldn't have stood against you…it was my fault you got hurt, and I never want that to happen again."

"Yeah," Ezra says. "We never meant for that to happen."

"Like I was saying, if you'd have killed Styx in a rage, Perses would've stepped up his plans." He points at the floor. "Seeing her, I figured out the what and why of his plan…but it took me a little while before I could figure out 'how' he intended to resurrect the other Titans."

Five takes on a smug grin. "And you have, haven't you?"

Ezra and Andre mirror their brother. Pearl scoffs a laugh and bows her head. "Always too smart for his own good."

"I'll take that," Andre says with a nod. "I'll always take that compliment."

****

Chapter 20: Slumber

"I'd just like to start again," Andre says. "...by saying that I'm truly sorry. If you'd have died...and it was might fault..." He holds his hands up near his chest.

Five nods and bows his head. I lean into him. "I like this new humble Andre."

"Don't get used to it. It won't last."

Surprised it's lasted this long.

I snicker. Andre glares at me and then at Ray. "If we're done with the running commentary," he complains. *See?*

"Should I apologize again, too?" Ezra asks, motioning to himself. Andre smacks him on the back of the head.

"Anyway," Andre says. "After doing some research and consulting some books on the occult, metallurgy, and even a few on alchemy...I think..."

"The occult?" I ask. "Why the oc...?" I trail off, noticing everyone's staring at me. I point at myself. "...mortal, remember?"

"A lot of Hecate's magic...information on her grimoires," Ramona starts. "...was reduced to superstitious mumbo jumbo...because unlike Hecate, anyone who tried to replicate her magic didn't have the power of a god making the spells go."

"Hecate...? What does she have to do with...?"

Five leans into me. "She's Perses's daughter...and Zeus...might've spoiled her..."

I nod. "Oh...so, if one of you could replicate her magic..."

"Possible," Pearl says. "...but we're not naturals at mage-craft like Hecate was, so it would take an extraordinary amount of power to activate even the most basic of her spells."

"Plus," Ramona picks up. "Our..." She looks at Ray, who returns her glance. "...cousin...was given a LOT of leeway." They both look at Five. He sighs.

"Can I continue?" Andre asks. "...if we're all done playing educate the mortal?"

"Petty," Alijiah says.

Super petty.

I hold up my hands in submission. Andre nods. "What my sister forgot to mention...is that for some of Hecate's spells and potions, special ingredients were required.

"As an example, she devised at least five...as many as ten, that I could find..." He puts his hand on a suddenly tense Ezra's shoulder. "...ways of sneaking into and out of the Underworld…and Tartarus, specifically without Ezra knowing about it."

"I thought only AZ or Styx could do that," Alijiah says. I frown.

"That was the way I set it up. I gave them permission to come and go as they please." Ezra shakes his head. "Hades gave them permission."

"Okay," I say. "…then the question is why Hecate would want to."

Ramona groans and rolls her eyes. "Why would we even worry about something like that now?"

"No," Andre says, pointing at me. "That is the question actually. You see, Hecate had different spells and potions for every reason and way she'd devised to get in and out of the underworld, including if she wanted company going in or coming out."

"So, she could swap," Ezra says. "The best way for me not to notice people were missing would be…"

"…to swap out an army for one very powerful being," Andre says. "Or, swap one very…" He looks at Five. "…very powerful being in exchange for an army. To that end, I found the spell that would allow her to force a doorway open into Tartarus directly…one that would be large enough and self-sustaining long enough to allow an army to march out on their own."

"Hecate with an army," Pearl says and then shivers. "As if she doesn't already get everything she wants."

"Exactly," Andre adds.

"Just how much did you spoil her?" I whisper.

"*Too much*," Five and Ray say together.

Andre walks around the table. "An army completely loyal to her, because she got them out of hell. This particular spell needed very specific ingredients…very hard to come by ingredients…"

"…back in the day," I suppose. "But now…"

"Thanks to modern manufacturing," Alijiah joins.

"…it's much easier to a get ahold of vast quantities of these materials…" Andre slips a small black book out of his jacket pocket. "…iron sulfide, silver nitrate, and sulfur dust," he reads.

"So," Five says. "With Styx's help, he pretty much has everything he needs to open the doors to Tartarus?"

"Not quite," Andre says.

"Opening a portal that large needs a lot of power," Ezra says. "But keeping it open…" His eyes grow cold and the skin around them darkens. "…probably requires a sacrifice of human souls…or at the very least, human life force."

"That's bleak," I say.

"Really bleak," Pearl agrees.

"Tartarus is Greek god hell, right?"

"Yeah," Ezra says.

"So…um…who's all in there? In Tartarus, I mean, and could they really come back?"

"The worst of the worst," Ezra says. "Hades divided the fallen and the Titans into three categories…" He lifts one finger. "…first those who were completely stripped of their powers were sent with the mortals in the afterlife, the Fields of Asphodel…" He lifts his second finger. "…the ones who fought alongside the Olympians went to Elysium, while some went to the Isles of the Blessed…" He thinks for a second. "…Valhalla is probably the closest thing you know to resemble it…" He lifts his third finger. "…and finally, those who fought against us…went to Tartarus…a whole world apart from the rest. It houses…like I said…the worst of the worst."

"Not the worst," Five says. "Our father isn't there."

Pearl, Andre, and Ezra shiver. I remember this story…originally, Five…Zeus was the youngest…his mother, Rhea, hid him from their father, Cronus…because he… I swallow a lump. …ate his five brothers and sisters prior.

The old Titan was paranoid…an oracle told him one of his children would be his downfall. I look at Ray. *It became a self-fulfilling prophecy when he started gobbling them up…until Rhea couldn't take it anymore.*

I guess that's the trouble with knowing the future. Ray nods.

"It's weird though," I say aloud. Everyone looks at me. "It's weird that Perses is the one who's driving all of this." I shake my head. "In all my research, he's mentioned very little in mythology."

"He was a minor god," Ramona says. "So, it makes sense."

"Yeah, but when you add to it that Styx is helping him…I mean, she was on your side originally, right?"

I think I can lend some insight to that, Ray says, projecting his thoughts to everyone. *I got a sense of her emotions after she left.*

"How?" Ramona asks. "You weren't even here when she attacked."

No, but her shadows cut through the sunlight…her emotions were so strong that they left an impression. Madness has driven her to side with her enemies against her former friends.

"Madness?" I ask.

"Styx was never in Tartarus," Pearl says. "And even if she'd gone, it could've never held her. The draw of her river is too strong. She always walked the line between life and death, but she never died or reincarnated into an earthly body. She has spent these millennia roaming the world."

"Probably hoping for someone like us to return," Alijiah says. She bows her head. "Or like her husband…"

Ezra frowns. "He can't." He lifts his head. "He can't…I put Pallas in a special cage for that very reason."

"That's awful," I sigh.

"She sided with us," Ezra says. "…but there was no guarantee that she'd remain loyal."

"And you did something that only made sure she'd turn against you some day." Ezra frowns. "I mean if something were keeping you away from the person you love…or even loved…" The corners of his mouth turn down, and his shadows swell. I stand, feeling a surge of anger. "…and furthermore…whoa…" I sit, suddenly feeling an energy drink/sugar-high type crash.

"Nicole?" Five says, sounding concerned. "Are you all right?"

"I don't know." I wobble. "I felt dizzy."

I'll check on her. Ray appears next to me or did he walk normally? *Does it matter? Hold still.* He puts his middle and index fingers on my forehead. He gasps, or at least, I think that's what it was. *It was, smart-ass.* I giggle or at least, try to giggle.

This isn't just weariness, he says to everyone. *This feeling has the influence of a god behind it.*

"He must have stepped up his plan," Andre growls.

"His plan?" I moan.

Pearl appears on the other side of me. She places her hand on my cheek. "Definitely a god. Draining her physical energy…"

…and mental strength simultaneously.

"Like I said," Andre starts. "His plan…nothing ever said he needed to open the portal and then drain humans…there'd be no point in opening it if he couldn't keep it open."

"I can't believe him," Five growls, slamming his palm on the table. Electricity sweeps across his hand and then moves from his left eye to his right. "Perses, I'll never forgive you for involving the mortals in this!" I touch his arm. The eye electricity fades away. He trembles. "It's why the Titan's had to go…" I nod and caress his cheek.

"Their fear of us," Pearl says.

"…their paranoia," Ezra adds.

"…his paranoia," Andre growls. "…drove him and all of them to pull insane plans like this…draining mortals to cover for their own weakness."

"It's a good thing that you're wearing those rings," Mordechai says, motioning to my hand on Five's cheek. "If not, you'd probably be in worse shape than you're in already."

"Yeah, you're probably…" I freeze. "…right…I would be…but what about…" I stand, wobble, and then run for the double doors.

"Nicole?" Five says. Half a dozen footsteps follow behind me. I reach the end of the hall, make the cross hallway for the dormitory side, and turn toward the boys' side. I run into the first room on the right.

"No," I moan and try to stay on my feet, clutching my stomach.

"What's wro-" Five stops instantly when he sees what stopped me. Xavier's laying on the floor, unconscious. He looks like he just fell over. His little arms sprawled out to his sides. "Xavier?" Five breathes.

I run over to him and kneel. "Is he...?" Ramona asks from the doorway.

"He's breathing," I sigh in relief at the sight of his shoulders rising and falling.

Five comes in and kneels beside me. He puts his pointer and middle fingers to the base of Xavier's jawline. He frowns. "His heartbeat's steady...it's weak, but steady." I tremble and hold him closer. "Give him to me," Five says. "I'll put him in the bed. I need you to check on..." I nod as Five stands with little Xavier in his arms.

"It's the same with all of them," Ramona says, stepping back into the doorway.

"All?" AZ says next to her. He swallows a lump and vanishes.

"The girls," Ramona says, running toward the girls' ward.

I turn back to Five, pulling the covers onto Xavier. "Go." I nod and run out. I follow Ramona down to the girls' side and quickly move to... I pause. Pearl and Alijiah stand at the next door with their hands over their mouths. I walk over as calmly as possible. It's Brandy's room.

I peak in...and AZ is on his knees, cradling Brandy against his chest. He trembles and holds her closer. "Why...?" he moans. "...why'd Perses do this?" Pearl shakes her head. "And Prometheus...he loved mortals...he loved them more than anyone..." Tears pour from his eyes. "...how could he go along with this?"

"We'll..." Alijiah starts, tugging on Pearl's arm. "...go and check on the others."

"Okay," I say, walking into Brandy's room.

"She doesn't deserve this!" AZ weeps. "She doesn't...she didn't do anything to them!" He lifts his tear-filled eyes and all doubt about which he is, boy or god, fall away. AZ is a boy...a boy crying over someone who he can't stand to lose.

"We should get her into bed," I say. He looks at me. "She'll be fine. We'll find Perses and Prometheus, and we'll stop them."

He nods and slips his arms under her. I turn down her covers, and he lays her down. I work to take her boots off as he slips off her jacket. He caresses her forehead, sweeping some of her dark hair to one side. Her eyes twitch, she releases a moan, and smiles. He sighs.

I pull the covers up on her. "You're sure?" I look at him, and his eyes meet mine. "You're sure that if we stop them…she'll be fine."

"I can't say for sure, but that makes sense, since they need the life energy of mortals to open the portal." I caress her cheek, and she leans into my hand. Strange, she's reacting so much more to outside stimuli than Xavier did…probably because she's older. "If we stop them from opening it, she…and everyone else should wake up."

"Good," he snarls. "Because I'm not going to stop Perses…I'm going to find him…and I'm going to kill him!"

****

Chapter 21: Door

I walk into the cafeteria, sliding my phone into my back pocket. Five's staring out the window with his back to me. The light from outside pours through, casting him in shadow. His shoulders hunch, his arms cross, and his stance is wide. If he were a military man, I'd guess he was pondering a dangerous deployment. Not much difference, I guess. I look down at the ring on my right middle finger…the little, golden lightning bolt staring back at me.

"Are you just going to stand there staring at me?"

"I was staring at my ring." I walk over to him as he turns to face me. "Are you alright?"

He steps forward, staring into my eyes…only half his face lit, but I still see both. "You tell me."

I check his left eye in the light, then his right in darkness, before taking in the two sides of his whole face. I shake my head with the corners of my mouth turning down. "This…is not your fault. You didn't do any of this. You didn't want any of this." He scoffs. "What?"

"You really do know me, don't you?"

I put my hands on his cheeks. "I've been staring at this handsome face every day for the last two months…I know it…I can read it like a book."

"Hah," he groans with a rattle to his voice. "The people who I promised to protect…"

"…need you now more than ever." I kiss him. "They need you, not overwrought, stressed out you…not even vengeful, wrath-bearing god you, but normal, doing things for the greater good you."

He puts his arms around my waist. "I might need you…" I smile. "…you know, to remind me of that every now and then." He puts his forehead against mine.

"As many times as you need me to."

He smiles that warm infectious smile of his, causing me to reciprocate. "What'd you find?"

"Nothing," Ramona says.

We found nothing on the grounds or anywhere around here, Raymond adds.

"We put all the children to bed," Mordechai says.

"They all seem to be sleeping soundly. No pain, just…against their will and deeply," Ezra adds.

"The girls are all in a similar state," Alijiah adds. Five's jaw clenches. She steps closer. "Brandy's fine. She doesn't seem to be as bad as the rest of the kids, in fact." Five nods.

"I could tear Perses apart with my bare hands," Pearl snarls.

"Only if I don't get to him first," AZ says.

"We'll have to find him first," Andre says, marching in past the others.

Five's hand vibrates with an electric spark. I take his hand…the sparking one…his electricity vanishes. He looks down at our hands. "The sooner we find him, the sooner we put a stop to this and save Brandy, Xavier, and all the others."

"The sooner the better," Andre says. "The longer Perses's victims are under, the more at risk they are." He walks to the nearest table and places a leather-bound book and several scrolls down there. The others gather around him.

He opens the book and motions to it. "From what I've read, a spell this far reaching needs a focal point…a way to channel the energy it's gathering."

"Like a funnel?" I ask.

"Exactly." He picks the book up. "Only this funnel needs to be made of stone and metal…" He flips through a few pages. "…specifically, some place heavy in granite, sandstone, and steel, but preferably iron."

"Can't be a lot of places like that around," Ramona says.

"Yes, except pretty much every building in the city," Mordechai counters.

"It needs to be more open than your average office building," Andre says.

"Parking deck?" I suggest.

"Maybe," Andre says. "But more than likely, the cars would throw the balance off too much."

"I can do some checking," I say. "…use *Georgia Now's* database to do a faster search."

"We don't have time to go to your office," Pearl says.

"My laptop. It's out in my car. I can connect to it from…"

"Keys?" AZ says, holding a hand in my face. I toss them up, and he plucks them out of the air as he vanishes.

"Did you get in touch with anyone?" Alijiah asks.

I take my phone out. "Nope. No one from the paper, no city officials, nobody. The entire towns asleep." I shake my head. "I even called the park rangers on the outskirts of town and still nothing."

"Here you go," AZ says, holding my laptop bag. "Just an FYI, Five might've cleaned up the neighborhood, but still not the best idea to leave your laptop in the car."

I touch his cheek, comfortingly. "I'll keep that in mind." He nods.

I take out my laptop and sit down with Andre's scrolls and book. "You said places with sandstone and granite…odd combination except, like

Mordechai said in buildings." The power comes up, and I connect to the VPN…knowing that if she were conscious Ronda would be ready to strangle me. Ugh, I just bummed myself out, wondering if she, Steven, and the others are okay.

"Baby," Five says.

"Yeah?" He smirks. I blush…answered to that way too quickly.

"Focus."

"Right." I start an advanced search for the materials Andre mentioned as well as a wide enough space to house an army. "Alright," I moan as the search engine throws back a list of possibilities at me. "I think we might be on the right track. I've turned up three textile mills…" I scroll down a little farther. "…correction one textile mill that fits the bill."

"Only one?" Ezra asks.

"Yeah, the other two were torn down, and the debris has been removed from the sites." I keep searching. "I need something to write on." Ramona slides a small notepad near my right arm, and Andre passes me a pen. "Thanks." I jot down the address for the textile mill. "It's Grover Mills over on Holiday. I'm writing down the address just in case.

"Next, is a construction company and a construction site downtown?"

"The building that exploded?" Five asks.

"No," Andre says. "That building only had damage done to its top three floors and even then, not enough to warrant bringing the building down. It would need to start on the lowest floor and with all the floors above it still intact, that one wouldn't work."

I nod. "So, Moors Construction over on Bleaker is doing the construction work on the new First National Bank building downtown and so far, all they have erected…" AZ and Ezra snicker, soon followed by Mordechai and Andre. I even hear a little bit of Ray's laughter in my head. "…ugh… boys…"

"What's so funny?" Ramona asks.

I turn and open my mouth. "Nope," Pearl says with a hand on top of my head, turning me back to face the screen.

Virgin goddess and generally naïve about these sorts of things, Ray explains quickly. I nod.

Pearl clears her throat. "You were saying about the bank?"

"Right. So far they've only er…um…put up a skeletal frame and a couple of the lowest levels."

"That'll work," Andre says. "But what about the company itself?"

"They have a large amount of land bordering the city limits, and they keep a lot of material onsite so that they're ready to go as soon as the paperwork is signed."

"Alright," Five says. "It sounds like we have a plan."

"It'll take all night to search all of those places," Alijiah says.

I touch my forehead. "She's right. Plus, if the way I feel is any indication, I think the drain is starting to feel worse."

"Is there something you can do to help, Pearl?" AZ asks. He shuffles. "The second you touched Brandy, she got some of the color back in her cheeks."

"I probably could use my power to help keep the people's physical strength up, but they'd still be suffering mentally."

And that's where I'd come in. Ray touches the lyre on his left forearm and the golden instrument appears in his left hand. *I'll play a song that will soothe the people's minds.*

"Do it," Five says. "Find the tallest building you can near the heart of town. It should help with your range."

Ray and Pearl nod and run out of the cafeteria.

"That still leaves the problem of three locations to search," Mordechai says.

"And my brother and Pearl are good, but they can only do so much for so long," Ramona adds.

"Then we should divide and conquer," I suggest, putting my laptop away. "There are only 3 of them and from what I've seen of Perses so far, he talks a good game, but he's not good at throwing bows."

Five laughs. "Love it when you talk slang."

"I use my slanguage sparingly."

He nods. "Andre, divide us up accordingly."

"Division of power," Andre says with a hand on his chin. "Alright." He tears the textile mill's address off the notepad. "Here." He gives it to Ramona. "I think you, Mordechai, and AZ should check there. Mordechai and Ramona can check the grounds outside, while AZ searches the inside with all of its nooks and crannies."

"That sounds gross," AZ suggests.

"You've never had an English Muffin before?" Mordechai asks. AZ shakes his head.

"Later, guys," Andre says. "Next." He tears off Moors Construction Company's address. "Ez and I will check out Moors Construction. It's a wider space, but level, and I'm sure most of the material is stored outside."

"Going off the pictures I saw, yeah," I tell him.

He nods. "Plus, there's a lake next door, so…"

"Right," Ezra says.

"Finally, Alijiah and Five can check the construction site downtown. The two of you should be able to handle them…" He looks at me. "…provided…"

"I'm going. End of story."

148 | Olympus Awakening

"Baby," Five says, stepping closer. "It'll be dangerous."

"Like they couldn't send some supernatural creature here, specifically looking for me to distract you," I say. Five bows his head.

"Don't worry," Alijiah says. "We'll protect her." Five looks at her. She smiles. "We will."

"All right, little one."

"Don't call me that," Alijiah whines.

"Everyone has their assignments," Five says, ignoring Alijiah's plea. "We all know what's at stake here…times have changed, so have we, but our enemy has not. The Titans have returned to spew their selfish agendas again, and again it falls on us to stop them. So, let's do what we do."

"Yes," Andre says. "Take out the trash."

"I like it," AZ says and vanishes.

"Ramona," Five says. He takes a set of keys out of his jacket pocket. "Take the Olympus van." She nods and plucks the keys out of mid-air. It was as if he handed them to her. She and Mordechai follow AZ.

"We have our bikes," Ezra says, walking out next.

"Take care of yourselves," Andre says. "And each other." The two of them walk out as nonchalantly as usual.

"You feel like driving?" Five says, following them.

"Sure." I drape my bag over my shoulder. "Wait a minute. If you have an Olympus van, why do you always walk?"

"Maybe it was to get sympathy from a certain pretty journalist," he suggests as we walk out the front door.

"Or," Alijiah says, while nudging him in the ribs with her tiny elbow. "…it could be that because of the constant static charge built up in his body…he starts to wreak havoc on a car's electrical systems if he's in one too long."

I pause, opening my driver's side door.

"No worries," Alijiah says. "It's not nearly as bad on hybrids…" I nod. "…but he absolutely destroys full electrics…that aren't nearly drained dry anyway."

Alijiah climbs into my tiny back seat and takes my bag. We're on our way soon after. As we pass through the whisper quiet streets, I can't help noticing the running cars stranded roadside with their driver's a sleep behind the wheels. I dart in and out of the right lane to void the 'traffic jam.'

"And…" Alijiah says, eyes glued to the tiny back window. "…you couldn't reach anyone?" I catch her staring back in the rearview. "No one at all?" I shake my head.

"I'm sure she's alright," Five says.

"She?"

"Alijiah's maternal grandmother moved here to be closer to her." I catch her eyes in the rearview again, just in time to see her wipe away a tear.

I come back to my rings. If not for them, I'd be unconscious, too…like Ronda, Brandy, Xavier, Steven, and Alijiah's grandmother. Five puts his hand on top of mine. I look at him. "We'll save them, baby. We'll save all of them." His right-hand clenches into a fist and electric sparks streak across his knuckles. He's definitely not the god from Greek mythology…he's the man I'm falling in love with. The man who's going to save an entire city.

****

Chapter 22: Key

"I guess it'd be asking too much for you to stay in the car."

I glare at him, while undoing my seatbelt. It slides across my lap, and I climb out. I hold the seat for Alijiah. She stands beside me and joins me in glowering at Five over the roof.

"You should've known better than to ask her that."

"It was more hoping than asking."

"You're gonna pay for that one," I warn, marching around the car.

"Can't wait."

The loose gravel under foot acts as a driveway onto the construction site. You can see the gray streaks moving across the road from dragged and crushed rocks. A fence encloses the entire construction site and a blue tarp covers that. The wind blows tossing a tiny dust cloud and the smell of dried earth over the fence. We walk over to the gate. "I don't suppose either of you knows how to pick a lock."

"Sure do," Alijiah chirps. She grabs the lock and snatches it off effortlessly. The heavy chain jingles and falls to the ground. She pushes both sides open and walks through.

"Should I pull the car through?"

Five shakes his head and follows her. "If we end up fighting, we don't need your car getting caught up in the fray."

I run to catch up. It looks like a normal construction site, except darker and so much creepier. I sigh. Five taps my hand, before taking it. "Stay close?" I ask.

"Yeah. Alijiah?" he stage-whispers.

"I don't see anything. No portal…no movement either though."

"Nicole, you have your phone, right?"

"Yeah."

"Call Andre and Mordechai. See if they've turned up anything."

"Okay." Alijiah wanders off searching the grounds.

"Yeah?" Andre growls through the phone.

"It's Nicole. Five wanted me to ask if you guys have seen or found anything yet."

"What? Are you his secretary now?"

"Stop being a jerk and answer the question."

"Sssshhh," Five issues still looking around.

I cover my phone. "Sorry."

"No, we haven't found anything. There's a couple of more places Ez wants to check before we call it a night."

"Alright. I'm gonna call Mordechai. I'll call back if they've found something."

"Right."

An icy wind whips through the skeletal building, giving me a shiver. Five steps in the path of the wind still looking around, although at this point, I wonder if he's searching for the portal or doing the overprotective thing. Although, I can't complain, because even my phone feels cold against my ear.

"Hello?" Mordechai's voice comes through the phone as warm and pleasant as it does in person.

"Who's calling at a time like this?" Ramona says in the background.

"Hey Morty, it's me."

"Oh, Nicole. Hello. How are you?"

"What are you two calling about afternoon tea?" she snarls. "We have a job to do here."

"I'm much better, thanks. I think whatever Ray and Pearl are doing is working."

"Good. Good. If you're calling about the portal, unfortunately, we haven't found anything yet...and AZ's been through the interior of this mill twice and nothing."

Five looks at me. I shake my head. "Okay, Morty...FYI, neither have we and the same goes for Andre and Ezra."

"Oy."

"Exactly. We'll call back if something pops off. We may need to widen our search parameters."

"I'll leave that up to you and the other Brainiac. Speak soon."

"Later, Morty." I end the call and slip my phone into my back pocket.

Alijiah returns. "Anything from the others?"

"Nothing so far."

"I wanna check the higher floors," Alijiah says, staring up at the frame.

Five steps closer and puts his hand on top of her head. "Alright, but be careful, little one."

She knocks his hand away. "I told you not to call me that." She pushes her left sleeve up to her elbow, revealing her mark, which looks like an owl. Weird. She touches it, and an owl comes out. It lands on her left forearm, only it looks like the mechanical owl from that cheesy movie from the 80s or was that the 70s...? Clash of the...something or other.

"What?" she asks, taking in my unimpressed face.

"It's just...Five's thunderbolt, Andre's trident, and Mordechai's mobile forge..." I shrug. "...compared to them, this owl seems...underwhelming."

"Oh, she's so gonna make you eat those words," Five whispers.

Alijiah taps the owl's head…it explodes into sheets of gold, moving around her. A flash of deep red swirls from the owl's center and wraps around her neck. The gold sheets cling to her body around her torso, forearms, shins, and head…when the swirling dies down…she looks like a Spartan warrior complete with gold breastplate, greaves, bracers, and helmet with a long red-bristled brush running along the top.

She wears a long red cape that clasps over her left collarbone with the owl's faceplate as a pin. There's a spear with a silver tip and a round-shield visibly affixed to her back. She holds a silver bow in her right hand.

I lift my hands in submission. "…consider my words…eaten." She nods.

"Be careful, little one," Five says.

"Don't call me that," Alijiah moans, leaping up to the third floor and vanishing over the edge.

"Why do you call her that? She clearly doesn't like it."

He sighs, staring at the third floor. "It's a holdover from when we were gods." He looks at me. "Alijiah was Athena…Athena was Zeus's child."

"Still doesn't explain why you keep calling her that…and besides…doesn't that go for like half of the Olympian gods?"

He groans and bows his head.

"We can talk about it later."

"One day," he says. "…and it wasn't half…only five of them…"

"Is that why…?"

"No."

I nod and take my phone out again. I turn on the flashlight and walk toward the structure.

"Careful."

"Yeah, but I was just thinking…this is supposed to be the building's ground floor, right?"

"Yeah. Looks like."

I check the chalk marks made on the girders and the concrete foundation. "Well, if this is going to be the ground floor…wouldn't they have to dig deep to make a basement and subbasement?"

Five walks over and lifts his right hand over my right shoulder. His hand sparks with electricity, lighting the entire area. The soft pale blue glow reveals rough cut, concrete stairs moving down straight ahead of us.

Five lifts his hand higher, and his eyes narrow. "Definitely worth a look." He lowers his hand. "We should wait for Alijah to come back though."

"Okay." He puts his arm around me, forearm resting at the base of my neck. My shoulder blades rest against his chest. "You're worried about them, aren't you?"

"Of course," he breathes into my hair. "…and a couple of other things. It's different this time. I'm different this time." I nod, my chin tapping his arm. "I don't want anyone but you, Nick. I need you to know that. You've made me different."

"I didn't do anything."

"You've been the bravest, most passionate, most amazing person I've ever met."

"Make a girl blush, why don't you."

"Oh, and you're gorgeous too."

I smile. "Yeah, that did it."

A boom comes from the roof. Five's other arm wraps around my waist, and we dart backward. We come out from under the building and look up. "Do you see anything?"

"No," he groans.

A crimson streak flies over the edge of the building. "Alijiah?"

She twists and turns in mid-air and fires one, two, three arrows back into the building at the same speed as automatic handgun fire. She lands next to us and brings her hand up to her bowstring. A silver arrow forms as she draws the string back, aimed at the edge of the building. She looks like a hunter, waiting for her prey.

Darkness pours over the building's edge. "Styx," Five growls.

"Yeah," Alijiah snarls, firing five arrows in rapid secession. A clang rings out for every arrow as Styx uses her shadows to deflect them one by one. "Go," Alijiah snaps, shoving Five and consequently me away. Styx lands and swings her sickle at Alijiah, who defends herself with her bow, using it as a blunt weapon.

Styx takes another swipe, and Alijiah rolls out of the way. Styx attacks again, and her sickle meets Alijiah's shield. Alijiah rises and her bow, disappears under her cape. She pulls out her spear and twirls it, causing Styx to retreat.

"Murderer!" Styx growls.

"It was a war!" Alijiah says, circling Styx like a lioness moving in for the kill. "…we gave your husband and you the same choice. He chose the wrong side. You understood that once. What's happened since then?"

"You can ask my husband…" She flips her sickle around so that it runs the length of her arm. "…when I send you to Tartarus." She runs her free hand along the handle, and it extends. The blade stretches out, and her sickle becomes a scythe. She rushes headlong, but her shadows circle around Alijiah and come at her like black daggers.

"Al-" Before I can finish, Alijiah spins, swiping the shadows, cutting off their tips. She comes back around, and her spear darts out toward Styx's head. She barely avoids the shot and retreats again, throwing layers of shadow in front of herself to gain some separation from Alijiah. It doesn't help. Alijiah's an unstoppable force of nature, moving like water flowing downhill through the shadows.

"She's…she's amazing," I tell Five.

"She always has been," he returns in a tense voice.

"What is it?"

"PROMETHEUS. PERSES. COME OUT AND FACE ME!" he bellows, his voice sounding like thunder, still rumbling in the distance after he finishes. His eyes dart around, taking in everything rapidly. He turns, putting himself between the building and me.

"What?" Perses says, stepping out of the shadows with his arms behind his back. His long black coat hanging open over his matching slacks and gray shirt. His hair dangles across his frost blue eyes that seem to hide something. "Were you looking for little old me?"

Perses brandishes a smile almost as deadly as the sword he pulls from behind his back. It twirls around, and he brings it up with his elbow bent, like a fencer. He stabs at Five, who keeps me behind him. I take a few more steps back so that Five feels free to fight him head on. Perses thrusts repeatedly, but Five avoids the jabs. I search through my phone for Andre's number and hit send…

"Can't have that just yet," Prometheus says, taking the phone from my hand.

"Prometheus?" He crushes it effortlessly and then wiggles his fingers to free them of any random phone bits.

"GET AWAY FROM HER!" Five roars as electricity flares up around him. Perses jumps back and holds his sword up to deflect several of the stray bolts. Five's discharge tears up tiny chunks of earth and sends pieces of gravel flying in every direction.

Five holds his left hand over the mark on his arm. It flashes pale blue and throws sparks off connecting with his hand. He pulls his thunderbolt free before twirling it like a staff. He points the tip at Prometheus.

I stare between them. It's weird, but I don't have the same feeling I had the first time they squared off. In fact, I'd say they're positions have switched completely with Five being the wronged party seeking retribution, and Prometheus feeling his actions drove his enemy too far.

"Prometheus?" He looks at me and that same sadness seems to move to me now. He grabs my wrist and pulls me closer. "Prometheus, what are you…?"

"LET HER GO!" Five barks and hefts his thunderbolt like a javelin. "Let her go," he repeats with a sinister growl. "Or, I'll kill you where you stand, and I will make sure you endure a living hell before you go."

"If you didn't want to put her life in danger," Prometheus says. "Then you should've kept her at home."

"I'm a person," I say, preparing to punch him with my free hand. "No one tells me to sit and stay like a dog."

"Clearly," Prometheus returns.

"Last chance," Five snarls. Electricity moves up his arm, dances along his fingers, and fills his thunderbolt. It flashes and glows paler blue, blurring the edges of its shaft.

"That's just what I've been waiting for," Perses says, extending a clear orb toward Five.

"Wha-?" Five manages, before the tiny transparent sphere taps his thunderbolt. Perses steps back, electricity flickers away from the thunderbolt and flows into the orb. It keeps drawing power away, and the weapon dims. Five lowers it and tries to move away, but it's as if the orb draws it back magnetically.

"YES!" Perses says as the thunderbolt loses the last of its electric glow and takes on the soft gleam of polished steel. "Hahaha," Perses chortles, throwing his head back. "MWAHAHAHAHA! I didn't think it could possibly be this easy!"

Five stares at his drained thunderbolt. "What'd you do?"

"Me?" Perses roars in truly overdramatic, over-acting fashion. "No, no, no, no, king of kings…what have you done?" He points at Five. "You've lorded this fantastic power over us. You've used this power to terrify and compel us to obey you…and I'm sick of it!"

He extends the orb. It looks like the sphere Mordechai originally gave Five. It's a thunderstorm in a bottle. "Now," Perses says. "You've handed me the key…and with it, you've sealed your destruction, Zeus…tonight…you and the other Olympians will face your final end!"

****

Perses stumbles like a drunk, hoping for one last drink. His stupid, maniacal laughter hasn't died down either. I try again to pull away from Prometheus, but he's a god. If he doesn't want me to move, I'm not going anywhere and considering that orb thing drained away Five's lightning…

Five holds his still empty thunderbolt horizontally across his chest, staring at it. "Perses, I don't know where you got that orb…"

"You know where I got it."

Five tenses up. He grips his thunderbolt tighter. "…but I recommend you be very careful with what you have there."

"Oh, I know exactly what I have here…and I know exactly what I intend to do with it."

"Good," Five says in a sexy bass that makes my insides feel…I don't know, nervous…but in a bad way. "It's good to have plans and know what you want out of life." He closes his eyes. "Everyone should be so lucky as to figure out what they want out of life…" He renews his grasp on his thunderbolt as his eyes snap open, filling both eyes and weapon with reinvigorated electric fire. The thunderbolt glows brighter than it did in fact. "…before they die."

Five vanishes and in his place, there's a spark of electricity, dancing in the tiny crater he left. "What the…?" Perses manages.

"Behind," Prometheus rumbles.

I gasp. Five is behind Perses with his thunderbolt raised, ready to strike…no, ready to kill. Perses ducks, barely avoiding losing his head. He dives out of the way, as Five comes down causing another crater, where Perses used to be…

"Whoa," I moan as gravel splashes away like a rock tossed into water.

Prometheus pulls me closer, wrapping a protective arm around me. "Stay close. You don't want to get caught up in what happens next."

"Which is?"

"NOW!" Perses yells, while jumping back…still cradling that thunderbolt-filled orb as if his life depends on it.

"YEEEEEEEEEEE," a figure squeals jumping out of the shadows. It's a black man, with long reddish-brown dreads that frame his face and hang down his back. He's wearing a black sleeveless hoodie, exposing his large arms. His black over gray and white camouflaged cargo pants meet his black boots at the ankles. He smiles, causing his bushy goatee to separate more. The light of Five's thunderbolt shines across his coppery skin. He twirls something silver in each hand.

"Epimetheus?" Five growls as the two twirling silver pieces collide with his thunderbolt.

"Epi...?"

"Epimetheus," Prometheus says more like a complaint. "He's my younger brother." I frown. Epimetheus pushes Five back with twin silver-notched maces pressed against his thunderbolt. Five plants his feet, stopping Epimetheus's progress. Five pushes off, causing both weapons to separate from his.

Epimetheus rolls and does a sort of whirling, spin in mid-air. His arms spread wide, maces pointed in opposite direction. Each hits Five's thunderbolt, stopping him from advancing. Epimetheus hits the ground, turns...spiraling on his head and shoulders, kicking both legs outward, and jumps up. Again, each mace crashes against Five's thunderbolt with a horrible metal on metal clank and then a scraping whine. The second Epimetheus's feet come down again, he springs forward and hits Five's thunderbolt again.

"He fights like..."

"...a wild man," Prometheus says. "...like a rabid dog. He fights like he doesn't have a thought in his head other than what's happening at the moment." I frown and look at Prometheus. "That's why fighting him would be so difficult for someone like Zeus or Athena, because they're such powerful and skilled warriors that fighting him would be...like trying to fight a cloud...or the wind...there's no rhyme or reason to his attacks."

"Come along," Perses says, walking past us, moving into the building. "Your idiot brother can only hold him off for so long...and bring the mortal."

"What?" Prometheus says. "That wasn't the plan...we were just supposed to use her to make Zeus angry...force him to use his thunderbolt at full power to warn us off."

"Indeed," Perses says. "...and that plan would have been considerably more effective had you brought her back with you...so that we could force Zeus to come here alone." I gasp and glare at Prometheus's face. He looks like a scolded child. It softens my expression. "Now, her continued presence will keep Zeus from using his thunderbolt at full power against us."

Prometheus sighs and ushers me toward the stairs after Perses. I try resisting again, but again...god. We move downstairs with Perses using Five's captured lightning as a lantern.

"So, that's why you were at Olympus?"

"Yes," he answers simply.

"You were going to kidnap me?"

"Yes."

We move down twenty steps before reaching a landing and turning to go down twenty more. The entire corridor smells like dust, feels damp, and it's a few degrees colder than outside.

"You're very brave," Prometheus compliments in the form of a whisper. I moan, questioningly…not exactly sure, if I'm actually ready to talk to him or not. "You didn't call out for Zeus as I carried you away."

"His name is Five," I return, just as quietly. "And if I'd called him, I might've distracted him…and he might've gotten hurt."

Prometheus makes an approving noise. "So, you protect him by not making him protect you."

"I don't need a knight in shining armor. I want a man who'll stand beside me…prop me up when I need, but knows I'll do the same for him."

"Someone to foster your ambitions?"

"Yes."

"And you theirs…? Athena said something similar to me once…I didn't understand it until I met you." I peer at him over my shoulder. Only the left side of his face his visible, but it holds more than enough sadness for both.

"Aren't you two getting chummy? Stockholm Syndrome, perhaps?" Perses says as we make a left, rounding a corner. He laughs. "It was so fortunate that Five brought his favorite pet with him."

"Not luck," Prometheus says. "I told you, he would. She's important to him and Zeus has always…will always keep the things he holds dear close."

"Yes, my man, you called it," Perses says in an eerily stiff voice. "And here I thought you were covering up for your own failure." Perses inhales deeply. "Well, water under the bridge…because I doubt we would've been able to hold him off without her."

"Why are you doing this?" I glance at Prometheus. "Why are you working with this lunatic? Everything I've read about you from Greek mythology said that you were a proponent of mankind, so why are you working with him?" He doesn't respond. "Andre said that if you're able to open this portal, linking Tartarus to this world, the humans you're using would die."

"I don't care about humanity anymore."

"Tell that to someone you didn't just try to keep close to you to keep her safe." He swallows a lump, and his hand on my shoulder twitches. "You're such a liar," I growl. "You don't care about humanity, but one girl…one girl had you doubting EVERYTHING!"

"I told you that you impressed me, not…"

"Not me. Brandy. That girl whose thoughts…the girl whose renewed spirit was so strong, you actually felt it." I glance at him again, and his eyes go to the floor. They shimmer in the tiny sparkles of pale blue light. "She's going to die if you're successful, Prometheus. Don't let your anger toward Five and the others, snuff out any chance she…and thousands like her have. Please."

"As a counter point," Perses says, stepping into a large open area. He kneels and turns on an electric lantern. Soft yellow light washes over the walls and the few loose pebbles that found their way down here. "I hope you remember the thousands of years you spent in your own special corner of Tartarus…having your innards pecked out by Zeus's diligently loyal eagle."

Prometheus rubs his stomach with his left hand, and his grip on my shoulder tightens. I groan, and he eases up a bit.

"It was Zeus himself who passed judgement on you and casted you into the pit, where his brother had a special prison ready for you. They chained you to a rock…left your eyes open so that you'd be forced to watch the eagle destroy you, time and time again." Perses switches on another lantern, this one glows pail blue on the opposite side of the room. "It was because of that mad god-king's rule that you, your parents, and all the Titans are stuck in Tartarus. All because he had an issue with his daddy."

"Issue?" I moan. "His father tried to eat him, just like he did to his brothers and sisters, before him…"

"Absorbed," Prometheus says. "Cronus absorbed the five originals, hoping to make their power his. Rhea, having fallen in love with Zeus at the very sight of him, hid her youngest child from her husband." Perses nods and kneels next to a large bowl. He places the lightning orb on a three-pronged garden stand…that looks suspiciously like the same metal as my left ring. "Rhea taught Zeus all about her husband's powers and his own…hoping that one day he'd be able to separate his siblings from their father."

Prometheus shakes his head. "In the end, Rhea brought about the downfall of her husband and all of the other Titans…a crime she's not been brought to answer for yet."

"Crime?" I ask.

"THE CRIME," Perses bellows, pointing a dust-covered, trembling finger at me. "…of bringing that self-righteous, self-centered bastard up to challenge his father!"

I turn to Prometheus. "That's not Five…that was Zeus."

"Same person. Different face."

"Different face. Different upbringing. An absentee father, but a mother who was every bit as loving and nurturing as Rhea was." He frowns. "You've walked this earth for the same 28 years that he has, Prometheus. You've seen how much this world can change a person for better or for worse." I put my hand on his heart. "Believe me when I tell you that it's changed Five for the better. I'm living proof of that.

"Five wants to work with the other Olympians to reach his ambitions, not in spite of them. He's hit some roadblocks, but unlike the Zeus you might've known, he never tried to use force to get his way."

"And what are they?" I frown. "Zeus's ambitions…what are they? Surely, he shared them with you."

"He wants to become powerful…"

"He is powerful," Prometheus growls.

I shake my head. "Not like that. He wants to go about it as a normal human would. He wants to climb through the ranks, starting out small and growing larger. He doesn't want to grab power but share it." I smile, remembering his face the night he told me…I think I fell in love with him all over again in that very moment. "He's seen the course that mankind is on, because he walked that same course…and he'll give anything…do anything to stop history from repeating."

Prometheus bows his head and releases me. As odd as it is, I can feel his gears turning. His mind is churning over what I've told him. Does he believe me or is this something else?

He lifts his eyes and looks at Perses, mixing ingredients in a large bowl. He pours in a deep blue-silver liquid and a yellow powder, smells like sulfur. He mixes the ingredients again and stands, taking a small box of matches from his pocket. He lights one and tosses it into the bowl. The mixture flashes deep blue, then red, before coming down to a pale-yellow flame and going out. A puff of smoke rises, and the smell of rotten eggs moves through the room. I cover my nose.

"It's ready," he says, claiming the bowl and the lightning orb. He walks around, pouring the mixture in a large circle on the floor. It looks like a bluish-gray gel, but with sparkly, powdery bits throughout it, making it lumpy. He finishes the circle.

Prometheus catches him by the bowl arm. They lock eyes. "What do you think you're doing?" Perses grumbles.

"If we do this," Prometheus starts. "You know what will happen. If the portal to Tartarus opens, war will erupt." Prometheus's face goes blank and his head cants slightly. Is this his foresight ability?

"Every Olympian still sleeping in their human body will awaken," he says mechanically. "…they will come to meet us with force, brother." His head tilts more. "Is that what you want? Do you not remember? Dionysus's madness? Hecate's torments…all while smiling?" Perses smirks. "Ares's path of destruction…that mad god alone cut a swathe through us, laughing maniacally the entire time. Is that what you want?"

Perses snatches his arm away and tosses the bowl to one side. It clangs against the wall, its contents flying and splattering in every direction. "I thought it was what we both wanted."

"I did, but that's before I thought through this."

Perses's eyes turn to me. "That mortal has turned your head as surely as she's turned Zeus's…" He tilts his head and glares at Prometheus. "…or is it some other part of you that she stirs?" My jaw clenches. "Has she bewitched you with her forked-tongue? Tempted you with bodily pleasures, brother?"

Prometheus shakes his head. "No brother. I simply remembered the torments of war…and I remembered that the Titans are not the only thing in Tartarus. The creatures of legend would surely sweep across the land decimating the humans. The cyclopes…the chimera, gryphons, leviathan, gorgons…the Medusa…

"And the Primordials, Perses." Prometheus covers his mouth, and his hand trembles. "My goodness brother…do you remember the stories about the void…and how the Primordials swept in, making that emptiness worse…" Prometheus's hand claws upward. "…what could be worse than nothing, brother?" Perses sucks his teeth. "Chaos. Gaia. Nyx…" I moan. That name tickles in the back of my head. It feels fuzzy, like a little itch that I can't scratch. "…Pontus and Thalassa. They're all there as well."

Perses lowers his eyes and turns toward the circle. He sighs and lifts the orb up to his chest. He begins chanting into it.

"BROTHER?" Perses ignores him and continues chanting in…ancient Greek, perhaps?

"What's he saying?"

"His daughter's spell," Prometheus says. "It's basically offering up a portion of a god's power to open the gates of hell."

"Prometheus?" He turns to me. "You can't let him do this. You're the Titan of Foresight, right? Then use your ability…think through what will happen to the world if he goes through with this."

"I already have." He returns to Perses and grabs him by the arm. He pulls him back away from the circle. Prometheus shoves him away and points at him. "…and I won't allow it!"

"TRAITOR!" Perses snarls.

"No, pragmatist." Prometheus reaches for the orb, and Perses holds it away. "There has to be a better way!" Perses pushes against Prometheus, who focuses solely on stealing the orb away. "Think brother. That same madness that gripped Styx…I experienced it as well when I first awakened. That madness will be ten…no, a hundred-fold with the others. They'll rage, and this world will burn."

Perses erupts with laughter. "DON'T YOU GET IT, BROTHER? THAT'S THE WHOLE POINT!" Prometheus gasps staggered by the revelation. Wait, what was that…? I heard a noise that sounded like tearing and… Now, I hear dripping.

Prometheus stumbles as Perses wrenches a sword from his abdomen with a horrible, wet ripping noise. Prometheus falls to his knees, clutching his stomach. He coughs, and blood spatters on the floor in front of him. He trembles and lifts pain-filled eyes to Perses.

Perses taps Prometheus's chin with the bloodied tip of his sword. "Titan of Destruction," he chirps happily. He hisses into a snarl of a laugh, before he steps closer and gives his sword a spin. "The spell requires a portion of a god's power as a catalyst for opening the portal." He raises the blade above his head, the tip pointing downward. "I wonder how powerful the portal will be if I give it your entire life!"

I'm in motion before I can tell my legs or arms to move. I step forward and punch Perses in the face with a right cross as hard as I can. He falls and rolls away. His sword clanks on the ground in front of Prometheus. There's a tiny clink. I look at my fist…I didn't think…right, my rings are made of Stygian Iron. I come back to Prometheus. He wobbles, eyes closing lazily.

"Come on," I moan, putting his arm over my shoulder.

"No. You should…get away…while you can."

"Not without you…" He stares at me in disbelief but nods and pushes himself up as best he can.

"Oh no," he moans. I look expecting to see Perses rushing us with his sword…but it's worse. The lightning orb, the cracked lightning orb is next to the portal. Perses must've dropped it when I punched him. It's rolling toward the edge of the powder. It makes contact, and a portion of lightning escapes through the crack. It explodes and…a spark of electricity sweeps across the powdery-gel mix…and then it bursts like a flare, moving around the surface burning bright red. I squint but pull Prometheus and myself away from it.

Next, it erupts in a burst of pale blue flames from the center. The pyre reaches the ceiling…I'm surprised we weren't incinerated it's so big and so intense.

"What should we do?" I ask Prometheus.

"GET BACK!" he growls and shoves me away…as Perses stabs him in the chest with a two-handed thrust. Everything seems to move in slow motion. I fly back, arms and legs flailing in front of me as if reaching for Prometheus. His hand outstretched toward me, still in the same position as when he pushed me. It falls to his side as the rest of his body slumps and bows with the weight of Perses's lunge. The Titan of Destruction bares his teeth and drools like a mad dog, satisfied with his meal.

Thunk… I hit something. The wall probably…thump! I hit the floor and ow! I see my hand…and gotta…try to…pink…horseshoe…clovers…

****

Chapter 24: Night

"Ugh." My eyes flutter open. Wait, did they? I blink. Yep, definitely open. It's just pitch black here. "Wherever here is."

I lift my head. "Ow." It's screaming out a samba. Worse, it has a rap song's heavy bass beat pushing it. I get my hands under me and push off. I stand. "Argh." That might've been a mistake. Head pounds out little drummer boy now.

I look around. For all the good, it does me. It's completely black here. I shiver, and it's cold. Colder than it was in the basement even. Wait, did I miss everything? What happened with Perses and Prometheus? Am I buried alive? Is that what happened? Or…I look down at the blackness where my hands should be. Am I dead? Is this what death like? Is that why I feel so cold?

"Am I dead?" My voice and heavy breathing echo in the darkness. Off what are they echoing? The echo came back at me from all four directions, but every direction sounded like a different distance…it took the longest to come back from in front of me. Maybe, I am dead, and this is my punishment for being a bad Christian or for falling in love with a Greek god. Still, you can't be faulted for whom you fall in love with, right? Especially someone as amazing as Five is.

"…but still to die like this?" I shiver and not from the cold this time. "Honestly, I never expected to survive this insanity. I figured I'd be killed by someone trying to take advantage of Five…" Tremble. "…but to go out like this…?"

I wish I'd gotten a chance to say goodbye to my dad…and Five, of course…maybe, Brandy, Xavier, and Ronda. I huff a laugh, maybe even Steven, Ray, Morty, and Alijiah. Ramona and Andre will probably laugh at me. "Stupid mortal…got herself killed." Pearl and Ezra will probably be indifferent about it. Ez might come to reap me himself though. Maybe, I'll be able to pass my goodbyes along through him.

I look around…and nothing's come into focus yet. I thought maybe my eyes would adjust to the darkness…and it's freezing in here…wherever here is. "I guess it's pretty lonely being dead, huh?" I complain, wrapping my coat tighter around myself and crossing my arms.

"Not as lonely as you might think," a voice calls back. It's weird, but it reminds me of Ray's voice…as if it's speaking directly into my mind. Only this is a woman's voice…puts me in the mind of Brandy…with less angsty snarl. It's more of a beautifully, melodic voice. "…but you should know that you're not dead."

"Who are you? Step out and show yourself."

"Now, what good would that do?"

Great, she's a smart ass, but she's right. If she stepped forward or backward or in any other direction, I'd never know. I can't see a thing.

"You said I'm not dead…what's your proof?"

"Well, I'm not dead, and I'm talking to you, so…"

"Yeah and that means about as much as the voice in my head reassuring me that I'm not crazy."

"Great, she's a smart ass," the voice calls back or she pulled it from my head the same as Ray does. "…but you're right." Okay, now she's just messing with me. "I suppose it would help if you could see me."

"Maybe." A big circle of light appears around me. It's so soft that it could easily be moonlight shining down on a cloudless night.

A woman steps forward, crossing into the light with me. She wears a dark cloak with the hood covering her head, showing only slight hints of her darker hair at the sides. Her long black dress moves down over her feet. It's sleeveless though and has a plunging neckline. I mean, I can seriously see her bellybutton. Furthermore, I think the dress is sheer, which would probably explain why she hangs out in the dark.

I move up from her bellybutton as she lifts her head and… I nearly gasp. …she's beautiful. Her pale skin seems to glow in the soft moonlight, especially those high cheekbones of hers.

She lowers her hood and pulls her hair out the back. It falls long over her shoulders and wafts in the no-breeze moving through here. As it does, it glimmers like a million stars twinkling in the midnight sky.

"Wow," I breathe.

"I take it you approve?" she asks, extending her hands to the side, presenting herself. I nod absently. She smiles. "Well, thank you. I do have to ask though, why were you lying to yourself earlier, dear?"

"Lying? About what?"

"When you said you didn't expect to live through this."

"So, you could hear me this whole time?"

"I can always hear you, dear…especially when you lie," she replies pleasantly, while calling me a liar to my face. "The truth is, you believed that together you and Five could take on anything thrown at you. Anything," she reiterates, turning to her right. She paces around the border of the moonlight circle, her bare feet smacking the ground as she walks.

"I'm just a mortal…" I throw my hand out, letting it flail. "…he's a god. I'd just slow him down."

"Do you truly believe that? Moreover, do you think for one second…?" She holds the appropriate finger up to driver her point home. "…he ever thought that?" She throws her hands out to her sides, showing her palms.

"Why do you think he allowed you to go to the construction site with him, even though he really wanted you to stay far away…to keep you safe?"

I shrug.

"Because he has faith in you. He believes exactly what you believe…the two of you together are stronger than apart. He values your opinion and your counsel in all things." I frown. "He sees you as his equal…as his mate."

"How could you possibly know all of that?" I rumble feeling violated. "Who are you?"

She intertwines her fingers in front of her stomach and inhales deeply through her nose. "Now, that is a very interesting question…" Her eyes drift over to me lazily. "…with a far more interesting answer…" She nods and points at me. "…oddly enough, this is the simplest answer…" She places her right hand over her heart. "…I am Nyx, the goddess of Night."

"Nyx?" I swallow a lump and step back. "…as in one of the Primordials?"

She snickers a laugh. "Whatever the Titans called us doesn't matter. I am simply…Nyx, and you are Nicole." I take another step back. "Careful, dear," she says with genuine concern. "Stay in the circle…" She looks past me. "…things…lurk in the dark."

I nod. She smiles. "Lovely, lovely Nicole," she says in sort of a gasping, whispery voice that seems to come from her mouth and my head at the same time. She steps…and in that one step, she moves from the opposite edge of the circle to stand directly in front of me. She cups my face in her right hand. Her skin feels warm, but also comforting and smooth as silk. "…so clever, so brave…so beautiful."

"Thank you," I say, unable to tear myself away from the chocolate pools of her eyes.

"You can relax," she says warmly. "I would NEVER hurt you, Nicole." I believe her. I don't actually know why, but I do. Her dress flows out from her as she steps back, and I realize it's not a dress and cloak at all. Shadows. She's wrapped herself entirely in shadows as clothing…no…they're not even shadows. She wears night as if it's a fabric.

"Once again," Nyx starts. "I want to reassure you that neither of us resides in Tartarus currently." I frown. "I know Prometheus told you that the other…" She motions to me. "…Primordials…?" I nod. "…and I were trapped in Tartarus, but this is simply not true."

"Okay. So, where are you? We?"

She smiles. "You are exactly where you were. I believe in the modern world what you're undergoing is called an 'out of body' experience. We, however, are where we've been since the rise of the Titans."

"Space?"

"Clever as always." Always? "No. We Primordial gods wait at the end of all things."

"Where is the end of all things? And why are you waiting there?"

She shakes her head. "Not where, but when, and we wait for the same reason we always have." She tips her head to me. I turn, and little dots of white and swirls of deep blue appear against the blackness. She moves up beside me and stares at it, seeming as fascinated as I am. "We Primordials are the Alpha and the Omega…the beginning and the end."

"So, you guys, collectively, are THE God."

"No," she says with a whimsical smile. "We are the beginning in the sense that the one, true God flings us into the void and allows us to play. Our revels bring life…bring destruction…the ebb and flow of the universe." She sweeps her hand across the darkness, and the visible star scape changes.

"So, you guys are like God's construction crew?

She laughs. "Not that God needs one, but yes, in a sense."

"You said that you were at the end, too. Is that why you're here? Because Perses opened the portal to Tartarus? Is the world about to end?"

She snickers quietly to herself. "My darling girl, the world will go on for millions of years…" Her eyes move to me. "…whether humans will go on with it is the only thing in question."

"Well, seeing as how I'm human…I kind of want that."

"So, do I."

"You're not what I expected from the goddess of Night."

"What were you expecting?"

I shrug and return to her star gazing wall. "I figured you might be a little more emo or something…" She laughs. "…but really, you're super cheery."

"I have a reason to be happy…Nicole."

"Which is?"

"Do you seek to pry, mortal?" Her eyes search my face, taking in every feature.

I hold my hands up innocently. "It was just a question." I shrug. "Answer it or don't."

"So inquisitive…so headstrong…so brave. I adore that in you." I nod, still watching the stars and alien galaxies pass by. "My time with you grows short, Nicole. Know that your part in this is far from over."

"My part in what?" She motions back to the stars. "Everything?"

She nods. "Prometheus was right. If the Titans return so will the Olympians and everything else from every dark corner of Tartarus. Both, Olympian and Titan, will be bound to earth. War will breakout and that war will be the end all things."

"All of humanity?"

She shakes her head slowly.

I swallow a lump. "You're talking way above my pay grade, Nyx."

She smiles as if amused. "I have no fear that you can handle it," she says, staring at the stars. I watch her, trace the line of her jaw, her cheekbones, and the perfection that are her eyebrows. She looks so familiar…as if I've seen her before, but I know I haven't. Her beautiful brown eyes come back to me. "Ahem," she says, pulling her 'hood' back up. "Sadly, even more than the return of the Titans, I fear the return of my own children."

"Your…your children?"

She nods. "I love them…so I cannot rein them in…not in the sense that they should be…and I am the only one who can…besides another of my children, but not one of them has the will to…not that I've seen."

I nod. "I have a couple of bratty cousins and trying to get them to control themselves is like trying to wash five cats at the same time."

"A delightful metaphor," she chirps with her hand over her mouth. Her mood drops all at once again. "My children…" She shakes her head. "…the war between the Titans and the Olympians very nearly caused their return. If Cronus walks the earth again…" She nods. "…this time, it would happen without fail."

"Okay. So, why are you telling me all of this? I mean, I get that my part's not over, and I'm close to Zeus but…"

"Ssshhhh," she issues with her finger over her mouth. "Oh, and you should know that his real name is Quinn…not Zeus, not Five, but Quinn."

"Quinn…as in quintuple…Five…"

"That's not the only reason he chose that name."

"Really? How do you know that? No one even knows what his real name is, except his brothers and sister and they're not telling anyone and even they don't know why he…"

"Ssshhhh." My mouth snaps shut as if locked. I try to talk, but not only does my mouth not open again…I think I've forgotten how to form words with it. She smiles and turns to me outright.

"My brave and clever girl," she says, putting her hands on my shoulders. "You will accomplish great things in this life…both as Zeus's love and as the woman known as Nicole Clark. To that end, I give you my protection." She cups my face in both hands and tilts my head down. She kisses me on the center of my forehead.

"What does that mean?" I ask as my eyes drift open, glad that I'm able to talk again.

Nyx smiles. "It means that I love you…and…" The light vanishes and so do Nyx's hands on my face.

"…and? Wait, what happened to the light? Nyx? NYX?"

****

Chapter 25: Moment

I take a deep breath and open my eyes, facing upward...I'm sitting up. "Oh, Nyx brought the stars back." I groan. "And the headache. Ow, ow, ow." Wait, no...the stars...we're not in the dark anymore...these aren't the stars she was showing me. How do I know that? I've never been able to recognize Orion's belt before tonight, but one conversation with Nyx and suddenly, I'm a star astronomer.

All astronomers are 'star' astronomers.

Ray?

Who else? And who were you having a conversation with?

What?

Never mind. When Andre couldn't get in touch with you, Five, or Alijiah, he started to worry. Yes, he even started worrying about you. They're on their way to where you are. Is Five okay? Alijiah? I haven't been able to communicate with them and you only just came back into focus.

I'm not surprised. They're fighting...Alijiah is fighting a very pissed off Nyx...

Who? I didn't hear that last part.

Sorry, I meant...Styx...and Five is fighting Epi...Epi...Prometheus's brother.

Ugh, I hate that guy.

Not a fan and as for me...no. No, I'm very not okay.

I'll say. I've been trying to get a read on you, and there are portions of your mind that I can't touch. It's as if night covers it. Is that right?

Never mind that...the portal is opening...burning bright and right in front of me.

I know. That's why I've been chatting you up, trying to keep you calm.

Right.

No wonder Pearl nearly passed out. Okay, I'm going to intensify my shielding efforts, but I'll let Andre and Mordechai know what's going on.

I nod...hope he could see that.

I did. Take care of yourself.

I will.

I squint. The fire's so bright...it's still burning with blue fire...it's like burning man...only blue. It's so warm, but not harsh. Why does that seem weird to me?

I tilt my head back; it rubs against the rough cinderblock wall behind me. Why can I see the sky? "Oh, the building's gone..." The fire must've destroyed the foundation above us. The ground around me...covered in metal splinters, pieces of concrete and mortar, and random bits of hollowed piping. It's all scattered in a perfect circle around me. Not one piece of debris came within two feet of me. "Wow."

"ANY MINUTE NOW!" Perses gloats to no one in particular, because I don't think he even realizes I'm still alive. He stands in front of the massive pyre, that's growing darker...it fazes from pale blue to violet and purple. Perses stares at it like a madman or a devoted follower preparing to worship it. His arms spread wide as if he were trying to take it all in and embrace it. I look up. The top of the flames easily reaches higher than the two basement levels we passed through.

I groan and push myself up with my back against the wall. I lean against it for support. My head is still reeling. I touch my forehead and...it's wet. I check my fingers. Crap, I'm bleeding. Probably dinged it pretty good when I hit the floor. I check the back. No blood, but a good-sized lump. Prometheus really rang my bell when he sho-

"Prometheus?" I gasp. "Prometheus," I whisper again, stepping out of my circle. My eyes dart to Perses, making sure he didn't hear me. The portal has his full attention. I could probably bring a marching band through here, and he wouldn't notice. "Prometheus?" I whisper again, stepping over a huge rock.

I lean over a jagged fallen pillar. "Prometheus?" I hear a groan from the other side, followed by a rustling sort of wheeze. I vault over the pillar and almost land on "Prometheus?" I move to his left side, because his right leg and arm are trapped under the pillar. A steel rod stands out of his left thigh. A few jagged pieces of rock and metal have imbedded themselves in his arm, leg, and chest...he even has a few lacerations on his face...none are nearly as damaging as the stab wound over his heart though.

Prometheus's eyes open slowly, and they've lost all luster, looking pale in the purple glow of the fire. Black blood spills out of both corners of his mouth. I kneel...ugh, might've been a mistake, my head reminds me that it just took two solid blows recently. I sigh, but how can I compare how I feel to...

His eyes move to me. "Ni...cole...?"

"I'm here," I reply, taking his left hand. He tries to squeeze my hand back, but his fingers won't even wrap around it.

"So-sorry..."

"It's okay, Prometheus...you don't have to..."

"Do..." He swallows...blood... "...may not...come back...this time..." He trembles and grits his bloodstained teeth. "...ugh...ah..." His breathing becomes even more erratic, panicked even. Blood fills his lungs...it's a horrible sloshing sort of wheeze. A tear falls onto our joined hands and then another. "...never...seen...anyone...die before...huh?"

I shake my head. "My dad wouldn't let me see my mom near the end and…so, far she's the only person I've ever lost…" I nod as more tears fall. "…you'll be the second."

"Not…losing me," he whispers.

"Feels that way."

He nods as best he can. "…sorry…"

"Don't."

"No…sorry…for my part…in this…hell. If…if you find…a way…to save…mor…tals…tell that girl…" He swallows again and quickly sniffs an inhale. "…tell Brandy…I saw it…in her…" He trembles. "…I changed…for her…"

"Why'd you change for her? What did you see?"

"Hope…" He nods, and tears streak his face, dragging the muck and blood spatters with them. I pull my sleeve over the base of my hand and wipe his eyes. "…compassion…in the end…" He smiles. "…Brandy…is hope…and potential…" He huffs a laugh, before coughing up more blood. "…gah…" He wheezes that choking, gurgle of a wheeze. "…infinite potential…" His eyes move to the sky. "…special…like…you…" His head slumps.

"Prometheus?" I shake him. "Prometheus?" I sob. I tremble. He's gone and why do I feel so…helpless? What could I have done to…? I shiver and hold his hand to my forehead. "I'm sorry…I'm sorry…I'm so sorry…" He died protecting me.

"What?" I gasp as his hand becomes rigid in mine. I look down, and his brown skin has turned gray…no, it's more than that…it's coarse, too. It feels like…stone. It moves up his arm and quickly spreads over his entire body including his clothes. I reach up and close his eyes, just before the stone covers his entire face. "Rest in peace."

Prometheus cracks… "No," I breathe. …and begins to crumble. Slowly, the pieces of him powder, and the tiny particles draw into the portal's fire. In seconds, Prometheus is gone…he's just gone.

"What just happened?"

THUMP! I look up, and Epimetheus lays at Perses's feet. That got his attention. Five lands beside me and pulls me to my feet. He stares at Perses like the villain he is. "This close to an opening to Tartarus…any god that badly injured would be drawn in."

"You saw?"

He nods, eyes still on Perses. "I figured in his last moment, seeing you would be better than seeing me." He looks at me. "You're bleeding."

"I'm fine." I nod. "Thanks to him." Five caresses my cheek and sweeps my tears away with his thumb. "Did you…did you kill his brother?"

"No. Epimetheus is still alive." He frowns, his hand does a spastic tremble against my cheek. He's furious and trying to keep his control because I'm close. "Perses on the other hand…" He turns to Perses, who's taken his sword out again. "…Perses, I plan on killing like a dog in the street."

Perses throws his head back and does that disturbing belly laugh. He comes back still chuckling. "You can't do anything to me," he boasts. "The portal is opening…" He extends the tip of his sword to it. It crosses into the flame, glows pale white, and the tip burns away. He withdraws the singed remains of his weapon. "…and you can't break the circle. Not without using your full power…" He points his tip-less blade at Five. "…and nothing short of your full power will ever close this portal."

He laughs again. "And I know that you'd NEVER use your full power so close to your beloved pet mortal." He puts the tips of his fingers to his lips and kisses them. "Mwah…thank you…silly little mortal…for being here…for being so fragile…" He laughs. "…for capturing Zeus's heart…in a way three wives…and countless consorts couldn't…"

Five swallows a lump. He trembles and electricity sparks at his right hand and runs the length of his arm. I grab that hand. He tries to pull away, but I hold tight. He looks down at my uninjured hand in amazement.

"If it means anything at all to you, I've been granted Nyx's protection…" He trembles again, and his eyes bulge. I nod. "…you won't hurt me. So, do what you do, Sparky."

He sighs. "Sparky?" he huffs. His eyes flash pale blue, and electricity ripples from one to the other. He lifts both his hands to my face…both with electricity flowing around them. "No matter what happens…know that I loved you," he whispers. "Really and truly loved you."

"You love me…present tense, Sparky." He nods. "Now, kiss me before you save the world."

I slip my hands over his as he kisses me. I inhale deeply as his lips tug at my lower lip. I feel his warm breath fill me…his hands leaving electric tingles across my skin…I purr. I love his kisses…and just like the first time…a little bit of that electric tingle moves through me…to my heart. I exhale loudly as we part.

He stares into my eyes. "Now, go get 'em…" I smirk. "…Sparky."

He nods and turns to Perses. He sweeps me behind him with a protective right arm. I take a step back. The fingers of his right-hand twitch and then wriggle. Lightning flows around them and there's a rumble of thunder from the sky. The air becomes rich with moisture…so much so, you can smell the airborne water.

Perses looks around before dropping his sword. He points at Five. "Zeus, wait…you can't…if-if-if you do this…you'll destroy her…"

Five tilts his head back as more electricity builds up around him. His mark becomes visible even through his coat.

"Don't you get it?" Perses snarls. "She's going to die. The woman you love…you will be the death of her…like Semele."

Five's hair turns white and glows as he lowers his head. He peers at me over his shoulder with white eyebrows, a white goatee, and the most heartbreaking expression I've seen since dad told me mom died. He mouths, 'I love you.'

I point at him and then hold up two fingers.

He smiles and returns to Perses. "You're right, Perses." He nods. "It will and it'll be my doing, but that's why I love her…because she's brave…far braver than you or me or any of us gods. Because she faces death, true death, and she's not backing down or blinking." Lightning flashes across the gathered clouds and thunder rumbles right on its heels. "Because she knows destroying that portal is more important than what we want."

I hear something else, after the thunder. *They're with you.*

I look up and see Andre, trident ready, and Ramona, emerald bow and matching arrow trained on Perses, standing on top of the wall behind me. I look to my left and AZ stands ready, staff in hand. I look right, and Mordechai has his hammer draped over his shoulder. Pearl is with Ray, protecting the people so…where's Ezra and…?

Alijiah comes down to Five's left with her spear pointed at Perses's heart.

"Brother," Andre says. "End this…now."

Five opens his right hand and his thunderbolt materializes there. He spins it around and lifts it like a javelin. Electricity rips from his body and his weapon in every direction. Alijiah jumps out of the way of the blast.

"NICOLE!" Alijiah barks as a stray bolt whips toward me. A shadowy sphere appears around me. The lightning flows over it, but it shields me. "What?" Alijiah lowers her spear. "I'm sorry. WHAT?"

Five's smirking face checks me over his shoulder. "You're so hot," I breathe.

"Tell me something I don't know, Nick," he says in a voice so earth-rattling deep it makes the thunder overhead seem like a phone vibrating.

"NO!!!" Styx screams, landing in front of the portal. "I can't let you do this," she says as her shadows subside. She stretches her arms out to block the portal. "Zeus, please," she pleads. "I've been denied access to Hades…I was alright as long as I could visit Pallas…but I've been cut off for nearly a thousand years." Tears streak down her face. "Please."

"Sorry," Five says in that thunderous voice.

Styx quivers, and her arms fall to her sides. "Then…kill me…too." She wobbles, before going down on her knees…completely defeated. "…kill me, too. Send me to him." She swallows a lump, closes her eyes, and tilts her head back, ready to accept her fate.

A blur of shadows sweeps in and throws Perses to the ground before wrapping Styx up. It moves away from the portal and to a ridge on the left.

"LET ME GO!" Styx snarls, fighting the shadow with her sickle. Ezra materializes out of the shadow, wearing a black helmet and holding his pitchfork. He roughly takes her by the chin with his free hand. He stares into her eyes, coming dangerously close to her face.

"Ez...?" Andre says.

All fight leaves Styx as if she's hypnotized. Wait, the same thing happened that day she attacked Five. Does Ezra have power over her? The shadow seems to consume them both and then flies away.

"Brother?" Andre says.

"A mystery for another day," Five says in that booming voice and with that stilted dialect. He prepares to throw his thunderbolt.

"It's not fair," Perses weeps, still on the floor. "I prepared for years for this...I fought and..." He points to the sky. "...I did everything I was told..." He grits his teeth and pounds the floor with his clenched fist. "...I DID AS I WAS TOLD!"

Five throws the thunderbolt at the portal. When he does, the sky seems to cut loose, too. A streak of lightning easily the size of the portal comes down as Five's thunderbolt strikes it.

I lose everything in the blinding flash and deafening clap of thunder. I wonder if it worked. I wonder if Nyx's protection was real or if she was just trying to convince Five to go all out to stop Perses. Either way, I guess I'll find out in a se-

****

Epilogue

"*…while we slept*," Ronda reads over the phone. "I have to say, every time I read that title, I love it more and more."

"Well, let's just hope our readership loves it as much," I reply.

"Well, if the online hits and likes are any indication, this issue's going to fly off the shelves. We bumped up our usual print order to 75,000."

"What? Why?"

"Are you serious? There's journalism award buzz for this piece already!"

"Really?"

"Yes, really," she replies happily. "So," she continues, her voice dropping to more of a serious tone. "Do you really believe Homeland Security's cover story?"

"Yeah, seems plausible," I say, especially when I'm the one who came up with it. An unknown group of terrorists released an aerosol-based agent in Bevelle, leaving its citizens' unconscious. During that time, they planted a device with the intention of detonating it after the construction project was completed. Most likely, an error made while storing the device caused it to explode prematurely, destroying the construction site. It also helped that Ray 'convinced' the Homeland Security Inspectors that that's what happened.

"Hmm," Ronda moans. "I'm still skeptical, but you're my star investigative reporter."

"Star reporter?"

"Yep…two award nods already…you're a star. All right, I gotta run. Talk soon and let me know how the move goes?"

"Bet," I reply and end the call.

I look around Five's room… I groan. …our room. Hard to believe, it's only been a week since Perses, the gate, and…Prometheus. Five insisted that I move in with him. Ugh, who am I kidding? This was the compromise to him sticking one of the Olympians with me 24/7. He's afraid that if Perses or Epimetheus survived, they'd come after me for payback.

A knock comes from the open door. I half-turn to Little Xavier. His sneakers are untied as usual.

"What's up?" I say, walking over to him. He points back down the hall. I kneel and start tying his left shoe. "The movers are here?" He nods. "Would you let them in for me?" I say as I finish tying the bow on his right shoe. He nods and runs back down the hall. "Xavier?" He stops and turns back to me. "Where's my smile?" He shakes his head and runs down to the corner. I swore I'd get him to smile one day.

I walk over to Five's…our bed…which is absolutely going to be replaced by mine…and search through my unpacked shirts, looking for a decent one to put on over my tank top.

"Ma'am," a husky voice says. I turn to the deep blue jumpsuit with a throat beard. His big brown eyes give me the once over, probably doesn't help that I'm still half-bent over the bed and wearing a tiny, tight tank. "Um…" He swallows a lump. My eyebrows go up as I turn to him with my blue on white plaid button up in hand. "…where do you want this stuff, ma'am?"

I point with my thumb. "Dresser over by the desk. Couch, replaces this couch…this couch goes wherever old dead couches go…same with the beds…and you can stack the boxes marked clothes near the closet…and the stuff marked kitchen well…I'll let you figure that part out."

He laughs. Yay, he's flirting. "Yeah, I was a little surprised that my boyfriend agreed to let me buy a new bed and couch and agreed to trash his old ones."

He frowns and mouths an 'oh.' "Yeah, he must really like you."

"Loves me actually." I smile.

He nods as two other jumpsuits walk in carrying my dresser, minus the mirror. "Over there," he says, pointing at the desk.

The man in front nods, and they carry it in. "Cool ink," the second guy says, staring at me.

"Thanks." I look at my right shoulder. It's not actually ink…it just sorta appeared after the portal. Five says it looks like Nyx's symbol…a crescent moon inside of a pyramid…but it has a lightning bolt running over it. It also has words etched along the moon that even Five can't read.

He said that more than likely it signified Nyx's protection and his 'claim' on me. It's like two halves came together to make a symbol of my own. It's weird though. Sometimes I feel it, sometimes I don't…like maybe there's power to it. Either way, I don't feel different. It's not as if I'm a god now or anything. I slip my arms into my sleeves and find my leather jacket under the pile of clothes.

The movers finish unloading my stuff quickly, which makes sense, since there were six of them. With everything in place, I tip them and they're on their way.

I sigh. I'm not in any hurry to put my stuff away. Five's been gone the last few days, and I've been sleeping on the couch. At least now, it'll be more comfortable with the new couch.

I walk down the hall heading for the crossway. I stop by AZ's room and peek in. "Ahem," I say, taking in Brandy laying across his bed with her head resting in his lap. They look at me. "…um, Brandy, it's almost 5. You know you're not allowed to be on the boy's side after dark."

She nods and sits up. She leans into him and steals a quick kiss. "I'll miss you," she purrs.

"I miss you already."

"You'll be right down the hall from each other and you'll probably text each other all night." They giggle as Brandy stands up. She waves at him and then turns to me. AZ shoots me a quick wink as Brandy turns her back. "Did you finish your paper on the Iraq War?"

"Yeah. You're gonna read it for me before I turn it in, right?"

"Of course." She wraps one arm around my neck and gives me a quick squeeze. She darts out of the room, throwing one more quick wave at AZ. "Oh, don't forget, you have an Algebra test on Wednesday."

"Yeah," she stretches out, while backing away. "It's hard to math."

"It is hard to math but get Pearl to help you. She's good at it." She nods and hurries down the hall. AZ walks past me, and I put a hand on his shoulder. "You know, you can't go to her side at all, right?"

He flashes a huge smile and laughs. "Can't blame a guy for trying." I shake my head. "Thank you."

"For what?"

"Just…being here. I can't explain it but…" He stares after Brandy. "…you being around, it makes her happier. Also, it makes Five less of a hard ass…" I point at him. "…tough father-figure type?" I nod. "Geez, mother-figure much?"

"Ugh, I just turned 26, and I've already got an 18-year-old son?"

"Technically, I'm a little older than that."

I laugh and head down the hall. I point at him, still standing in his doorway. "Don't even think about it?"

"Me? Think? Never!" He ducks back inside. I continue around the corner, and I hear a distinct whistle behind me.

"NO SIR!" Pearl snarls. That same whistle whizzes by me again heading in the other direction. I laugh.

AZ drapes his arm over my shoulders. "Sooooooo, we're going outside, huh?" I laugh harder as we head out the backdoors. AZ runs out ahead and joins Alijiah and Ray, leading a game of kickball with the smaller kids.

Xavier sits at the bottom step, watching the game. I rub the top of his head. "You should go play, too. Still another hour before dinner's ready." He shakes his head. "…even if the bunny asks?" He frowns. I hold up a peace sign, letting it double as a bunny. I make the bunny hop toward him and tickle him. He sighs but doesn't laugh. "One day, Xavier…" I show him the bunny. "…me and the bunny will get you to smile. I promise." He shrugs.

I walk toward home plate and spot Ramona leading a group of girls in archery practice. A clang sounds out behind me. Another and another. Mordechai puts the final additions on a four-swing and jungle gym-slide combo. He sighs and brushes his hands against one another. I'm glad he decided to stay. He waves. I smile and wave back.

I guess this is home for me now, too. Living at Mt. Olympus with Greek gods. Yeah, cause that doesn't sound insane or anything. My phone buzzes. I slip it out of my back pocket and step away from the game.

"Hello?"

"Hey, baby…"

Wow, even the sound of his voice causes that little tingle in my heart now. "Hey yourself, Sparky. I thought you said you'd be back by now."

"I know, I know, and I'm sorry. Are you still sleeping on the couch?"

"No."

"Nick?"

"Yes. It's not the same sleeping in your bed without you."

"I know. I can't seem to sleep much without you beside me either."

"Well, we could be doing more than sleeping, if someone wasn't afraid of hurting me."

He laughs through the phone, and I blush, not exactly believing I just said that. "One day, I promise, Nick."

"Nick?"

"Don't like it?"

"No, I do…but only coming from you, Sparky."

"Understood."

"When are you coming home? I miss you."

"I'll be back soon. Promise. I think I finally got a lead on Ezra and Styx, and I think Andre's found the reincarnation of Dionysus."

Someone taps me on the shoulder. I turn to…Andre. He smiles in that awkward, condescending way he does toward me. "Um…somehow, I doubt that."

"He's there isn't he?"

"Uh huh."

"Tell him, we'll talk later."

I lower the phone away from my mouth. "You. Five. Serious talking to." He shrugs. I replace the phone. "He doesn't seem to care."

Five groans, and I imagine him pinching the bridge of his nose, the way Alijiah and he do most of the time when they talk to Andre. "It'll be fine…" He moans a yes. "…but you don't believe that, do you?"

"I've sensed two more awakenings since the portal…and that was after Dionysus and…" He hums. "…Ares, I think."

"Oooohhhh," I moan. "No wonder you're so worried about finding Ezra."

He sighs. "He won't betray me again."

"You trust him that much?"

He laughs. "We grew up together…twice."

"Once."

"Forgot, my girl's kind of a research genius."

"Woman and don't you forget either of those facts, Sparky."

"Yes, ma'am." There's a tone in the background on his end.

"Where are you?"

"Pulling into Lincoln, Nebraska now."

"Be careful."

"Always."

"Liar."

"Yep. I can't wait to see what you did to our room, Nick. Love you."

"I…" I choke.

"Bye."

"Bye." The phone beeps twice. I slip it into my back pocket. I choked again. I still haven't been able to just come out and tell him I love him back yet.

"Ugh." My shoulder… I slip my jacket off my right shoulder and do the same with my shirt. "Weird," I groan, realizing that the crescent moon on my shoulder is glowing. I reach for it. The pyramid radiates, and electricity passes between my hand and my mark… I gasp. …did I just call it…*my mark*?

****